The Hidden

Louise Doherty

ii

For my mother and father
Elizabeth and John Doherty

I would also like to thank Mary Theresa Doherty,
formerly of Rockdale Street, for her love and
kindness throughout my childhood.

Author Biography

Louise Doherty was born in 1968 in Belfast. She has worked as a journalist, teacher and songwriter.

Author's Note:
This is a work of fiction

The Hidden

A Novel

Prologue
The Silent Night

The leaves were brown and wet and rotting and the streetlamps, still lit, seemed only to draw attention to the debris. There were soiled paper bags, empty beer tins and cigarette butts strewn about the pavement, remnants from the Saturday night carousers who had left the street, shoddy and cold and empty, shortly after the public houses closed. But a child's dummy also lay there. It dangled half on and half off the kerb, and was crushed as though it had been pushed into the ground by a heavy boot. Instinctively Mary stopped walking and bent over to pick it up.

She balanced a child on her left arm so that, far from being an encumbrance, he looked to be a natural extension of her being, as an arm or a leg might look. But as her hand was fully stretched and within reach of the crushed dummy she hastily retracted it, and leaving the filthy thing to lie where it was she stood up, pulling the child back into her breast.

1

'I'm sorry,' she whispered as a teardrop broke and trickled into her mouth. The baby stared back at her and spewed up wind. She lifted Alexander and placed him over her shoulder.

'I can't keep you,' she argued as she continued to rub his back and clean the spew intermittently from his mouth.

She wrapped the white cotton blanket closely around his face, and layered this with the coarse grey alpaca blanket; it was trimmed with a soft silver-grey cloth, cross-stitched to the blanket using braided beige cord. The neatly spaced needlework was her own for she had purchased cloth from The Spinning Wheel in Rosemary Street so as to make the blanket, though thick and warm, less harsh around the edges where it might touch Alexander's skin. She examined the needlework and felt content as she sat down on the low redbrick wall that Alexander was snug.

As she rocked him back and forth she began to say the words of the song she had sung to him when he was born, 'I loved a laddie, a bonnie, bonnie laddie, he's as fair a laddie as can be,' and then she hummed the words and then she tried to sing the words but the song would not come.

'The nuns will look after you,' she said as she looked down at the bit of paper on which she'd printed his name, and in parenthesis below it appended 'The Great'. But the addition to his name mocked her as she read it, for it seemed stupid and childish. She wanted to unpin the tag and replace it, but it was too late.

For a while she imagined that she would at some time in the future, when she was married, if she met a good man, return to claim him, but the coldness of the wall beneath her, a seeping malign coldness that her very bones absorbed, returned her to the present.

She walked a little further to where the top of the Ravenhill Road met the top of the Ormeau Road: a fork in the road upon which Nazareth House was built. She looked at the child again and pulled him into her.

'Forgive me,' she tendered as she laid him down on the concrete steps before lifting the heavily polished nickel-coated knocker.

The din as the knocker fell rang out as she ran back down the path to hide behind a row of hedges. Through this, where she found a small gap, she watched the front of the building, oblivious to the light from an upstairs room that had been switched on and hastily switched off again.

Meanwhile Alexander lay quiet and still, in no-man's-land, between his mother who crouched beneath the hovering streetlamp and Sister Augustine who watched from the window.

Sister Augustine studied the silhouette. She toyed with the large silver crucifix that draped her neck and, as the wait continued, withdrew heavy shiny rosary beads from the pocket of her habit.

She had moved to the ninth bead upon which the polish was particularly worn, as though it was the most lingered upon prayer, when she heard from below the window the cry of a child. It was a muffled cry, as though the lungs were not fully developed. She left the window and walked steadily and quietly, so as not to disturb the rest of the house, to the front door.

'I can see you,' said Sister Augustine as she lifted the bundle from the steps. 'Reveal yourself.' Mary came out from behind the hedge and stood at the bottom of the path.

'Come towards me,' said the nun. Mary shook her head. 'You won't!' Again Mary shook her head. 'There are forms and documents to fill in. What time is this to leave a child here?' The nun stepped towards her, putting her open hand over her brow in an attempt to see the shadowy figure more clearly. 'Next time you'll think, won't you?' said the nun.

Mary nodded, as she remembered how quickly, how much without thought, she had conceived the child.

'You can hide,' said the nun, 'but not from God.'

'His name's Alexander.'

'I see that,' said the nun as she turned his nametag over.

'You'll keep his name?'

'And it's the only thing you'll ever give him?'

'I gave him birth.'

'For your shame.'

'He's a good child.'

'They're all good children. It's their mothers who aren't.'

Mary bit into her lower lip. She bowed her head too, as a penitent might – shamefully and completely.

Sister Augustine took another step forward, but Mary once more stepped back, knocking the wooden gate that marked the entrance to the pathway and which swung perilously in both directions.

'Go then, if you're going.'

'You'll look after him?' Mary asked.

'What choice do we have?' said the nun.

'Choice?' Mary asked plaintively, as though she had not heard the word before and did not therefore comprehend it.

4

'Go,' shouted the nun, 'you've done enough harm.'

But Mary did not go. Her hands involuntarily reached out into the empty space in front of her so that her palms lay upwards, suspended in their vacancy. She did not kneel, but her head was bent forward so that her poise was all that a supplicant's might be.

'Go,' the nun repeated so that Mary's hands, held out in painful reverie, fell down and flapped violently back against her fragile body.

She retreated onto the pavement, taking backward footsteps that, though delicately taken, seemed to resound so that their eerie resonance permeated the stillness of the night.

And hesitant still Mary paused, so that all was quiet. For there was no bird to break the deadness, the rain had temporarily hushed and the leaves on the ground were stagnant. She paused to wonder at what was, at what might yet be; perhaps it was not too late after all, perhaps she could keep him. And in that silence, for a moment, there was still hope.

But as Sister Augustine stepped forward the shifting wary weary order of the night, the silent night, broke. Mary turned and fled.

'Run,' shouted the nun. 'Run if you want to, but you can't run from God.'

****

And the night and the wind, as though it had with bated breath suspended its inclemency, poured forth its vehement worst: the street became dark, without shadow to give it earthly form or moonlight to lighten it. The rain beat down and the wind howled seeming to feed itself with

5

its own angry torrents, so that even the undead, if they existed, on this suddenly merciless night sought shelter. But for Mary there was no refuge, for as she ran the wind seemed to lift and carry the spirit of Alexander with it, except his spirit was no longer benign; instead his small and delicate hands reached out to grab her, to catch her, to shake her. She kept running as tears drifted off her cheek and into the cold night air; but still he hovered over her and around her so that her breath began to choke and to suffocate. Stop, she thought, and face it. If you stop and turn it'll go away; but she could not stop, for his hands touched her now: icy fingertips grappling her neck, hands that could not forgive and that, though flesh of her flesh, though small and finely wrought, seemed to seek revenge.

Her strength to run soon waned. She gasped for breath, but her breath coughed and stuttered and broke in upon her causing her to stop and to move into the shade of a narrow porch. She faced the wall, feeling the unnatural coldness of what lay behind her, but was too full of fear: of the night, of the dark, of the spirit of the child who had followed her to turn around.

Yet hadn't she held him and rocked him and sung to him, she reasoned. Hadn't she suffered the pains of birth to bring him here? Why would he hurt her?

Slowly she turned, but there in the night was only the night: the cold wet wintry night. There was no spirit, no fiend waiting to harm her.

She sank against the wall of the porch and fell onto the ground. The rain beat diagonally into the recess saturating her clothes, but she did not rise to go. She remembered, as the cold seemed to move and shift so that she did not feel it any more, that she had dreamed of gathering enough money to leave the city when Alexander was born and go someplace where no-one would know them.

She remembered dreaming of a cottage in the hills, perhaps overlooking the sea where she might tend a vegetable garden and where Alexander might grow and where she could love him and protect him.

In the preceding months she had eaten meagrely so as to save as much as she could, and had exchanged her winter coat for the grey blanket so that the rain beat against her and the cold seeped into her unencumbered.

She was glad that she had put her savings into an envelope and pinned it under his nametag. At least she had left him something.

****

The council's city street cleaners rose early in the morning, as they always did. They had swept most of the city clean before they found her lying in a corner of the porch.

'Wake up love,' said one of the street cleaners as he shook her. But she was cold he realised, and dead.

He stood back and, for a moment, looked dumbly on.

'When I first saw her lying in the porch,' he later reflected, 'I thought she was holding something, but when I got closer there was nothing there. Her arms were strangely cradled,' he said, 'as though she'd been holding a baby.'

Sister Augustine read of her death in The Irish News. 'A young woman,' the paper said, 'as yet unnamed, was found in tragic circumstances…'

Children were left in the home often enough and Sister Augustine understood that questions would not be asked,

7

and that the connection between the young mother and orphaned child would never be made.

Despite appeals, in the week that followed, even as they buried her, in the year of Our Lord nineteen hundred and sixty-seven, no-one came to claim Mary as their child: no brother, no sister, no family or friend at all. And so the identity of Alexander's mother remained hidden from the world and he, as his mother before him, was left truly alone.

Chapter 1

St. Joseph's, the baby unit of the Poor Sisters of Nazareth's children's home, kept Alexander until his fourth birthday. He remembered hiding in the cubbyhole and hiding in the henhouse, or stealing a black banana from the shed in the garden, but he had no other recollection of these earliest years. His earliest memory came later, shortly after he was transferred to Nazareth Lodge. It was a full memory, unlike the earlier snapshots, and began in the dining room where he sat with the other boys, waiting for Grace to be over and dinner to be served.

Sister Augustine stood at the far table where the nuns ate their dinner. She was a tall figure, as Alexander remembered, and stout. She extended her right arm outwards and blessed herself; the boys copied her so that they looked like altar boys. When she'd finished the boys quickly blessed themselves, for it was Sunday and though scant in quantity they had corned beef and potatoes to eat. It was Alexander's favourite dinner, but instead of tucking in he felt only discomfort, for he badly needed to pee.

He knew he was not allowed to leave the dining room so he eased himself under the table, hoping that he would not be seen, but he had only taken a few steps across the parquet floor when Sister Augustine called his name. He returned to the table immediately and lowered his left hand beneath it so as to hold onto himself.

'Are you not eating that?' said one of the elder boys. Alexander nodded but Michael scooped most of Alexander's food onto his own plate, leaving only a spoonful of potatoes. 'Too late,' the elder boy muttered as Alexander watched the boy's Adam's apple jut out as though it might pierce the skin on his neck, and sink back in as he swallowed the meat.

'Imagine you not wanting your dinner,' Michael said as he smirked.

Alexander looked at him dolefully and ate what was left.

'Aye, see,' said Michael, 'you'll soon learn to eat it when it's in front of you; you skinny wee drip.'

Left without any dinner to eat, Alexander resolved to take whatever punishment the nuns would give him and got up from the table a second time, and though Sister Augustine spotted him immediately and called for him to return, he continued to walk towards the door.

Michael raised an eyebrow, surprised by the younger boy's defiance, as Sister Augustine stood up and bellowed, 'Stop that boy.'

The dining room, though relatively quiet up to that point, assumed a deadly silence: the forks and knives ceased to scrape their dinner plates and every mouth held its contents in animated suspension; all eyes moved from the plates to the volcanic indignance of Sister Augustine. Alexander came to an abrupt halt.

He turned around to face Sister Augustine, but as he turned his arms fell in attention to his side, and having lifted the lid off the long and pressurized pee it burst into song so that a huge patch of wet formed on the front of his trousers. The eyes of the boys moved back and forth from Alexander to Sister Augustine, from Sister Augustine to Alexander.

The boys nudged each other and began to point at the puddle that was slowly forming around Alexander's feet, but when the clock in the dining room chimed for the Angelus and Alexander jumped, for he was not yet accustomed to its sound, they began to laugh and to stamp their feet.

The nuns stood up. Sister Augustine called the children to order, but her voice was lost in the din; she began to feel light-headed and sat down. Some said afterwards that she fell backwards, on the chair behind her.

Her fall fuelled the clamour so that the boys leapt up from their seats; some jumped onto the tables, others squealed, all banged whatever it was they could bang, competing with each other for every risen and rising decibel.

Alexander did not know why they screamed, yelled and yahooed. He only knew that like a baby he had soiled his clothes in front of them, and the mortification of that soaked into his already too wet flesh. As he closed his eyes and stuck his fingers into his ears to block out the noise two nuns grabbed his arms and hoisted him off his feet.

They carried him up the long and winding staircase and deposited him in the washroom where they stripped him of his clothes and put him into the bathtub. They turned on the tap and as the cold water splashed against Alexander's bare flesh he began to cry.

11

'Now sit,' they said as the bath began to fill. They placed his clothes beside him, ducking them under the water with a wooden spoon, and poured a vile blue liquid into the bathtub. The stench made Alexander's throat ache and his stomach, perhaps because it was all but empty, heaved at the smell.

He took the scrubbing brush they handed to him and was trying to wash the clothes when Sister Augustine appeared in the doorway.

'Enough,' she said. 'The boy had an accident. It was not his fault.'

The nuns obeyed Sister Augustine's instruction and took him out of the bathtub; they told him to sit on the toilet and not to move. When they did come back, a half hour, perhaps an hour later, they asked him to kneel with them on the floor of the washroom to say an Our Father and to ask for God's forgiveness.

As Alexander walked back to the dormitory he thought of Jesus's walk up the hill of Cavalry. He had a lot in common with Jesus, except that Jesus knew who his father was and who his mother was and knew that he was going to heaven whereas Alexander did not know who his father was or who his mother was, and if the nuns had anything to do with it he was going straight to hell.

He turned the round black Bakelite handle of the dormitory door and went in on his tiptoes; as he pulled back the blankets of his own bed he heard someone say, 'Do you smell Jeyes?' 'Pisspot,' muttered a second boy and someone else counted 'One, two, three,' out loud so that all the boys, who must have faked sleep as he entered the room, began to chant, 'Clean the floor, clean your ass, cleanse your soul...'

12

Alexander jumped into bed and pulled the covers up over him; he plugged both his ears as he had done earlier, hoping that the chanting and the mockery would stop, but as he lay curled up like a hedgehog two boys pulled the blankets from him.

'We're just kidding,' said the elder boy. 'We had more fun today in the dining room than we've had in a long time and we've you to thank for that.'

Alexander looked up at them and felt confused.

'When they wouldn't let you go to the toilet and you just peed yourself. Well, that'll teach them.'

Alexander still felt confused.

'And then the way he smiled, as if to say stuff you.'

He knew that he hadn't deliberately smiled, but if the boys believed he had wet himself in order to provoke the nuns then...

'You're a hero,' said Michael, lifting him up onto his shoulders. But Alexander did not trust this turn of events, did not trust Michael who, after all, was the same boy who had earlier stolen his dinner. His instinct was to kick, to insist that Michael release him, but what good would it do? Michael was twelve years old, bigger and stronger; and so Alexander found himself paraded around the dormitory and, as they stalled at the foot of each bed, saluted before Michael released Alexander from his stirrup-like armpits and set him down carefully. 'Look,' he said, pointing to a huge gobstopper that lay on Alexander's pillow. 'Best we could do.'

As Alexander opened the wrapper and popped the gobstopper into his mouth, and as he tasted its sweet shell of orange, he knew that the boys truly believed he was a hero. In fact, as time moved on, Alexander remembered

13

their version of events as being the most true. He remembered too that the gobstopper had lasted a whole week.

****

Alexander's heroic status was cemented that summer when Sister Augustine left and Elsie, whom the boys took an instant shine to, joined the orphanage – for Elsie was young and motherly and treated them with kindness.

Her eyes, the boys said, were blue, like the sea, like the ocean, even though some of them, though the coast was a short distance from the children's home, had never seen the sea never mind an ocean. But they were blue. They all agreed too that she liked Alexander the best: this was 'Okay,' they said, for hadn't he, albeit indirectly, delivered her to them.

Elsie worked most days and sometimes visited them on her days off. She'd been working in the home for nearly a year and a half when Alexander hoped that she'd invite him to spend Christmas with her, at home in her own house. The younger boys encouraged him: 'Of course she'll bring you home,' they said. But some of the older boys shrugged their shoulders and argued that there was few boarded out for the vacation the year before.

During the early days of December, after he said his prayers, Alexander had more often than not fallen asleep with his fingers crossed, hoping against hope that Elsie would soon ask him to come home with her, but today he had had a bad day at school and he could think of nothing else but school: 'Time and again,' the schoolmaster said, 'I have told you to write with your right hand; and you will write with the hand that the good Lord gave you to write with, for I'll not have a cloot in my class.'

Alexander nodded as he stood humbly in front of the dais. 'Now hold out your hand.' Alexander proffered his right hand. 'Not the right, you must write with that hand. Don't you understand? The left,' the master roared. 'Give me the left.'

He stretched out his left hand and lifted his eyes to glimpse the threatening birch before quickly shutting them. The birch whipped through the air and struck his left hand.

'Again,' the master said. He put out his right hand. 'Damn it boy. The left, the left.' But the left was burning and stung more fiercely than when it had been struck. 'Straighten it,' said the master, 'unless you want to end up a cripple.' The birch fell for a second time, breaking the skin.

Alexander was determined not to cry but he could feel tears well up into his eyes. 'It's for your own good,' the master said.

As he turned and walked back to his seat, the boys did not look at him. Instead, they buried their heads into their books so that he felt betrayed and conspired against. He got to his desk, sat down and lifted the pencil with his right hand.

'Now copy out the alphabet,' the master instructed.

It was the work of a primary one pupil and the other boys laughed.

'Silence,' the master ordered.

Alexander tried to form the letters as accurately as he could; he tried to make them neat, he tried desperately, but the sprawled toddler's alphabet looked back at him mockingly and made him feel stupid. He would never

15

write properly; he would never get a proper education; he would never be any good.

****

That night, as Alexander lay in bed, he extended out his thumbs to measure one against the other. His left thumb, he saw, was longer than his right. Despite the cold he pulled down the blankets and stared at his toes. The left toe, he saw with incredulity, was also longer than his right; and instead of reasoning that nature had no regard for symmetry he concluded that here lay the reason for his left-handedness: he had been made wrong, or at least, made badly; and having been made badly he understood the hopelessness of his endeavours to write properly.

He would always be a cloot and God had made him so. And if God had made him so, then the schoolmaster was wrong to have caned him; in the morning he would let Elsie know what had happened. Once he explained this newfound wisdom, she would fix it so that he would not be caned again, and as he thought about her he forgot the pain in his left hand and nursed instead the image of the blue-eyed woman whom he had grown fond of, perhaps even grown to love.

The following day Alexander got up early and lingered anxiously in the hallway for Elsie, but she did not come and he had to go to school without seeing her. That evening he asked the other boys had they seen her, but none had. Perhaps, he thought, she had changed her day off.

The next day he again got up earlier than usual so as to wait for her, but again she did not come. That night he cried, and on the second and third day of her absence Alexander woke with wet sheets.

The Christmas tree, donated to the orphanage by the authorities in Belvoir Forest Park, had already arrived, but Alexander had no enthusiasm for it. He was glad that it sat in the hallway, still wrapped up, for he did not want Christmas to come.

Sister Well always took charge of the tree. Why had she let it lie in the hallway for so long? He didn't want it to be up, not without Elsie, but his curiosity got the better of him.

'Well,' she said, scratching her chin. Alexander was in no mood for laughter, but he couldn't help but laugh when she poked her chin out and continued to scratch it.

'Well what?' he said.

'I was waiting for one of Santa's little helpers to come along.'

'There's no such thing Sister Well,' said Alexander.

'Are you sure?' said Sister Well.

Alexander started to flick his fingers in an agitated, anxious fashion. 'Well, maybe,' he said, as he stared at the floor.

'And wouldn't you be one of the little helpers who put the tree up last year?' said Sister Well.

'Maybe,' said Alexander, looking up.

'And might you be one of Santa's little helpers this year too?' she said, smiling.

'Might be,' said Alexander, as he took Sister Well's hand.

They went into the hallway together to get the Christmas tree, lifted it into the dining room and unwrapped it, but as Alexander hung tinsel, shiny coloured

17

balls and the Santa's they'd made from toilet rolls, red paint and cotton wool, on the bigger than usual tree he began once more to think of Elsie, and of how she had deserted him, as his own mother before her had deserted him. She was not, as he had thought, an angel of God, but a temptress, a Delilah, and as he decorated the tree he resolved never to love again.

When the tree was finished Sister Well asked Alexander to remove his bedclothes and bring them to the washroom. He went up to the dormitory, stripped the clothes and went into the laundry room expecting to meet Sister Well there, but he found himself alone.

He pulled the clothes in the commercial washing machine out onto the floor and stuffed his bedlinen into the machine, but he did not know how to operate it and so he sat down on the floor and waited for Sister Well to come and help him.

As he waited he noticed that one of the cupboards had been left open, so he climbed up on the toilet seat to shut it. But the cupboard was further away than he had first judged and, despite his elevated position, he could barely reach it.

He moved to the edge of the seat and stood up on his tiptoes. This gave him an extended reach, enabling his curiosity.

On the second shelf he found a pair of scissors, but as he leaned further to grasp the handle his foot slipped so that he fell, bashing the side of his head on the cupboard, but it did not hurt that much and when he looked and saw the scissors, cleverly held out from his body as he fell, he smiled, got up and began searching for a mirror. But there was no mirror so he wiped the condensation off the tiles

18

hoping to see his reflection. There was a shadow of sorts, reflecting his outline, but not enough. His eyes lit up when he realised that he could see his reflection, albeit vaguely, in the window; and so he began to cut, just a little bit at first and then some more and some more of his hair. He looked at its colour as it dropped into the bath as though seeing it for the first time; it was redder than he'd thought. When he had the left side completed to his satisfaction and barely begun on the right side he heard Elsie's voice.

'Looks good,' she said. He looked down at the scissors and pulled them behind his back. 'Perhaps,' she said, 'I'll just finish it off for you though, because you've missed a bit.' He handed the scissors to her thinking that she would be cross, but she placed her hand gently around his waist to turn him sideways and told him only to stand still.

As she sculpted his hair, he wanted to ask her where she'd been. She was free to go where she pleased he supposed, and he wondered what it must be like – to have a place of your own, a fire of your own, a room of your own. He wondered what it must be like to eat without being watched, to sleep without other boys snoring and coughing around you. He couldn't fully imagine that sort of aloneness.

She turned him around to face her when she had finished. He could see a small tear well up in her eyes and so he reached his hand across to her, cupping the side of her cheek. 'I'm sorry,' she said, 'for going away. I had things to do and there just wasn't…'

As Elsie stumbled out her apology, Alexander thought she was going to tell him that she was going away for good so he withdrew his hand and held it into his chest,

19

close to his own heart, feeling, perhaps for the first time in his life, the dread of being truly alone.

'No,' she said, reaching for his hand, for she saw his bright and freckled face fall into shadow. 'I'm not going away.' The shadow lifted and he raised his dulled head expectantly.

'Would you be happy,' she asked, 'to come home with me for Christmas?'

He leaned back away from her and looked puzzled so that, for a moment, she wondered whether she was mistaken in the bond she thought they'd forged.

But slowly, a smile welled from the pit of his stomach. 'Yes,' he said in a strangely adult tone, as though there was something predetermined and fateful in her ask, as though finally the world had come to him and invited him into it.

Chapter 2

Elsie was only thirty-four years of age but she felt too old ever to get married. Her first job had been in the local mill where Lily, her best friend, also worked.

They had been best friends as long as Elsie could remember: they looked out for each other, shared each other's woes, shared sometimes even each other's enemies. They were, it was said by the other mill-hands, the head and tail of a sixpence; nothing would ever separate them, and so when Lily was asked out by one of the managers, he offered to bring a mate, '...if you want to bring Elsie,' he said, ''cause everyone knows what you two are like.'

The much talked about Beast with Five Fingers was showing in The Ritz, and when Lily asked Elsie to go along with her on the double date she readily agreed. It was only Wednesday but they began almost instantly to plan what to wear. When Friday night came Elsie was the first to be ready and to call.

'The periwinkles look great,' said Lily as Elsie stood waiting at the door.

'Wow,' said Elsie, 'just look at you in that skirt.'

21

'Like it?' said Lily. The taffeta skirt flared out and swished as she burled. 'Just finished making it about half an hour ago.'

'Love the petticoat too.' Lily smiled and took another burl. Elsie watched and laughed and then held out her arm, 'Smell,' she said. Lily leant forward and sniffed. 'You know I've washed myself over and over but I still don't think that I've got rid of the smell of that mill. Can you still smell it?'

'I don't smell anything,' said Lily.

'Nothing?'

'What do you expect? I work there too. But as for that, so does Jimmy and Tommy; no-one's going to notice.'

'I suppose,' said Elsie.

'We've the same smell and the same fringe cut too,' said Lily, flicking her head to one side. The heavily lacquered fringe didn't move. 'I'll just be a minute,' she said. She went into the house, grabbed her handbag and returned outside. 'Jimmy said to meet them at the corner,' she said as she linked Elsie's arm.

****

The Ritz was packed tight when they got in. Tommy paid for the tickets and went back to wait for Elsie who was having trouble with her new shoes. She took the left shoe off, for it pinched and cut into her toes, and stuffed a ripped piece of tissue paper into the front of it. Tommy held out his arm to help her to balance. She leant against him as she put the shoe back on. 'Sorry,' she said. Tommy smiled. 'They look good though,' he said, letting go of her arm as she hobbled into the auditorium.

22

Tommy sat beside her; he did not smoke but as the lights dipped he opened a pack of Embassy Regal, withdrew the wrapping, and handed one of the cigarettes to her. Jimmy held up an empty packet and as Tommy leant across her to give him a few cigarettes Elsie caught a waft of Old Spice aftershave; she chuckled inwardly: he'd made an effort to impress.

It was mid-way through the film when Lily and Jimmy shared their first snog. Elsie felt a bit like a gooseberry, for Tommy hadn't made any advances. She let her left hand dangle close to his, hoping that he'd hold it; it was a horror movie after all.

But no, not even when Hilary Cummins, the personal secretary of an invalid concert pianist, cut the hand off his employer's corpse did Tommy make a move. As the hand inherited a life of its own and relentlessly stalked the wild-eyed Peter Lorre, Elsie began to feel uncomfortable with her own hand dangling in the dark of the smoke-filled auditorium, so she tucked it back into her lap.

At first she'd thought that Tommy was a bit shy, but as the film continued she began to worry that he didn't fancy her at all: this made her feel awkward and lean, ever so slightly, away from him into the available space that Lily's own leanings had created.

When the film was over they took the Trolleybus back up The Falls Road. Jimmy and Lily lingered behind as Tommy walked Elsie to her door. When they got there and Tommy took her hand to ask could he see her again she felt relieved.

The weeks rolled into months so that Tommy and Elsie, Lily and Jimmy became known by the other mill-hands as items. They spent every weekend together and Elsie told Tommy of her plans to become a nurse.

It made him glad to think of his girl being something more than a mill-hand, but he worried too about not being good enough for her if she did qualify.

They were going out together four months when Elsie met him at the usual spot outside the chippie. She waved a letter joyously in the air.

'I've been accepted,' she said, 'I'm going to be a nurse.'

Tommy tried to pluck up a smile.

'What's wrong?' she asked.

'You'll have to go away,' he murmured.

'I've worked in the mill Tommy since I was ten, as a half-timer and as a doffer until I was thirteen when I went full-time. I like the camaraderie, yes, the women are great and if anyone's going through hard times there's always a whip round, but it's dusty all the time and the smell of the flax fibres gets right up my nose.'

'There's plenty that work in the mills,' he said.

'I know that.'

'Almost half of Belfast.'

'But I don't want to be in that half. I don't want to end up like Helen Blunden.'

'Who?'

'Helen Blunden. You must have heard the stories. You know they say her ghost still haunts the mill.'

'Conway Mill?'

'No, I don't know what mill she worked in; it was a long time ago. It's all the same though. She fell down the stairs.'

'Anyone could fall down stairs.'

'Yes, but she was a Millie, like me. Working her guts off in her bare feet since she was no age and singing her religious songs for all the good they did her. And she's stuck there in the mill, dead and haunting the place.'

'You're not going to die working in the mill.'

'How do you know? There's still plenty of injuries and plenty of women too that end up half-deaf with the noise of the place. But you're dead right, I'm not going to die in the mill, ''cause I'm not going to work there anymore.'

'I don't want you to go away,' said Tommy.

'You mean better myself.' She'd had these arguments at home and was fed up with the world trying to hold her back.

'No, go away,' he said, throwing back a little of the venom she'd spat into the air.

'Well,' she said, angry that even Tommy didn't understand that nursing was all she'd ever wanted to do, that she'd worked hard, nights in the college after her long days at the mill, in order to achieve her one ambition in life.

'We can stay in touch,' she said.

'Letters?' he said.

'Why not?'

'I've never written a letter in my life and I'm not about to start.'

'You could visit,' she added, seeing now that he was clearly upset at the thought of her leaving.

'I don't want you to go,' he said. 'In fact, I forbid you to go.'

'Do you think you're my father or something?' she said. 'Nobody forbids me to do anything, least of all you.'

'Not good enough for you now,' he said. 'Nurse Elsie in the little white pinafore. You're not even a nurse yet and already you've got airs about you. At least I know my place.'

'You know nothing,' she shouted.

'I'm right then. Not good enough for you. Well, if that be the case, you know what to do.'

'What?'

'End it.'

'What?'

'End it,' he said again.

Elsie couldn't believe that he'd said the words twice.

'Alright,' she said.

Tommy waited, wanting her to take back the words.

'It's over then,' she said.

'Suits me,' he replied, so that Elsie turned and ran home crying.

Tommy stalled on the pavement and watched her, but instead of following he went to The Rock for a drink. He'd make it up with her later; it was a stupid argument anyhow, and they'd never argued before.

In The Rock he realised that he should have followed, but that his pride had got in the way.

He would go to her tomorrow and tell her that he was sorry. If only the letter had come a week later, he thought, lifting out the engagement ring he had bought and intended to surprise her with that evening, then she'd have this now and we'd be engaged; but the next day he did not go to her: he reckoned he'd wait, until she calmed down.

****

26

Conway Mill had three stories and an attic. In front of the mill there was a one-storey building designated as a weaving factory and a number of two-storey buildings at the back that were used for storage and machinery. It was one of eight mills located on or near The Falls Road, with twenty-eight mills in the city altogether. The flax was durable and flexible so that it was reconstituted not just as linen clothing but also as ropes or even hosepipes. The linen mills, as Tommy said, were the city's main employer; at one point they employed forty per cent of the population.

There was the stigma, yes, of being a Millie. Tommy had heard the taunts, but he also felt proud of the women who worked there, his own mother included. For when his father lost his job after the war his mother had not just been the main breadwinner, she'd been the only one. It was true that some of the mills had closed in recent years and that they might not always provide employment. But flax, the blue flowering plant out of which linen was made, had put bread on the table for many, and an honest day's work, no matter what you did, was something to be proud of.

But Tommy understood too that Elsie had ambition: she'd never lied to him about wanting to become a nurse and he'd never wanted to hold her back; it was just the way it had happened. He would bring her the ring and let her go and do the nursing. He could visit. He would wait for her. If only she'd come and tell him that she was sorry for finishing it.

A week passed but she did not come to him. He'd been avoiding her at work; it had been easy for he worked largely in the machinery room, separate from her. But as he queued up on Friday afternoon to collect his wages, for the mill closed early on Fridays, he looked for her, but he saw Lily first. 'Where is she?' he said. Lily shrugged. 'Like that is it.' He was annoyed with Lily's rebuttal but he realised too that he would have to swallow his pride and call.

Tommy headed home and went straight upstairs to his bedroom. He sat on the bed and took off his shoes, putting them neatly together as a pair before lying down on top of the bed. He propped up the pillow against the headboard and lay down to think. He didn't know whether he should take her out and propose, or whether on one knee he should ask her to marry him there and then on the doorstep when he called.

He stood up and opened the wardrobe door, took the engagement ring out of his jacket pocket and lay back down on the bed. He opened the box and looked at the ring. It was a single diamond, set in eighteen-carat gold. Elsie always said she liked a single diamond, a ring without too much fuss as she'd put it; it had cost him all of his savings. Once they were engaged he could start saving again so they could set up home together. He closed the box and put it back in his jacket pocket, laying the jacket on the end of the bed carefully so as not to crease it. He decided that he would propose at her door; it would surprise her; it would be better.

He went downstairs, lifted the white enamel-coated tin basin with the blue rim and poured hot water into it so that it was half-full before adding running cold water from the tap. He'd have preferred to have had a bath in the tub in front of the fire, but there wasn't time for he wanted to be at Elsie's house sooner rather than later. He took out the

28

shoe polish from under the stairs and rubbed it thickly onto his brogues in circular motions. The shoes were heavily studded at the bottom – for the studs helped the soles to wear longer; Tommy also liked the sound they made on the pavement. He buffed the shoes and ran upstairs with them.

He was glad there were freshly ironed shirts in the wardrobe, for time was wearing on. He pulled out his best white cotton shirt and his best navy tie and hung them on the back of the bedroom door, but he couldn't resist looking at the ring again – the lining of the box was cream and puffed up so that the ring sat tilted forward. He couldn't wait to see Elsie's face.

It was a spring evening and the sun was setting on The Black Mountain when he left the house. It was low in the sky so that the streets and houses and buildings were cast in half-shadow.

He stopped at the corner shop to buy flowers. The road was quieter than it had been earlier in the day though it was hard to imagine it as it had once been – a mere country lane leading out from the city centre and up towards Hannahstown Hill and the mountain.

Tommy crossed the road and turned into Rockdale Street. The rag and bone man had parked his cart and aging docile horse, but Tommy, who always liked to banter with the ragman, was singularly focused and didn't pay any attention to him. He checked for the ring, straightened his tie, and rapped the door.

Elsie's mum opened it. She looked at Tommy and at the flowers and shook her head from side to side.

'She's started her nursing training in England,' she said.

'Gone? But she wasn't meant to have gone until October.'

'She asked could she start early. A vacancy arose.'

'But,' said Tommy as he reached into the inner pocket of his jacket where his hand touched and lingered on the engagement ring.

'Tommy,' Elsie's mother said, 'I didn't want her to go, if that's any consolation. Here,' she said, holding out an address, 'she asked me to give it to you if you called'.

'Thank you,' said Tommy, 'but I won't be needing that. Here,' he said, handing her the flowers, 'you might as well have these.'

She held out the address. 'Take it,' she said.

Chapter 3

'Why are you not married?' said Alexander as he looked up at Elsie.

'Too old, I guess,' she said laughing.

'Really though, why aren't you?'

'Never mind that.'

'You could marry me,' he volunteered as he squeezed her hand, 'I mean, when I grow up.'

'Maybe I will,' she said as she winked at him.

'We'll miss you both over Christmas,' said Sister Well as she slipped in front of them to open the door.

Elsie stooped down to pick up Alexander's white plastic bag of belongings.

'Oh,' she said out loud, 'I nearly forgot.' She put the carrier bag back onto the floor, unbuttoned her outdoor coat and withdrew a small parcel from her apron pocket; it was wrapped in Christmas paper and tied with a red ribbon. 'Don't be telling anyone else,' she said in a hushed voice, 'for I never bought for everyone.'

'Tell what?' said Sister Well as she took the parcel and concealed it within the folds of her habit before waving them goodbye.

Once outside Elsie walked with her head held slightly higher than usual, but she was nervous too and at first gripped Alexander's hand a little too tightly. When they had strode a half-mile or so down the Ormeau Road her grasp relaxed so that eventually she was able to let go. Alexander ran slightly ahead of her to look at the shops, at the sky, at the world with a newfound zeal that manifested itself in the occasional hop, skip and jump.

'Careful,' she admonished when he jumped up and kicked his heels. Alexander laughed but ran back to take her hand. 'Now,' she said, 'I've made the little room up for you, but I'll leave the door open and if you wake up in the night you can come into my room.'

Alexander's eyes lit up. 'I'll have my own room?' he said.

Elsie laughed, 'Yes, your room, for as long as you want it.'

'Then that'll be just about forever,' he said.

'And I've got fish fingers for tea. You like them, don't you?' Alexander nodded. 'Now,' she continued, 'there's a rock at the top of the street and you can go and play on that with the other kids. There's Robert, Lily's son, he's a good boy and some other boys too, but you mustn't go to the bottom of the street. It's a big road and there's too much heavy traffic.'

Alexander was still thinking of the room that was waiting for him and now he tried to envisage the rock and how big it was, how big a rock must be to be able to play on it.

They got a Trolleybus into the city centre and took another bus up The Falls Road.

When they got off Elsie took his hand; he could feel that she was tense. It was dark and the headlights of the traffic glared fiercely at them as it zoomed past. Alexander rubbed his eyes. 'We're nearly there,' she said as they turned into Rockdale Street.

32

'That's clever,' said Alexander, smiling up at her as she put her hand through the letterbox of number forty-nine and pulled out a long string with a key attached to the end of it.

'You look tired,' she said as she opened the front door, standing back to let Alexander go in first. He shrugged his shoulders and held back, but when she pushed open the inner door and it released a chime Alexander smiled, for the noise reminded him of the door of Nazareth Lodge.

It was cold inside. Elsie raked the slate off the top of the fire and the flames soon rose, forming shadows on the walls. She moved to the scullery as he sat with his duffel coat on, toying with the wooden buttons that he couldn't quite manage to push through the loops.

'Elsie,' he shouted through to her. She came running from the scullery. 'It's only the buttons,' he said, 'I can't get them through the loops and I need to pee.'

She undid his overcoat and led him through the scullery, out down two steep concrete steps and into the yard. The toilet was beside the coal shed, at right angles to the yard door.

'Someday,' she said, holding the door slightly ajar as he peed, 'I'm going to have an indoor bathroom, with a toilet and a washbasin and a bath where you can just lie in silky bubbles for hours and hours and hours. And not even answer the door if it knocks.'

'Silky bubbles?' he said as he came out from behind the toilet door.

'Yep,' she said, raising her eyebrows and rolling her big blue eyes around her head.

'Can I have silky bubbles too?' he said, looking up at her as she opened the coal shed door that seemed to have

33

more coal in it than there was space to have and that, as she opened it, tumbled out at her feet.

'Course,' she said. 'You will have silky bubbles and silk pyjamas and even,' she added, 'a silken robe.'

'Wow,' he said, suddenly remembering that she'd got fish fingers for tea.

Elsie shovelled coal into the black plastic bucket and as she closed the latch on the wooden door Alexander offered to carry it. She stood back while he bent forward as a heavyweight lifter might: stretching his fingers in preparation for the big lift before bending to heave at the bucket, but it refused to budge.

'Together?' she said.

Alexander smiled, rolling his eyes in imitation of hers as they carried the bucket into the house and set it down on the hearth. He held out his blackened hands, palm upwards.

'You've a bit on your nose too,' she said, threatening him playfully with her own blackened hands. Alexander giggled.

She took his hand and led him into the scullery and propped him up on the drainer beside the sink. She washed her own hands under the running tap and then filled a basin with lukewarm water, soaped the flannel and passed it to him.

'Bubbles,' he said, trying to blow at the little ones before he laid his hands flat in the basin to watch more bubbles float to the surface. 'We'll have lots of bubbles,' he said, 'when we get the bath.' She tousled the top of his head and helped him to wash his hands properly.

When she put him to bed and made him kneel beside her on the floor to say their prayers, she thanked God with every fibre of her being for bringing them together. In her heart she knew that he fitted here with her as nothing in her life had ever seemed to fit: not the mill where she'd worked, not the nursing that she'd tried and failed at, not even Tommy whom she'd loved, whom she'd lost. And as she kneeled on the cold linoleum floor she promised God that Alexander would want for nothing that it was in her power to give; she promised that she would protect him always, blessed herself and tucked him into bed.

At the door of his bedroom she left a yellow plastic bucket. 'In the night,' she said, 'if you need to pee.'

Alexander chuckled as he felt the warmth of the hot water bottle at his feet. 'Goodnight,' she said, leaving the door ajar and the landing light on.

****

In the morning when Alexander went into Elsie's bedroom the curtains were drawn and the bedclothes pulled back. 'Is that you?' he heard Elsie shout upstairs.

He turned and walked along the landing where he saw Elsie at the top of the staircase carrying a tray with breakfast things upon it.

'You're up now,' she said, looking from him to the tray.

Alexander nodded as he wiped the sleep from his eyes. She put the tray on the ground and lifted him down the remaining stairs. The fire was lit and the room was warm, even so, she put a blanket around him before retrieving his breakfast from the staircase.

'Nothing special,' she said as he held the tray on his knees. 'It's too cold for the wee room where there's a

35

table, but there's a man coming out today to see if he can get the chimney in that room fixed.'

Elsie watched as Alexander ate the bowl of Weetabix and drank back the full glass of Del Monte orange juice. He slurped his cereal and apologized when he spilt a bit. 'As long as you eat it all up,' she said, returning from the kitchen to give him hot toasted Ormeau bread with butter and Hartley's blackberry jam on it.

'Did you sleep well?' she asked. Alexander nodded.

Elsie had been up since six-thirty; the scullery was scrubbed, the carpet in the living room brushed and Alexander's white cotton vest and underpants washed out: they were drying over the edge of the mantelpiece, weighted down at the edge with heavy ornaments. The fire blazed but she managed to squeeze another shovel full of coal into it.

'So,' she said turning. 'What would you like to do today?'

Alexander shrugged. He could think of nothing he wanted to do more than sit with her in front of the fire.

'Cat got your tongue?' she said laughing.

He remembered the rock that she said he could climb and the name of the boy Robert, Lily's son. 'Would it be alright to call on Robert?' he said. But as he spoke Robert stood on the other side of the front door, anxious to meet the friend that he too had been promised.

'You'd better answer that,' said Elsie as she removed the tray from his lap. Alexander stretched his legs to the floor, stood up and opened the inner door. He reached up to the latch on the front door, standing on his tiptoes, but he was too small. Elsie leaned over the top of him and opened it.

'Hello,' said Robert, curiously eyeing up his newfound friend.

'I'm Alexander,' said Alexander as he extended his hand out to shake Robert's hand.

'Right,' said Robert, failing to retrieve his own hands from his trouser pockets. Alexander felt embarrassed.

'Go on now and play,' said Elsie. 'But mind the road.'

Elsie grabbed the duffel coat off the balustrade and followed them into the street. 'It's cold,' she said. Alexander noticed that Robert didn't have a coat on.

'Can we climb the rock?' said Alexander to Robert.

'I can climb it,' said Robert, tapping his chest twice with his closed hand. 'But it's hard, especially the difficult bit.'

'Are they alright?' shouted Lily as she leant out the window of number fifty.

'Best friends already,' said Elsie.

'He's lovely,' said Lily. Elsie bit on her lower lip, attempting to disguise the proud, nervous smile that lurked there.

****

The four days passed too quickly. As Elsie took Alexander by the hand onto the Trolleybus to bring him back to Nazareth Lodge the rain came down and a bitter wind blew. She was glad that they'd gone shopping on the Saturday and that his new duffle coat that covered his bum and legs and stretched slightly long off his wrists, kept him warm. There was nothing particularly wrong with the other duffel coat, but the clothes in the children's home were shared and she wanted him to have his own coat that

37

he could keep. She wondered too why she had been so anxious about his stay. He was, as she had always known, an easy child to look after.

Alexander looked forward to going back to the children's home. He had stories to tell, real stories, of the rock and the difficult bit he'd climbed, even though, as Robert had said, only boys of nine or ten could usually climb that bit. He remembered the goat that hid behind the hedge at the top of the rock and how it had frightened him when it bayed: this he would not tell. In fact he might say to the other kids that it was a horse and that he'd got to sit on it.

He thought of Christmas morning – ripping open the present that Elsie had wrapped up for him and placed under the tree. She'd pointed to a half-finished glass of milk on the hearth and a half-eaten biscuit as evidence that Santa had definitely been and gone. When he ripped open the paper he found a cowboy hat and a silver gun inside.

Robert got the same present and they'd played every day on the rock, shooting pellets at the goat and at each other, pretending they were cowboys in the Wild West. He was sorry that he'd had to leave the gun in Elsie's house, but he still wore the black felt cowboy hat and he kind of liked the new duffel coat too, even though he had to stretch his hand out from under it every time he wanted to pick something up. Elsie said he would grow into it. He liked the thought of that.

Alexander listened to the stories of the other boys and soon realised that not everyone had had a happy Christmas. In some of the houses there had been arguments; one boy had witnessed a full-blown fight, but most of the boys had had a pleasant time and engaged in exaggerated storytelling. It was listening to the other stories that made Alexander feel that he didn't, despite his plans, need to tell them how great Christmas had been. It had been more than great – his first real Christmas, in a proper house, with proper presents and with Elsie.

In the dormitory that night he propped the cowboy hat upon his pillow, remembering all the fun he'd had. But what excited him as he fell asleep was the knowledge that he would go to Elsie's house again. She had promised him that he wouldn't have to wait until the next Christmas for a home visit, though she hadn't told him when he might go home with her again. Perhaps Easter, he thought, trying to count how many weeks there'd be between then and now.

Chapter 4

Elsie spent the four days on which she was absent from the children's home getting the house organized for Alexander's visit, and making plans for adoption procedures. She had had to procure personal documentation: her mortgage deeds, proof of income and birth certificate. It had taken the guts of an afternoon queuing for the birth certificate alone, and when they finally posted it to her, a week later, she discovered that she was born not on the sixth of the month but on the third. It made her laugh to think that she'd always celebrated the day of her christening as her birthday.

On one of the days she had gone to see Bishop Wiseman, but she had been turned away. She would have to ring the diocese office to make an appointment, the housekeeper said. 'The bishop is a busy man. He can't have callers whenever it suits them.' Chagrined and frustrated by her wasted journey, Elsie left the door and rang the diocese office from a telephone booth in the city centre to make the appointment.

When the day of the appointment came she was nervous for, even though she'd been told that any decision rested with the adoption board, she knew that the bishop's consent paved the way.

The grim housekeeper answered the door and asked her to wait in the hallway. The bishop came out from the library and waved for her to come forward. She felt uncomfortable in the large room, running her eyes up and down the mahogany bookshelves that stretched from the floor to the ceiling. A fire roared in the large cast iron fireplace, but the room itself was big and cold and the paint had peeled on the windowsills so that you could see the black rotten timber beneath it.

When she told him of her plans the bishop commended her.

'It's a charitable act,' he said, pontificating on the irresponsibility of those parents who had abandoned their children. He asked her about her circumstances.

She told him that she worked in the children's home herself and had formed a strong bond with the child. She told him that she owned her own home and that she could provide for him.

'All good,' he said.

She told him of the street she lived in and the good neighbours, some of whose children Alexander had already met. She told him that she attended church regularly and assured him that it was her intention to bring him up solidly in the faith.

The bishop nodded and smiled. She felt his gaze strongly, hoping only that he might approve of what he saw. He asked whether she had any children of her own. She shook her head. He noticed that her hands were charred, and the skin in places broken.

'Don't the children in the home keep you busy enough?'

'I intend to leave the home,' she said.

'Oh, I see,' said the bishop.

'So that I can be a good mother,' she added.

'Oh, I do see,' he said. 'Of course, you would need the time.' The bishop got up from his chair. 'I'll do all that I can to support you and your husband's application. Certainly some of those children could be doing with a good home. Now if you'll excuse me,' he said, exiting the room.

Elsie reached for the wedding ring on her finger as the large clock in the hallway chimed; she had not intended to mislead him. She looked through the window and saw the bishop in a long black coat that despite its length did not hide his soutane or petticoat; he wore black gloves and held a black umbrella. Elsie waited, twisting her mother's wedding ring on her finger. The housemaid came into the library and handed her a form.

'The bishop said to give you this,' she said in an irritated manner. 'He's been called away all of a sudden and I've just made his dinner. He'll eat it cold when he gets back,' she said.

Elsie thanked the housemaid and was shown to the front door; it closed promptly behind her, almost cuffing her heels.

Outside the rain had stopped and the shadow of a rainbow begun to emerge. She tucked the application into her clutch bag and walked up The Ravenhill Road. With the bishop's consent she could take Alexander out of the home almost immediately, as a long-term fosterer until the adoption papers were signed.

As she walked she imagined her future with Alexander. She had her part-time job in the doctor's surgery: it brought in a weekly income, though in itself it was insufficient for the two of them to live on, but coupled with part-time work in the corner newsagents she could make ends meet. It would be hard but she had her savings to lean on in times of necessity, but suddenly a gust of wind blew, disrupting her thoughts as well as lifting the top page off the application. The wind carried it upwards so that it seemed to float mid-air. Elsie grabbed at it but without luck. It swirled, rising, falling. She grabbed at it again but it moved beyond her reach and began to fall downwards in the direction of a puddle. She reached for it, one last time, and managed to catch it before it hit the ground.

She checked her watch; it had a white face with Roman numerals and a silver, though tarnished, rim. She had replaced the brown leather strap and swore by the time upon it, for her father's watch had never let her down. The visit to the bishop had been quicker than she'd expected and she arrived at the children's home early. She entered the hallway, placed her umbrella in the basket and changed from her outdoor shoes to her flat indoor ones, took her apron from the clothes rack under the hallway stairs and was just wrapping it around her waist when she heard the bishop's voice.

At first she thought that she was mistaken, but as she looked up she saw that it was the bishop; he was talking to one of the nuns further down the hallway. At that moment she realised that she would have to tell him that she was not married. She brushed her hands down the front of her apron and walked towards him. As she approached, the bishop and nun hushed their conversation and moved apart, turning away from her.

43

As he went out through the large stained glass door, she heard the death-knell of her future with Alexander. The nun had clearly told him.

She approached the nun, expecting to have to explain her dishonesty. 'Not now,' the nun said as she strode past, leaving Elsie adrift. She would have to wait until Sister was ready to speak, but how could she wait and how could she work and see Alexander, knowing that she could not keep her promise to him.

Sister Well had seen what had happened as she descended the staircase, but she did not wish to upset Elsie further by asking questions. 'Can you help me?' she said instead, as she put the large bucket of coal she carried down on the parquet floor. 'It's the weather,' she added, holding out her leather strapped arthritic hand. 'Or perhaps my age.'

Elsie lifted the bucket.

'Into the dining room with it,' said the nun. 'For somehow all the buckets have got mixed up, so I'm just rearranging them.'

Sister Well was less than five foot tall; her neck and forehead were heavily creased with wrinkles. When Elsie had begun working in the home, she had asked the other nuns what age Sister Well actually was. 'Old,' they had said. 'Older than any of us.' But she didn't seem old, for she was always busy.

Elsie put the bucket down on the hearth, looked up at Sister Well, and tried to smile.

'There won't be a problem,' said Sister Well.

'What?' said Elsie.

'Fill in the adoption papers, and trust in God.'

'But how did you know?'

'Never you mind,' said Sister Well as she tapped her own nose with her arthritic hand.

Elsie wanted to put her arms around Sister Well and hug her, but even though she was not as distant as the other nuns Elsie knew not to. Her real name was Sister Bruno, but the children had nick-named her Sister Well because she nursed them when they were ill, and because she always seemed to have a bucket in her hand, whether of water or of coal.

'Now help me take these decorations down, for it's January the sixth and bad luck for them to be up any longer.'

'Sister!' said Elsie.

'Nothing wrong with a good old bit of superstition,' said Sister Well. 'Besides, the needles are rapidly falling off. It was a good tree this year though, wasn't it?'

'More than good,' said Elsie as Sister Well laid her hand on Elsie's arm and gently squeezed it.

Elsie could see that even this act of tenderness caused her hands to hurt. She did not know how Sister Well managed to stay so kind and so full of humour when she was in so much pain, for even her ankles and knees were heavily bandaged.

****

When Elsie got home that night the house felt unusually quiet. She was used to being alone and the quiet and the solitude rarely irked her. She cleaned out the ashes in the fireplace and set the fire for the following day. In the scullery she lit the gas stove with the last match from the box of Bo-peep matches. The box was daubed with black coal-dust fingerprints; she always meant to have two boxes, one for the stove and one for the fireplace but it never quite worked out that way.

The kettle was half-boiled when the gas went out, so she moved to the meter underneath the staircase and put some money into it. She reached for the emergency lighter she kept on the top of the cooker and re-lit the stove, holding her hands close to warm them as she waited for the kettle to boil, almost too close, for her cuff came precariously near to the flame and a single loose thread caught the flame; it burnt out.

Having carefully measured out a medium spoonful of tea into the teapot she threw thrift to the wind and spooned out another on top. It was a cold night after all and given her visit to the bishop and all that had gone wrong it seemed a small comfort to allow herself; she lifted the kettle to pour the hot bubbling water into the teapot but became once more distracted by the day's events so that she tilted it too quickly: the water bubbled out and hit the top of her hand. She shoved the kettle back on the stove, turned on the cold-water tap and put her hand under it.

As the water poured from the tap, gradually numbing her hand, she began to cry. How can I mother a child, she thought, if I can't even make a cup of tea?

She dried her hands with the tea towel and applied some Sudocream before moving into the living room.

As she drank the tea the wooden clock ticked loudly; it was a comforting sound. It was clichéd, she knew, but tomorrow was another day and she'd go to the bishop and rectify the misunderstanding. Perhaps, as Sister Well suggested, there was still hope.

The moon shone through the landing window when she went upstairs, and along the hallway where the front bedroom lay. It had been her mother and father's bedroom and the double wooden wardrobe and large wooden chest of drawers had belonged to her mother and father too.

A silver-plated crucifix hung on the wall above the bed. Elsie had bought it to replace the one her father, shortly after Rosie's death, had lifted from the wall and hurled through the window onto the street where it had landed and fragmented. He forbid prayers, icons, even prayer books to be in the house, for her father could not forgive the world, or God, for taking another child from him. He never set foot in a church again.

Elsie did not blame him when he took to the drink, for her mother and father had borne four children and Elsie alone had survived. When he died Elsie maintained that it was not of the drink but of a broken heart.

She had come across the crucifix in Smithfield years later. It was identical to the one that had been smashed, and even though her mother and father were both dead, she had hesitated before buying it. But it was there in front of her, an icon only, but in its purchase an act of reconciliation too.

As a child Elsie sometimes saw Rosie at night, sitting on the end of the bed, watching her. But as she'd grown Elsie saw her little sister less and less. Tonight though, as she fell asleep, she knew that she was not alone: Rosie had come and was at her side, comforting her. Elsie knew that the dead don't die and she didn't care what anyone else thought. Hadn't she seen the dead, talked with the dead, lived with the dead as well as with the living. No, the dead don't die. And as she fell asleep it occurred to Elsie too that Alexander was seven, the same age Rosie was when she was taken from them; but she saw, as it was

47

wont for Elsie to see, only good in this, for she did not believe in coincidence and she did not believe that life could be cruel enough to take Alexander away too.

In the morning Elsie rose early and put on her Sunday best: a blue and white flowered dress that curved around her delicate neck and accentuated her slim frame.

She checked the length in the mirror. Just right, she thought, just below the knees. She applied make-up, then took it off in case the bishop would disapprove, but she looked pale and didn't feel dressed without it so she re-applied a very light foundation and a paler shade of lipstick which was more in tone with her natural skin colour.

As she waited on the bus at the bottom of the street, Lily waved to her from across the road. The bus was stuck in traffic just a few metres from the stop and Elsie hoped that it would get there before Lily, for she did not want to have to explain why she was dressed up on a weekday.

But Lily manoeuvred deftly through the jammed traffic and arrived at the bus stop before the bus. She carried a loaf of bread, The Daily Telegraph under her left arm and a pint of milk in her right. 'Feed the five thousand,' she said, looking Elsie up and down in anticipation of an explanation. None came. 'None of my business I suppose,' said Lily.

'Don't be like that,' said Elsie as the bus pulled into the stop, 'I'll explain to you later.'

The traffic was slow and the time on Elsie's watch slower still. She wiped the condensation from the window with her hand and looked out, trying to distract herself from the meeting with the bishop, but her mind would not focus on anything else. She envisaged the bishop's wrath, his stern gaze condemning her deception, condemning her future. But it was too late to change what had gone before; she must confront him and make amends. If he withdrew his approval, she could go to the board.

She unclasped her clutch bag and took out a pocket mirror to double-check her make-up. The lipstick was bland and she did not like it. She'd only put it on to please the bishop.

'Bloody awful,' she said out loud as she looked at it again, so she took out a paper hanky and wiped it off. He'll find me as I am, she decided, as she rubbed on the brighter plum-coloured lipstick she usually wore.

Despite the early start she'd made it was just before ten in the morning, the time of her appointment, when she arrived at the bishop's house.

'I'll see if he's in,' said the housekeeper, leaving her on the doorstep.

Of course she knows whether he's in or not, thought Elsie as she held the appointment card in her hand. It had been sent to her from the diocese office through the post.

The starch-faced housekeeper returned sooner than Elsie expected.

'He says to go through,' she said, temporarily barring the way despite the invitation.

The bishop sat at the dark-stained worn desk with his back to her; it was pushed into the bay of the window and the top was cluttered with pamphlets and leaflets that had been pushed haphazardly to either side to create a small space in-between where the bishop worked.

'I won't be a minute,' he said as he licked the seal of an envelope, turned it over and laid it on the table. As he filled in the address, Elsie stayed near the door, trying not

49

to watch him, not knowing whether to sit or to stay where she was. 'Please,' he said, waving his hand behind him. 'Take a seat.'

Finally he rose to greet her, apologizing for the absence of a fire.

'Can't get the staff these days,' he joked.

'There's been a misunderstanding,' she said.

The bishop saw how pale she was. He rang the bell.

'I'm afraid you've rather lost me. Perhaps you might explain,' he said. 'But first, if I may?'

Elsie nodded, though she'd wanted to speak first. If he didn't let her, perhaps she would lose the courage to tell him that she was not married, perhaps she would allow the misunderstanding to fatefully go forward, come what may.

'I have spoken to the sisters at the children's home,' the bishop continued. 'You might have seen me there yesterday yourself?' Elsie choked out a yes. 'They speak very highly of you, and of the special bond you and the young boy have.'

The housekeeper entered.

'We'll be needing some tea,' the bishop said. She looked up at the clock. 'Yes,' he said, 'I know it's early. But if you could.'

'Certainly,' she said abruptly as she folded her arms and left the room, leaving the door ajar. The bishop apologised, got up from his chair and closed it.

'As far as I'm concerned you'd make a very suitable guardian for the child. Alexander's his name. Yes?' Elsie nodded. 'You can take him home at any time.'

The bishop looked at Elsie and was more puzzled than ever, for instead of seeing her relief, delight even, he saw her pale complexion turn grey and her features strain.

50

'You still wish to adopt him?' he said, raising his left bushy eyebrow.

'Of course,' she said.

The housekeeper opened the door; she set the tray she carried down on the low table between the two armchairs before walking to the window and drawing the curtains open. 'That'll be all,' said the bishop. As she left the room she again left the door ajar.

The bishop closed the door and returning to the chair poured the tea; he scratched his head as he handed Elsie a cup and saucer. 'Before,' he said. 'You were trying to tell me something?'

The opportunity to speak, at last, caused Elsie's composure to flail and her breath and speech to panic. 'I'm not married,' she blurted out, setting the cup and saucer unsteadily on the table so that it rattled.

The bishop leaned back in his chair. 'I know that,' he said, 'it was my mistake. So, that's what you mean by the misunderstanding.' The bishop rose from his chair and laughed. 'I'm so sorry,' he said as he took one of her gloved hands in his. Elsie stood up. He held onto her hand. 'We are not ogres,' he said. 'It is better for the child to have a mother. You know yourself that once they are over five years of age, the chances of finding them a proper home is next to nil. And he's not, well, how shall I say? Not the perfect child.'

Elsie pulled her hand away from him and tried not to scowl.

'Good Lord,' said the bishop.

He lifted the poker from the compendium and slowly, awkwardly, knelt down on the hearth with his back to her so as to rake the ashes.

He looked lonely there, his black garment melting his figure into the cast-iron surround. A lock of hair fell forward; he pushed it back and turned his gaze around to her. 'Isn't that how most of these adoptive parents are?' he said plaintively. 'The rash he develops on his skin is enough to put them off.'

Elsie shrugged, accepting too that this was true. She had witnessed how the children, lined up sometimes in front of would-be parents, were chosen, or not chosen.

'I'm not saying anything that you don't know already,' he murmured. She did not answer and he turned, once more, to look up at her. 'Please, please sit. He's a lucky child,' the bishop said, 'to have you'.

He laid the poker horizontally on the hearth and reached behind him to use the armchair for support. As Elsie watched she saw, perhaps for the first time, how thin he was, how worn. He was older than she had at first thought, older and perhaps a little defeated too, not by her, but by life, as though he had given it his all and as though it had bled him instead of nourishing him. He did not want to fight and she had no quarrel with him, and so she sat down and paused before speaking, for she wanted her tone to be gentle.

'I can adopt him?' she said.

'It's not my decision. It'll have to go in front of the board.

Elsie nodded, still unsure as to whether she had his support, or not.

'But it's a mere formality.'

Elsie bit the side of her lip.

'There's no need to worry,' he reassured as he got up and held out his hand to her, but she did not want to shake

52

his hand, though she took it and held it, for her instinct was to hug him, but she could not hug him for he was a bishop.

Chapter 5

It was a week to the day of her meeting with the bishop when Elsie brought Alexander home. She had hoped to have the stained-glass window of the inner front door repaired and put in; it had been damaged and blackened by the chip pan fire three years before, along with a great deal of the rest of the house and it had taken time and money to repair the damage, but luckily Elsie had a good insurance policy and they had paid out.

The house had stayed largely fresh after its redecoration: the wallpaper was unmarked and because she liked to keep things orderly the house was immaculate in every respect. But she wanted it spotless for Alexander's arrival and cleaned and dusted every nook and cranny; she even deck-scrubbed the yard and whitewashed the walls of the toilet. And though everything but the linen drawers that she wanted to freshen up was clean, she felt anxious.

The family's linen had served them well over the years – in matrimony and in death. As Elsie stood in the steam-filled scullery, washing the linen, wringing it through the twin-tub and hanging it out to dry she remembered how peaceful Rosie had looked when they had laid her out. As she put the last peg on the line she looked up to the sky, as if God was listening, and thanked him for looking after her little sister.

Still though, it was a pity that there wasn't enough time to have the stained-glass window repaired. It had been badly damaged in the fire and the insurance hadn't been enough to cover the cost of fixing it. Elsie sighed, 'temporary', she knew, was always longer than you thought.

Rosie had loved the window, the blood reds and yellows and the halo around Christ's head. She liked to sit at the foot of the stairs and copy the figure of Christ. She never got the hands right and so they always appeared disproportionate. When Elsie had asked her why she always drew small hands, like those of a child, Rosie giggled and told her, in utmost confidence, that the hands were not Christ's but her own and that she liked the picture so much that she wanted to be in it.

Elsie pushed the twin-tub back against the wall and tidied up before going upstairs to finish sorting the small bedroom. She unwrapped the toy train and laid it on top of the bedclothes, but the room still looked empty. She lifted the train and put it on the side locker; it had cost her more than she'd ever spent on a present and even as she'd purchased it in Robinson and Cleaver's toy department she'd wondered whether it was an extravagance that could not be justified. On the Trolleybus home she'd carried it delicately, as you might carry a basin of boiling water: with both hands and a watchful eye.

But Alexander would love it and she would love him loving it, though now in the small double room the magnificent looking train made the bedclothes and the paintwork look dull. The net curtains on the window that overlooked Beechmount Grove had not washed as well as she'd hoped, despite the second boil wash she'd given them. Elsie jangled the few coppers left in her apron pocket. There wasn't much money left, certainly not for new curtains. By the time she'd pay for the bus and there was some shopping she had to get and she still hadn't bought flowers for Rosie's grave. She sighed and scratched her head. Why was it that ends never met as well as you hoped they would? Still though, she couldn't regret buying the train.

The inner door chimed, 'You in?' shouted Lily.

'Up here. Come on up.' Lily climbed the stairs.

'I can't stop,' she said. 'Just brought a wee box of cakes for you. You've the place spick and span. It's today, isn't it? The wean comes home today?'

Elsie burst into tears and flung her arms around Lily's neck.

'There, there,' said Lily, patting Elsie's back as though she was a child. 'It's all just got to you. It'll be alright. You'll see. You'll make a great mum.'

'You think I won't?' said Elsie jumping back from Lily's embrace.

Lily rolled her eyes and tilted her head forward. 'Didn't I just say that you'd make a great mum?'

'But that's not what you meant.'

'I did.'

'No, you didn't. You think that I'm worried about being a good mum?'

'No.'

'Well why did you say that then? As if I haven't got enough to worry about without you implying I'd be no good at mothering. As if you've got all the know-how and I don't.'

'You're not being reasonable,' said Lily. 'It's the stress.'

'What stress? said Elsie. 'I'm not stressed.' Lily turned and walked down the stairs.

'Don't you walk away from me Lily Mahon,' said Elsie.

'Shist your whist,' said Lily, raising her hands in the air as she continued to walk down the stairs. 'I'm telling you now that you better stop this nonsense and pull yourself together. As for walking away, I'm going nowhere fast except to the scullery to make a pot of tea. And when I do you'll sit down and drink it.'

'I don't want any tea,' said Elsie.

'You'll do as you're told,' said Lily as she turned around at the foot of the staircase, placing her hands indignantly on either side of her hips, 'for I am two months older than you,' she said.

Elsie sat down on the staircase. When she heard the teapot whistle she got up and went downstairs.

'You'll have it stewed stupid,' she said, nudging Lily aside in order to switch off the gas ring.

'It's not the only thing that's stewed stupid this day,' said Lily.

'I'm two months older than you,' said Elsie managing to smile.

'Well, I am,' said Lily laughing.

'You haven't said that since we were kids and you used to say it all the bloody time.'

'I did,' said Lily buckling over.

'You're a bloody eejit, Lily Mahon.'

'Aye, and your best friend.' Elsie nodded.

'I figured we could go to the cemetery together. And before you say you'd like to go alone I'm telling you that I'm going with you and I'll give you your space too.'

****

Elsie could not understand why the graveyard around her was so unkempt. She was glad that Lily had offered to go with her, for it was strange that the day of Rosie's anniversary should coincide with Alexander's homecoming. Lily held her hand as they recited an Our Father and a Hail Mary. The sun shone and the air was calm but a sudden wind broke the silence as Elsie replaced the withered flowers with fresh ones.

'It's Rosie,' said Elsie.

Lily smiled. 'I'll take the tools home,' she said, 'for time's running on and you don't want to be late for the wee one.'

'I'm doing the right thing?' Elsie asked.

'You're the best mother a child could ever hope for,' said Lily. 'The very best.'

Lily took the small spade and trowel and put them back in the plastic bag. When they got to the gates of the cemetery Elsie pulled at Lily's sleeve, halting her. 'If,' said Elsie, 'something should happen to me. I don't mean today or tomorrow but in the future. Would you take him in?'

Lily nodded.

'I didn't want to say that but I'd thought about it. The same goes for me Elsie. If something ever happened to me I'd like to think that you'd be a mother to Robert.'

'Agreed?' they both said.

58

'Agreed.'

But Elsie's stomach was in knots. She had the journey to Nazareth Lodge in front of her and she was fearful that Alexander would not wish to leave. What, she thought, in the grand scheme of things had she to offer him? It was not as if she was rich and she had no husband either. Didn't they say that boys need a father figure?

It was as if Lily had just read her thoughts: 'You know that Tommy will be happy to step in as a father figure. He told me to tell you.'

Elsie nodded, glad to have Lily and Tommy's support but, even so, her knotted stomach ached with fear.

****

Elsie was due at the children's home at two o'clock. The traffic as she sat on the bus seemed slow but her father's watch, reliable as always, indicated that she would be early. She looked out the window thinking of the future and of the second chance she had been given, but she thought too of the day she had returned to Belfast from her nursing training.

Her mother had gone to the docks to meet her, but when Elsie got off the Stella Liner the reception was more utilitarian than welcoming. Her mother took her one small suitcase and set it on the ground. She lifted Elsie's hands that were covered in raw cuts and scars left by her psoriasis. She pulled at Elsie's blouse, though they were in public, as if to parade the further sores and scarring on her neck and upper back. Elsie remembered wanting to get back on the boat. She'd hoped that her mother would be glad to have her home but all she sensed was her mother's disappointment. And when she asked after Tommy, her mother snapped at her, 'It's too late,' she said. 'You left your home, you left me, and you left Tommy. And what for? To come home looking like that?'

But it wasn't too late, for Tommy came to her the day after her return and told her that he still loved her.

The traffic ground to a halt. If I'd married Tommy, Elsie thought, I'd not only have lost my best friend but I wouldn't have found Alexander.

A further five minutes passed, but the bus did not move. 'There's been a crash further on up,' said a pedestrian to the busman through the open door. Elsie blessed herself. It was on this same road that Rosie was knocked down by a lorry. Its front wheels had gone over her legs and all but severed them. She had bled to death as the medics tried to stitch her together where she lay.

Elsie chose to get off the bus and walk the remaining half-mile into the city. The crash in the road had shaken her.

She walked quickly so that she arrived in Castle Street within ten minutes.

It was full of market street traders with their stalls set up on either side of the road – a fruit and veg; a fish stall with fresh pike and salmon; another laid out with cheap cellophane-wrapped plastic toys; an electrical stall that sold toasters and kettles and parts for vacuum cleaners too at knock-off prices, or so they said. The wrapping littered the street and pavement.

One stall sold flowers; it had silver-coated buckets lining its periphery, taking up part of the pavement so that Elsie had to step around them.

Another of the market holders sold carpet cuttings and rugs. The stallholder unfurled a narrow, though long, peach-flowered carpet roll. It would have suited a hallway. 'Just look at that,' he shouted above the thrall, 'as good a rug as you'll find anywhere. Hardwearing too. I'll give you a guarantee,' he said to a passer-by who had stopped to look, 'it'll never go threadbare on you. My word of honour,' he said, striking his breast. 'I'll give it to you for a bargain. In fact, I'll give it to you for nothing.'

The customer's eyes opened wide.

'Did I say that?' he said. 'Yes, keep my word I will. I'll give it to you for nothing. All you need to do is buy this one.'

He unfurled another rug, burgundy with a neat yellowish beige edge; it was clearly a superior rug. The customer looked at the price tag, shook her head and walked on. The carpet man shouted after her, 'I'll give it to you cheap,' he said. She laughed and waved her hand in the air. He turned to his next customer, 'Giving it away today I am,' he said. 'What are you after?'

As Elsie turned left into Chapel Lane she reached into her pocket and took out the coppers. An old unshaven man sat on the ground. He leant against the middle rung of his crutch with his left elbow. His pale blue trousers were torn on one side in jagged edges and hung loosely over the stump of his amputated right leg.

Elsie leant down and placed the coins on top of his cap that he'd placed upside down on the cobbled stones so that they fell softly into the rust-coloured lining.

'God bless you,' he said, grabbing the tail of her coat. Elsie didn't flinch. She'd seen the 'ol critter many's a time and knew that he was harmless.

'There's plenty of good 'uns in the world,' the old man said as he jumped up from the ground with an agility that Elsie couldn't quite fathom. 'Plenty of good 'uns still.'

Elsie smiled.

'Now If I was younger,' he said, swaying to one side, 'We'd have got married. Oh yes,' he said, 'For one like you, I'd have stopped the drink. Sure I would, for one like you. We could have gone to the dances,' he said, holding his arm out as if to link with someone else's though he'd moved a metre or more away from Elsie into the middle of the street. 'I'd have brought you to the dances alright. We'd have danced and danced,' he said, swaying from side to side, 'and I'd have walked you home and given you a wee kiss I would.' He pursed his lips though he stood at a distance from her and closed his eyes. 'Like that,' he said. 'I wouldn't even have looked.' Elsie smiled. He tipped his cap and bowed in front of her before taking a half bottle of whiskey, covered in a brown paper bag, from his jacket pocket and swigging it. 'Oh, if I was younger,' he said winking.

Elsie walked a little further up the cobbled lane and turned left into St. Mary's; it was dark in the foyer. She dipped her right hand into the font and blessed herself. As she went through into the church she could smell the remnants of burnt incense. She put a shilling in the box and lit a candle.

The first was for Rosie. She delved into her purse and retrieved another shilling, withdrew a second candle and lit it using the flame from Rosie's so that the two tallow candles burnt brightly side-by-side. She went into a pew at the back of the chapel and knelt down on the brown tattered footrest to say a prayer.

62

As she left she genuflected, dipped her hand in the font and blessed herself. The quietness of the chapel had calmed her and she felt grateful for that.

Despite the delays she arrived at the children's home early. Alexander was waiting in the hallway and smiled up at her, 'What will I call you?' he asked.

'The same as always,' she said. He nestled into her skirt. 'You happy,' she said.

'As ever I was, or ever will be'.

Late that night when she had put Alexander to bed, tucked him in and read him a story, she knelt in front of the crucifix and said a rosary. She prayed that God would forgive her sins and she asked only that he would protect Alexander and guide her.

Chapter 6

It was nine o'clock before Alexander headed home and already dark. As he turned into Rockdale Street he looked up towards the floodlit three-foot statue of the Virgin Mary. He felt guilty because he owed Elsie for the electricity bill and he felt the Virgin's eyes boring into him.

As if in defiance, he sat on the doorstep of number forty-nine and stared at it. It was set into a rift in the middle of the rock that he and Robert had played on as children. His eyes moved from the statue to survey the street; he imagined it as it was when he was a child, with a hopscotch drawn, scooters flying, younger boys in short pants and older boys playing handball against the gable walls at the bottom of the street. But the life of the street was gone, for most of the neighbours were old and their children had left home. Instead, the narrow street was lined with parked cars.

It was just after nine-thirty when Alexander put his hand through the letterbox. The string was now brown in parts and yellowed. As he went through into the house he saw that Elsie was asleep on the armchair. He lifted the blanket that had slipped off her knees and put it back around her.

'Those fire-lighters are no damn good,' she said.

'You're awake then.'

'Who sleeps during the day?'

Elsie looked up at the clock, pushed the blanket away and got up. She took the clock off the wall, wound it up seven times and placed it carefully back on the beige tiled mantelpiece. Alexander bent down and lifted the poker. He raked the grate and folded the ashes compactly into an old newspaper.

'I didn't mean to stay in the pub,' he said, as he looked down at the floor.

'I'm not angry with you. A young lad needs to have a social life. I'm just worried, that's all.'

'I don't want you to worry,' he said.

'That's what mothers do. It's too late for the fire, but you can set it for the morning if you like.'

Alexander left the ashes out and went back into the front room; he lifted the ornaments on the mantelpiece, most of which were from school trips or outings he'd had as a child. His favourite was the nativity scene, set inside a globed ball, when you shook it blizzard-like snow fell. He looked around the room. Thick wooden rosary beads hung over the banister post at the foot of the stairs, directly facing you as you walked through the inner door. They had always hung there, though he'd never actually seen Elsie use them.

But the room badly needed redecorating: the old grey settee, coated in a silvery sheen that wiped easily with a cloth, was still functional but nothing more, and the carpet, in patches most walked upon, was threadbare. He wished he had the money to refurbish the entire room.

Elsie went into the scullery and lifted the plate of cold meat, coleslaw and bread she'd prepared earlier in the evening, before she fell asleep; it was covered with a crisp red and white tea cloth. She handed the plate to Alexander and told him to take it down to Mrs. Cullen.

'It's late,' she said, scratching her head and throwing her arms wide so that they dropped despondently at her side. 'And sit with her awhile, won't you?'

****

Mrs. Cullen was eighty-nine years old. Her thin dark grey hair was patchy in parts, revealing a motley-coloured scalp of red and purple and white. She sat in a hard plastic wheelchair with a chequered blanket tightly tucked around her too thin legs; they had long since withered in disproportion to the frame of her body.

'It's just me,' said Alexander, entering the house. He went straight through to the scullery, filled the kettle up and plugged it in.

'It's too late for tea,' mumbled Mrs. Cullen.

'What?' said Alexander, coming into the living room.

She fumbled underneath her embroidered shawl and retrieved her teeth, turning her head slightly to one side as she slipped them into her mouth. 'That's better,' she said. 'Is everything all right with Elsie? It's not like her to be late.'

'She fell asleep,' said Alexander settling himself on the arm of the settee facing her.

'That's not what I asked,' said Mrs. Cullen. 'I asked was everything alright.'

66

It hadn't occurred to Alexander that anything might be wrong. He shrugged off the question a second time and went back to the scullery to finish making the tea. He brought two cups in and settled into the armchair.

The fire was still lit in the grate and emitted sufficient light, for Mrs. Cullen had never got used to electricity and barely used it. The room was full of dark, worm-eaten furniture and a black and white portable television lay disused in the corner underneath the dining table beside a rack of old newspapers.

'How's the new home help?' he said.

'Ach,' said Mrs. Cullen. 'She's a nice woman but she's no sooner in than gone. No time.'

'Aye,' said Alexander, handing her a cup of tea.

Mrs. Cullen stretched up and placed her cup beside the ticking clock, tucking her arms back underneath the purple shawl.

As far back as Alexander could remember Mrs. Cullen was old. He had never seen her outside of the house and she didn't talk about herself. Elsie said that she had been married once during the war but that her husband had gone missing, but Mrs. Cullen didn't talk about him, though a black and white picture of a man in uniform sat beside the clock on the otherwise bare mantelpiece. Alexander presumed it was her dead husband.

'Shall I put more coal on the fire?' he said.

'No, no,' said Mrs. Cullen. 'That'll be enough for tonight.' She folded her arms underneath the blanket and leant her head against one side of the back of the wheelchair. Within minutes Alexander heard a gentle snore. He lifted the two cups, brought them into the scullery and rinsed them out.

He returned to the front room and sat back into the chair. Elsie had said to sit for a while so he sat on, listening in the dark room to the quietness and to the slowly dying embers.

'You still here,' mumbled Mrs. Cullen when she woke. 'Bring that plate of food into me. I'm ready for it now.' He arranged the tray in front of her and suggested that he make more tea. She declined but thanked him.

'I'll be going then,' he said.

'Aye, thanks son,' said Mrs. Cullen. 'Tell Elsie I'll see her tomorrow.'

'I will. Goodnight.'

'Goodnight.'

'I've taken the latch off,' he shouted through.

'Aye'

'Night then.'

'Night.'

It was cold outside, but Alexander welcomed the fresh air though he wondered whether Mrs. Cullen managed to get up the stairs at night or whether she slept in the chair. He wondered too how long she'd left to live. If there was a God, he thought, looking up at the eyes of the Virgin Mary, people wouldn't live alone like that, people wouldn't die like that.

The front door of his own house was open, but as he turned to close the inner stained-glass door he saw the edge of a letter underneath the doormat. It was addressed to him on behalf of Her Majesty's Government; he opened it.

His dole had been put on hold pending attendance at an interview the following day; the letter had clearly lain concealed for several days. He would not get his dole

68

check in the morning and he still owed Elsie for the electricity bill.

Alexander sighed, put the letter in his pocket and closed the inner door. Despite there being no fire the house was unusually cold. As Alexander went into the scullery he saw that the back door leading into the yard was wide open, but Elsie usually left it ajar when she went to the toilet and so he presumed that that's where she was, but it was cold so he closed it over slightly.

He wished that she had an indoor bathroom; she'd been dreaming of one for so long and though she'd been saving and the government had fifty per cent grants on offer, she still couldn't afford it.

He switched on the kettle, remembering the money he'd squandered in London when he was younger: twenty, even thirty quid a night on drink, maybe more.

As the kettle began to boil he heard Elsie shout. Alexander rushed outside. The toilet door was half open and Elsie's strong hand gripped the edge of it.

'I'm stuck,' she said. 'Get Lily.'

'Can I help?' said Alexander, 'I'll close my eyes.'

'You'll do no such thing,' said Elsie. 'Now get Lily. Be quick,' she said, 'I don't know how long my back will hold out.'

Alexander ran across to Lily's. Tommy answered the door and shouted up to her so that she came rushing down the stairs; she untied the strings on her apron and flung it over the banister rail.

'Stuck are you?' said Lily outside the toilet door.

'Aye,' said Elsie.

Lily eased herself around the door though there was barely enough space inside for two.

She tried to get Elsie to stand up, but her back wouldn't budge and when she did manage to get Elsie upon her feet they couldn't get the door open wide enough to squeeze through it, for it opened inwards, so Lily put the toilet seat down and stood up on it.

Elsie opened the door and Lily tried to climb down, but as she descended she leant on Elsie's shoulder for support. Elsie squealed and Lily jumped back so that she banged her own head off the cistern. She too squealed.

'A right pair,' said Elsie.

Lily laughed, touching the side of her head with one hand to check for any blood.

'I thought you were here to help and you've bloody well done my back in for good.'

'Shist your wist,' said Lily, 'or you'll have to walk around with your knickers round your ankles for I'll not pull them up for you and, by the looks of you, you won't be able to bend to pull them up either.'

Elsie looked down. She'd forgotten that they were still around her ankles.

'You think so,' she said as she stepped out of her crisp white underpants while gripping her lower back with her left arm.

'Trust you,' said Lily laughing. 'Now can we get out of here?' Lily was still perched on top of the toilet seat where she saw a very large black coal-shed spider creep into a hole in the mortar.

Elsie took a tentative step forward and then a second step before straightening up. 'I'm alright now,' she said as she climbed up the steps into the scullery with ease.

Alexander led her into the front room where he wrapped the blanket around her. He lit the fire despite the

70

late hour of the evening, boiled up a pot of tea and brought two cups into Elsie and Lily who were now laughing and reminiscing about old times.

'That's a picture,' he said as he stood smiling in front of them before bending down to kiss Elsie on the cheek.

'Where's my kiss?' said Lily, holding out her cheek. Alexander blushed, but bent and kissed her on the cheek anyhow.

'I'm away on up to bed,' he said. Elsie and Lily nodded, and watched him as he made his way upstairs. He lay down, with his hands behind his head, on the single bed in the small back room, and listened to their laughter, sighed contentedly and drifted off to sleep.

****

Alexander woke. It had been snowing outside and a red robin was perched on the window ledge, even though it was April. It was too early to get up, so he lifted his library book off the top shelf of his bedside locker. It was about an old man called Jacob Glasgow who brings a child who was murdered in her previous life back from the dead. Alexander wondered whether in the future they'd be able to genetically engineer replicas of people; he wondered too whether that would be a good or a bad thing.

He heard Elsie get up and jumped out of bed, pulled on his striped pyjama bottoms, grabbed his suit that hung on the back of the door and met her on the landing. 'I was thinking,' he said scratching his head.

'Did it hurt?' she said, holding her hand up to his forehead as she pretended to check his temperature.

'You're awful bloody funny. You'll see,' he said.

'What?'

'I'm going to get rich.'

'Are you now?' said Elsie.

'I am,' said Alexander.

'Do you want some breakfast or do you plan to get rich before then?'

'Did you see the snow this morning?'

'No snow,' she answered.

'And a red robin was perched on my windowsill.'

'In April? You don't get robins in April.'

'It had a red breast.'

'Chaffinch perhaps. What do you want with the suit?'

'Will you iron it for me?' he asked. 'I've to go to the dole office for an interview and then to the library, but I also want to get onto that new project for starting up your own business.'

'What business?'

Alexander ran up the stairs and grabbed his library book, 'Second Chances,' he said, waving the book in the air. I realised what it was about and it gave me an idea. I thought of it when I saw the robin.'

'Chaffinch,' Elsie said.

'Aye, and the snow.'

'I'm none the wiser,' she said as she set up the ironing board.

****

In the dole office Alexander took a ticket and waited to be seen. He held the letter in his hand but did not dread the appointment as he had the day before. If they'd discovered that he'd been working in The Rock they would stop his dole and ask him to pay the money back.

That was all. Once his business was up and running he could pay it back easily.

The boy behind the desk was chubby and keen to please. He apologised to Alexander for calling him in: lots of letters had gone out to the wrong addresses because of a computer mix-up. There was no need for Alexander to be there; if he wanted to fill in the form he could, perhaps, reclaim his bus fare.

'Interview?' the boy behind the desk asked as he looked at Alexander's suit.

Alexander stood up, stretching to his full height. 'You could say that,' he replied, as he dusted the lapel of his jacket. The boy apologised for a second time as Alexander turned and left.

He went from the dole office to the Carnegie Library. Inside an old man sat reading a newspaper; otherwise the library was empty, except for a new attendant. Alexander couldn't believe his luck. He approached the desk.

'Have you the list for me?' he said to the young girl with dark curly hair.

'What list?' she said.

'The list of overdue books. Colm said he'd leave it for me.'

She fumbled at the desk, took off her glasses and rubbed her eyes.

'No list,' she said.

'Don't worry about it. He'll have forgotten to leave it. Just print off a list. It'll be on the computer.'

The girl hesitated.

Alexander came around the desk offering to show her how to access it. 'I need it today,' he said, 'so that I can begin the collections.'

'I know how to get to it,' she said. She accessed the list and printed it off.

Alexander said a polite thank you and was just about to leave when he saw Colm, the manager in charge of the library, watching him from the doorway; they had been at school together.

'What's all this?' said Colm, approaching the desk.

'Nothing,' said Alexander.

Colm grabbed the computer printout from Alexander's hand.

'What do you want this for?'

'I thought I'd collect them for you,' said Alexander, trying not to be submissive.

'And maybe charge a fine or two in the process?' said Colm.

Alexander feigned indignance, 'I was doing you a favour,' he replied.

'You mean you were trying out one of your infamous scams.'

Alexander shrugged. 'Never mind,' he said. 'You can't help anyone these days.'

'Get yourself a proper job Alexander,' shouted Colm as Alexander left. 'A proper one.'

Alexander laughed. 'You have a nice day,' he said. Colm was furious and waved his fist frantically at Alexander. This made Alexander laugh even more.

Outside, The Falls Road was busy with traffic, as always. Alexander still had the book 'Second Chances' in his hand, but he had to leave it back to Central Library. He preferred using the city library, for the local one was small, parochial, and besides, he'd already shared too much space at school with Colm – the unimaginative class

74

swot. The sun was shining, faintly warm as it fell against his skin.

He liked to walk, though the traffic alongside him lay bumper to bumper so that the road was noisy: drivers tooting their horns at other impatient drivers who tried to get ahead by changing lanes. It was the world, it was the way people were: busy with their lives. But when did they stop and think?

Philosophy meant 'lover of wisdom' but if you didn't think how could you ever be wise? But to think you had to make time; Alexander knew that, he hadn't always been on the dole. But people didn't make time and the park clearly seen through the iron railings from the busy road lay empty. Alexander imagined Socrates sitting there, beckoning his disciples Plato and Aristotle to sit with him.

'What is wisdom?' Socrates would say to the gathering mob. 'What is beauty?' he would ask.

When he got to the city centre it was bustling with shoppers carrying one, two, maybe three shopping bags. He was glad as he walked through Smithfield and cut into Royal Avenue to see the library within sight.

The library had a black granite base and a Dumfries red sandstone exterior, with a slightly Italianate feel, setting it apart from the surrounding buildings. Miraculously, it had survived through the Belfast Blitz of World War II.

He climbed the steps up to it, and pushed at the revolving door. The door had always felt like a time machine, conveying you from the hustle and bustle of modern life into the world of thought, into the world of books: metamorphosing the very feel of time. He passed through the pillared foyer and walked eagerly up the sweeping staircase to the domed first floor reading room.

75

Alexander loved the library. It was full of ordinary people – eccentric people, old people, students, lonely people, researchers, archivists, novelists, housewives, road diggers. It was beyond class or culture or religion and yet it was also all of these – the best of what has been said and done and sometimes not quite the best either. He loved being able to order whatever books he wanted and as long as he returned them on time it was free too; he'd always wanted to work in a library but he'd no qualifications.

Alexander left his book on the counter. 'It was good,' he said. 'It gave me lots of ideas.' The thin librarian looked up and tried to smile but her countenance remained stern. She left the desk to retrieve the books, returned and set them on the counter. 'Thank you,' he said, lifting the books. He brought them to a table at the far end of the room and sat down to read as the gentle sun through the domed ceiling cast its bright light.

****

When Alexander got home Robert was sitting in the front room talking to Elsie.

'What's with the suit?' he said.

'Nothing,' said Alexander.

They had made plans to go to the pub but Alexander had no money; he went upstairs and rooted through old trouser pockets and coat pockets hoping to find some change. He took off his suit, put on a pair of jeans and a baggy shirt and returned downstairs. As he was going out the front door Elsie slipped a fiver into his side pocket, but he took it out and handed it back to her.

At the bottom of the street two younger fellows were playing handball against the gable wall. In the hope of making some money, Alexander suggested that they have a game. Bets of two quid a head were placed. Winner takes all.

Robert won the first game and stayed on to play the second lad. He won this game too before it was Alexander's turn to play.

Robert was slightly taller but that was not an advantage. If you were smaller you could bend and pick up even a low ball. It was true that Robert was generally better at sports, but over the years Alexander had become equally good at handball, perhaps even better now that Robert spent most of his days sitting behind a desk. Alexander spat on both his hands and rubbed the spittle in.

As the game progressed the score was neck and neck but Alexander still believed that he would win.

Robert served a standard low soft ball. Alexander whacked it so that it bounced and hit the facing gable wall. Robert had time to strategically place the next hit to the edge of the gable wall, at an angle. Alexander had to be quick to reach it. He raced towards it but a car turned into the street and stalled in his pathway.

Robert stood back and put his hands in his pockets, believing that Alexander wouldn't be able to make the hit. But Alexander put one hand on the edge of the bonnet of the car and leapt over it. He dived at the ball and managed to scoop it up before it hit the ground.

The ball shot through the air, but it dipped at the last minute, falling a centimetre short of the baseline mark.

'Sorry mate,' said Robert. 'That was bad luck.'

77

Alexander got up from the ground and dusted his shirt. 'Good game,' he said, shaking Robert's hand, and giving him two quid.

'That rule about obstacles sucks,' said Robert.

'It's a good rule,' said Alexander, picking out a piece of fine gravel that had lodged itself in the palm of his left hand. 'Except when you lose,' he added.

On the way to The Rock Robert stopped outside the bookies. 'Mary would kill me but one bet wouldn't do any harm. Would it?' he said.

Alexander was surprised, for ordinarily Robert hated gambling.

'It'll never win,' he said, as Robert put down a fiver on a fifteen to one horse.

'Don't care,' said Robert. 'I'm feeling a bit reckless.'

Alexander jangled the four-pound coins he had remaining around his pocket. Perhaps his luck would change.

He glanced at the listings in The Daily Mirror and on the runner board and decided on a modest eight to one bet that an old man next to him said was a sure bet. He put a quid down and slipped the receipt into his pocket.

In the pub Robert ordered two pints and set one down in front of Alexander. 'I know the loser's meant to buy, but that was bad luck with the car. Call it a draw,' he said as they took a seat in front of the television set.

The race was due to run in fifteen minutes but when it did Alexander's horse fell at the first hurdle. Robert's held out giving him a run for his money, but came in third. Alexander ripped up his ticket as Robert retrieved his from his pocket. 'Each way,' he said, holding the ticket up and kissing it.

78

'Why is it,' Alexander asked, 'you're such a lucky bastard?'

'Birthright,' replied Robert. 'Anyway, don't be so mean. The next drink's on me.'

Alexander was called behind the bar and asked to work a shift. He was meant to be out for the evening with Robert, but he'd no money anyway, so he agreed to work. He also asked for an advance.

The bar manager shook his head, 'You should know better than to ask.' Alexander pulled out the three quid left in his pocket and laid it down on the bar.

'Put the rest to it and I'll pay you later.'

The manager lifted the money and put it in his pocket. 'It's the last time Alexander,' he said. 'Rules are rules and I can't keep breaking them for you and not for others.' Alexander nodded and thanked him.

'Paid for already,' said Alexander to Robert as the barman set down two pints on the table.

'What?' said Robert.

'I can only stay for two,' said Alexander, 'I've been asked to work a shift.'

'Shame,' said Robert. 'I was looking forward to having a few. I thought we were out for the night.'

'I can't afford to turn down the work,' replied Alexander.

'Y'know, I don't have all the luck,' said Robert reflectively.

'Yes you do. Always bloody well did.'

'I don't.'

'The boy with the white teeth and the swarthy skin gets the girl, gets the job, gets the house, gets the kids and lives happily ever after.'

79

'What's eating you?' said Robert.

'Nothing,' said Alexander. 'Forget about it.'

'It's not perfect,' said Robert. 'To be truthful, I'm fed up with work, fed up sitting at a desk and watching the same bloody clock turn at a snail's pace. I reckon that I've spent more time there than I have with my own family.'

'Now who's moaning,' said Alexander.

'You started it.'

'Forget it,' said Alexander.

'Was it the job? Is that what's annoyed you?'

'What job?' asked Alexander.

'The suit. You must have been for a job interview.'

Alexander didn't answer. When they got three quarters of the way through their drinks he apologised for being out of humour. Robert talked about the tree house he planned to build for his youngest son Peter and about Emily's last school report, all A's. As he was leaving he invited Alexander to dinner on Sunday, 'Mary asked me to ask you.' Alexander smiled. 'Sometimes I think you're still sweet on her,' said Robert.

'Don't be daft,' Alexander said. He worked his shift after Robert left and when he got home Elsie was already in bed, so he laid his wages down on the mantelpiece on top of the electricity bill.

Chapter 7

St. John's had always been full, even for early morning mass, but as Elsie looked around there was only twenty or thirty people in the pews and most of those were pensioners like herself. She missed the old church, it was damp, that was true, but it had more character. The new St. John's hadn't even got a spire on the outside, just a cross stuck on top of a concrete wall.

Elsie walked up the aisle and queued to take communion. She held out her tongue for she didn't like the new way of taking the body of Christ on your hand. She walked back down the aisle and felt a sharp twinge in her side, causing her to stall at the edge of the pew in front of her own. She rubbed her side and moved to her own seat, marked with the missal she had left there, genuflected and entered.

Instead of kneeling she sat down and opened her clutch bag as gently as she could, but the silver clasp clicked loudly. The older man, behind her, tutted. She massaged her stomach, hoping that the indigestion tablet would start to work quickly. The pain was more severe than usual and on the way home she paused several times to rub her side; it didn't seem to hurt so much if she wasn't moving.

When she got home Alexander was dressed in his suit. She thought, at first, that he was going to church and smiled at him approvingly; but when he told her that he didn't want dinner because he was going to Robert and Mary's she scowled at him.

'You don't need to wear your good suit to go to their house,' she said.

'I like to look well. Robert's always dressed up on a Sunday and if I go in my casuals it doesn't feel right. Mary's always dressed up too.'

'And why's that?' she asked him. 'Because they go to church. They don't dress for you but for church and you'd be better going there yourself instead of ...'

'What?' said Alexander.

'It doesn't matter,' said Elsie, gripping her side. 'Give me my bag.'

Alexander reached for the clutch bag she used on Sundays only, or on special occasions. She took out an indigestion tablet and popped it into her mouth. 'Wear your bloody suit if you like but wear it because you want to and not to impress some married man's wife.'

'I'm not trying to impress her. They've been married twelve years.'

'Yes, and you've been single for most of those. Why is that Alexander? Can you tell me why?'

'So you think I still fancy her?'

'I didn't say that.'

'You might as well have.'

'Well, do you?'

Alexander stepped back.

'I haven't done anything Elsie except put a suit on and I don't understand.'

82

'I'm not getting any younger Alexander and it's time you moved on, found yourself a girl and settled down.'

'I'll take the suit off if it pleases you,' he said. Elsie didn't answer; he went upstairs anyhow and changed into his casual trousers. He returned downstairs and lingered in the living room, hoping that she might stop fussing with the ornaments on the mantelpiece and talk to him. But she didn't talk, and as he closed the inner door he heard her mutter, 'It'll come to no good.'

Alexander stepped off the bus with a bouquet of flowers in his hand. The lilt in his step and the way he kept swiping at his trouser legs and jackets to remove dust that was not visible to the naked eye made him look, to the plump elderly lady who also carried flowers, like a young lover. She smiled up at him, but as he passed by a bag of Bonbons fell out of his jacket pocket. She bent down, picked them up, and handed them to him. 'For the kids?' she said. Alexander nodded.

'And you?' he said, pointing towards her own bunch of flowers.

'For my husband. Not that he'll notice. He never liked them unless they were in the garden. Said flowers weren't beautiful unless they had roots in the ground.'

'Said?'

'He's dead. I'm on my way to the cemetery. It's nice and quiet there as long as the rain holds off. Is she a good cook your wife?' Alexander shook his head from side to side. The old woman looked at his left hand.

'You young'uns these days! You shack up together, buy a house, have the kids and think about getting married almost as an afterthought.' Alexander smiled, not wanting to contradict the plump lady's mistake.

'Ah,' she continued, 'as well you might smile. But look.'

She opened up the lid of her trolley and pulled out a rusted Ogden's tobacco tin, pulled the lid off and held it up in front of him. Alexander saw a mass of stubbed out cigarette butts.

'In the bird-shed,' she said. 'Always smoked those damned things in the bird-shed. For I wasn't for having none of that smell in the house. Out in the bird-shed morning, noon and night. Well, I told him, again and again,' she said, 'they'd get to him in the end.'

'But these butts aren't his. I dumped his on his grave the week he died. Now I pick them up from the street.' She produced a polythene glove from her left pocket and waved it from left to right. 'Wouldn't touch the darn things myself. And every month on a Sunday, for he died on a Sunday,' she said, leaning confidentially towards Alexander, 'I bring him two presents: his rusted tin full of butts and I dump them on the grave, cover them over with soil, of course, and then I take out the old flowers and put fresh ones in.'

The plump lady placed her hand on her stomach as she began to laugh. She laughed so much that her belly moved up and down and a laughter tear fell from her right eye.

'Oh Jesus,' she said, taking a handkerchief out of her right pocket. 'I don't know why I'm telling you all this. But you see, it was like that, he complained about the cut flowers and I complained about the smell of the cigarettes, and he still got the cigarettes and I got the cut flowers and that was just the way it was. So that's the way it has to go on. Once a month I get the flowers and bring them to him, just to annoy him, and then dump the butts on the grave,

84

just to say, I told you so, and because I loved the old bugger and once,' she said, leaning closer into Alexander, 'I even bought his favourite's, hard to get, Blues: they don't have a filter on them, and I left the packet with him. Just in case,' she said. 'I mean I know that the dead can't eat or drink or anything but you never know. You just never know.'

The plump lady replaced the lid of the rusted tobacco tin and put it back into the top compartment of the trolley, pulling the tartan cover over it. She wiped her eyes with the handkerchief and blew her nose, before pushing the handkerchief into the cuff of the sleeve of her pale yellow cardigan. As the bus pulled up, Alexander took her hand and helped her onto it, lifting the trolley up the step.

'Thanks son,' she said. 'You be good to your wife. It's a short time. A short time for all of us.'

Alexander nodded and as the bus pulled off he felt the urge to wave at the little plump lady who was still in conversation with her dead husband; but he felt jealous too: of the dead man whose wife loved him so much.

****

As Alexander walked up Queen Street into Lough Beg Park, Emily came skating towards him. She was only nine years old and had blonde curly locks. She sucked on a lollipop and wore, what seemed to Alexander a ballerina's costume; it was pink and white and laced around the collar. She stopped skilfully in front of him.

'Sweets,' she said, spying the Bonbons.

'Pink, your favourite,' said Alexander. Emily took the sweets, kissed him on the cheek and skated off with the

85

Bonbons clutched in her right hand. She made it to the front door of her parents' house and yelled inside that Alexander had arrived.

Robert sat, as usual, in the burgundy armchair playing with the remote control. 'I'm going to get Sky one of these days,' he said.

'Hello Alexander, nice to see you. What have you been doing with yourself?' said Alexander.

'I am.'

'What?'

'Going to get all the sports channels. It's only fourteen quid a month to start with.'

'What's it like,' said Alexander, 'to speak in monologue?'

'What?' said Robert.

'You're not listening to me at all.'

'Nope.'

Alexander swiped at his friend's head. Robert ducked. Mary shouted from the kitchen for one of them to set the table. Alexander volunteered but Robert eased himself out of the armchair and said that he'd better do it. When he'd set the table he came back into the sitting room and handed Alexander a can of Carlsberg. 'It'll be a wee while yet for dinner,' he said, 'she forgot to light the spuds; but there's something in the garage I want to show you anyway.'

Robert opened the garage door and pointed at the pile of wood he'd bought for the tree house. The wood was weighted down in the middle and at either end with red bricks to stop it from warping, for he didn't know when he'd actually get around to using it.

'It'll go up there,' he said, looking through the garage window into the garden, 'between the two firs.'

'Never built a tree house,' said Alexander.

'Well, if you had've, I expect I'd have known about it,' said Robert. 'What age were you when you came from the home?'

'I don't talk about the home,' said Alexander. 'You know that.'

'I know, but what age were you?'

'Seven,' said Alexander, biting his lip.

'Sorry Alexander. I didn't mean to pry. Was it that bad?'

'No, it wasn't bad at all. I just don't like talking about it. My home was with Elsie. As far as I'm concerned I've never had any other home. At least, that's the way I like to think about it.'

'Fair enough,' said Robert.

As they were making notes on the design of the tree house Peter came up the tarmac driveway sobbing out loud; he held onto the side of his head.

'She hit me,' he said, when he got to the open garage door.

'Who?' said Robert.

'Emily. She said that I wasn't her brother and that even if I was that she didn't play with boys and then she hit me with something and it hurts.'

Alexander handed Peter the large bag of jellies from his jacket pocket.

'Alexander's going to help us with the tree house.'

'I am?' said Alexander.

'Please,' said Peter, ''cause then I might have it before Christmas.'

'If you're good,' said Robert.

'I'm always good,' said Peter.

He pulled open the bag of jellies. Two tumbled to the ground; he picked them up, blessed them and popped them into his mouth.

****

Throughout dinner Alexander kept thinking of the little old plump lady. He took little or no interest in either Emily or Peter and ate his dinner quietly, issuing the occasional comment on Mary's cooking, but even this reminded him of the little plump lady's comments on whether or not his wife was a good cook. What was he doing here on a Sunday afternoon except living, as he so often did, in other people's lives?

He stayed for a short while after dinner and decided to walk home, though it was six miles, to clear his head. But he was only halfway through the journey when his polished black brogues began to cut into his feet; he only ever wore them with his suit but had kept them on when he'd changed. He watched the black clouds gather and when he finally arrived back in Rockdale Street he was soaked through so that the water dripped off the shoulders of his navy corduroy half-jacket like that from the broken ends of a gutter pipe.

'You're home early,' said Elsie. It was more of a question. Alexander bent down and kissed her on the forehead.

'You're right,' he said as he held his arm out for her to lean on. She got up from the armchair and returned with a towel. He knelt in front of the fire as she wrapped the towel around his head.

'You'd think I was just a kid,' he said.

'You are,' she said.

She finished tousling his hair, draped the towel around his shoulders, went into the scullery and returned with a pot of tea and a packet of digestives.

The room was dark and the flames created shadows on the walls of the living room that seemed to dance.

'Tell me,' he said, as his pallor warmed, 'about the day you went to see the bishop.'

Elsie laughed, and told him.

'You didn't tell me before that the strap on your shoe broke just before you went in.'

'Didn't I?'

'No.'

'Tell me,' he said, still sitting on the floor in front of her 'about Rosie.' He'd heard all the stories before but he never tired of listening to them: there always seemed to be some new detail that caught his imagination. 'Do you still see her?' he asked.

Elsie sighed, 'You think I'm an old fool, don't you?'

'No.' Alexander shook his head. 'But do you still see her?' he said.

'Not so much see her,' she admitted, 'but I know she's there.'

Alexander looked into the fire and at the dancing walls and at the staircase that swept up from one side of the living room to the bedrooms upstairs.

'I don't think you're an old fool,' he said.

'No?'

'I never told you this before, partly because I used to think it was just the stories you told me and that it was the stories I remembered.'

89

'Tell me what?'

Alexander lifted the poker and began to play with the fire. 'I saw her too,' he said, 'on the first night I came to live with you: the day of Rosie's anniversary. You'd left the train for me on that night.'

'When I went to bed,' he continued, 'I lay awake for a while. I wanted to go into your room to check that you were really there, that it wasn't all a dream. I was just about to get out of bed so I'd sat up and there at the end of the bed was a young girl, just the way you describe Rosie; she was pale-skinned with dark curly hair and her eyes were blue, like yours. She sat smiling at me. I wasn't frightened at all for I could feel that she was happy for me. She held out her hand; it fitted almost perfectly into mine and she climbed into the bed with me, still holding my hand. We fell asleep. In the morning she was gone. I never saw her again after that, though sometimes I could feel that she was there.'

'Why didn't you tell me?'

'I don't know. I was the outsider. I didn't want to come between the two of you.'

'And did Rosie make you feel that way?'

'No.'

'Well then. You're talking a load of nonsense.' Elsie got up from the chair. 'It's time for bed,' she said. 'Rake that fire out before you go and don't forget to put the fireguard on.'

'I didn't mean to upset you Elsie.'

'You haven't,' she said as she went upstairs without saying goodnight.

Chapter 8

Robert worked in the city centre filing law documents. He worked hard, was punctual, was, once upon a time, full of ambition, but he always said what he thought and this more often than not got him into trouble.

In his youth he'd dreamt of fast cars, fancy apartments, women on tap and a lifestyle of travel and wealth. Instead he had a corner of an open plan office floor and was surrounded by younger clerks. Someday, he thought as he sat at the desk, they too would arrive at mediocrity and wonder how or why they got there. He scrawled the word 'mediocrity' on a sheet of paper, followed by the word 'lacklustre', 'forgettable', 'unexceptional', 'prosaic' – he liked that one – 'ordinary', 'no great shakes', 'so-so', and finally arrived at the word 'boring'.

Robert tried to imagine the kind of freedom Alexander had: he could get up each day and do as he pleased, go where he wanted; a bachelor had no responsibilities – no wife or children to look after and no mortgage to pay.

He looked up at the calendar on the office wall. Beside it a sign on the bulletin board read: 'Stuckness is only a new beginning.'

Robert wished with all his heart that the aphorism was true, but he'd felt stuck for some time and the morning, as usual, past slowly so that when a faint alarm he'd set himself sounded on his computer he felt relieved. He saved the document he was working on mid-sentence, lifted his lunchbox and draped his coat over his arm.

Once outside he pulled off his tie and opened the top button of his shirt before heading to the Cathedral Quarter. He had to pass by the Albert Clock on the way; it was built on wooden piles on marshy reclaimed land and the River Farset ran under it and around it so that the clock's poor foundations caused it to progressively lilt; it now leaned four foot off the perpendicular. Robert adjusted his gait as he past it, for he had fallen into the habit of stooping forward as he walked instead of standing tall.

But as he past it he remembered the Celtic myth that inanimate objects sometimes held captive the souls of the departed, until they were called and released, so that he looked intently at the tilting clock. But whose soul lay in its foundations? For so many had passed there, civilians and soldiers and sailors and prostitutes alike.

He turned left into High Street and left again up Skipper Street, jumping aside onto the narrow pavement as a lorry spat up muddy water from the road, before arriving at the cobble-stoned entrance of The Duke of York – a pub he favoured, like his grandfather before him. He ordered a pint of Carlsberg and sat at a table in the corner.

The afternoon at work passed as tediously as the morning and Robert wondered how many more years he could sit there before all of him died.

On the way home he drove his Citroen Picasso a little faster than usual and when he got there he rummaged through his video collection.

Mary laid the table and opened a tin of Brandy to feed Samson. She asked Robert to help Emily and her friend with the scarecrow they were making in the back garden.

'But I was going to watch a video,' he said, before relinquishing. 'There's nothing here anyway,' he muttered as he tumbled the videos he held in his hand back into the drawer.

'And bring these out to them,' said Mary. She handed Robert an old pair of trousers.

'I like these,' he said as he held them up against himself.

'Don't be daft. You haven't worn those in donkeys. Besides,' she said, as she turned one of the trouser legs around and poked her finger through a hole. 'Mothballs.'

Emily took the trousers Robert gave her and put them on the legs of the scarecrow. 'But Daddy,' she said. 'We wanted a female scarecrow.'

'Umm,' her father said. He knew Mary was busy getting the dinner ready and he didn't want to bother her.

'Please,' said Emily. Her father nodded.

'Take the old blue one,' Mary said. 'The buttons have been missing for ages and I'll never get around to mending them. Besides, it's faded.'

Robert went upstairs, returning almost immediately with the skirt. But it was the wrong blue skirt so Mary switched off the rings on the electric cooker and went upstairs to fetch the one she'd asked him to bring.

'Sorry,' he said as she handed the skirt to him.

'It's okay.'

'I'm a bit useless today. But we'll make a good scarecrow.' Mary nodded.

93

'Right then,' he said to the two children. 'It's a female scarecrow you want.' The children giggled.

Robert pushed the wooden legs, made of two brush stems, deeper into the ground and wedged a couple of bricks on either side.

'She's a tramp,' said Emily. 'That's why she doesn't look very pretty.'

'And that's why,' her friend added. 'She's got no shoes.' The two of them giggled.

'We'll call her Aunt Sally,' said Emily. Leanne clapped her hands together to applaud the name Emily had chosen.

'Dinner's ready,' shouted her mother through the open window of the kitchen.

Emily's friend waved goodbye and climbed up on her bicycle.

'See you tomorrow,' said Emily.

Peter came up the pathway gasping and sobbing.

'Here's cry baby,' said Emily.

'Enough of that,' Robert said. He turned to Peter, 'What's wrong?'

'I wanted to be in the football team, but they said I was too young and that I couldn't play football anyway. But I can play football, can't I Daddy?'

'It's their loss,' said Robert, wishing that his son didn't have two left feet.

'And Emily told me I was a sissy,' said Peter.

'I didn't,' said Emily.

'You did,' said Peter

'Did you or didn't you?' said Mary who had come out from the kitchen to find out what all the crying was about. 'The truth,' she warned with pointed finger.

'Well, we were making a female scarecrow and so I told him to go and play with the boys. It's not our fault that he can't play football.'

'You did then,' said her mother.

Emily nodded.

During dinner Emily stretched her legs under the table and kicked Peter on the shinbone. He yelled out, dropped his spoon full of food onto the floor, got off the chair, picked the spoon up and smiled, for the food hadn't spilled.

When he stood up he catapulted its contents across the table, missing Emily marginally.

'Enough,' shouted their mother.

Emily complained, but when they were sent straight to bed after their dinner as their mother had promised Emily switched on the side-lamp and read contentedly; it was the story of The Happy Prince, her favourite. In the next room Peter cried himself to sleep.

After Robert and Mary tidied up they decided that they would also have an early night. As Robert got into bed he felt more tired than he'd ever felt in his life; Mary climbed in beside him and cuddled into his back. Before long they drifted off to sleep.

In the morning Mary was up early as usual. Robert slept late, woken only by the sound of the vacuum cleaner on the staircase. He went in for a shower and shave, but as he looked into the mirror he saw a single grey hair: his first.

He checked through the rest of his hair, pulling it from side to side and, using the small shaving mirror, he checked for further greys around the back of his head. There were no others, at least none that he could see. It seemed to him that that one Friday in the office had aged him more than the last five years; it also seemed to him that the particular colour of grey was exactly the same as his father's: a dirty lanky shiny grey. He plucked it out and threw it into the waste bin. He wiped the dust off a bottle of gel that lay on the top of the bathroom cabinet, opened the lid and peered in at its contents before dipping his forefinger and thumb in; it was tacky and perhaps out of date, but he rubbed it between his fingers anyway and applied it to his hair, spiking it up. He looked in the mirror and flattened it back down a little, rubbing more gel into his hair in an attempt to remove the line of its usual parting; the shade eventually blurred and then disappeared.

He applied more gel, spiked it up again and turned his head to the side to check out his profile, but he was dissatisfied with the new look and got back into the shower to wash the gel out. He leant his left hand against the tiles as the water rushed in a stream down his neck and back and for a while there was only himself, the hot gushing water and a day long ago when Alexander and himself and his other mates were swimming in The Cooler:

It was a hot dry summer. Hosepipes were banned due to a lack of rainfall and the dust and dirt lay thick on the ground. The black taxi's that serviced the busy Falls Road wore a thick mask of grey dust and the fumes of the traffic in general gathered and hung in the air making it feel stale. When Robert suggested to Alexander that they head up to the swimming baths in The Falls Park, known locally as The Cooler, it didn't take much persuasion to gather together a gang of four boys and four girls.

96

The girls put their swimsuits on underneath their clothes before leaving home but the boys wrapped their togs in a towel, carrying them underneath their arms.

The boys walked ahead, bunched together, and turning occasionally to the group of girls who walked behind them.

Both groups giggled and laughed, for the equal number of girls and boys leant itself to speculation: who would pair with whom?

All of the boys fancied Mary. She was, as someone said, 'A proper mama,' with full breasts and a pert bum.

'You could just lie down and suck on them forever,' said Alexander as he lay down on the pavement and began an impromptu imitation of breastfeeding.

The girls looked on and laughed at his frolicking. When Alexander got up, Robert tapped him on the shoulder.

'Too bad,' he said, 'she fancies me.'

'They always fancy you,' said Alexander. 'But at least I make them laugh.'

'You can have the laughter,' said Robert, 'as long as I have all the snogs.' He pursed his lips and taunted Alexander with the threat of kissing him.

'Get off you queer git,' said Alexander, laughing.

They walked past The City Cemetery; it lay parallel to the park, sloping upwards from The Falls, to the right of The Black Mountain. Both cemetery and park had been created many years before when a hundred and one acres of land were purchased by the local authorities from the Sinclair family.

They entered through a parting in the thick iron gates of the park, walked past the carefully maintained flowerbeds that were in full bloom and further up past the

97

closely shorn bowling lawn that, despite the lack of water, remained radiantly fresh and green; the stream that flanked the left side of the park was shallow, retaining nevertheless sufficient depth for small children to paddle in.

The Cooler, built in 1924, was at the top end of the park; it was surrounded by beautiful lawns though some of these, unlike the bowling green, had burnt up in the heat so that patches of grass had dried and lost its colour. The walls of the open-air pool were painted a pale blue; it was divided into three sections. The middle was the deepest and had a couple of diving boards stretching out from the pool's grassy banks over the water.

When they arrived at The Cooler Alexander was the first to dive off one of the boards into the water. He rose to the surface, gasped for breath and dived back underwater to show off his ability to turn handstands. While upside down in the water he kicked his feet in the air before holding them straight as he pointed his toes like a gymnast. The girls, who'd sat on the grassy banks to paddle their feet, applauded. When Alexander came to the surface he squawked like a seal and clambered up out of the pool and onto the diving board to initiate a second performance.

A row of mature European beech trees lined one side of the pool: they were huge dark trees, not native to Ireland, that blocked out the woodland understory and provided relief from the scorching heat.

Robert laid his towel on the opposite grassy verge and leant back on one elbow as he struck up a Marlborough cigarette; he inhaled deeply.

The girls looked at Alexander in the water and laughed, but out of the side of her eye Teresa watched Robert: he

98

was sun-tanned, almost Italian looking and his body sharply contrasted with Alexander's freckled lanky frame. She nudged Mary. 'Come with me,' she said.

The girls moved over to Robert and laid their towels out beside him. Robert finished his cigarette and sipped his beer before getting into the water to swim lengths. When he got out he lay back on the towel to soak up the sun and further tan his body.

As the afternoon wore on it became clear who might pair off with whom. Robert had it worked out in his head: Teresa with Jimmy, Claire with John, Kathleen with Alexander and Mary with himself.

As he walked her home Mary admitted that she'd wanted to go out with Alexander, because he made her laugh so much. 'It's alright now,' she said. 'I don't mind.'

'Why didn't you ask him?' Robert said.

'Kathleen fancies him and she hasn't had a boyfriend in a while.'

Robert could see the regret in her eyes, despite what she'd said.

It was two years later when he'd got together with Mary. Within weeks they got married. They were both in their second year of university. Mary was enrolled as an undergraduate for straight English and Robert was in his second year of a computer technology degree. He'd had to repeat one of his modules and had found the course boring and his peers nerdy. So when Mary discovered she was pregnant he gave the degree up without regret and took a job as a sales rep.

The work went well so that he superseded his quotas week after week. It seemed that every student and every household were either wanting or buying a PC; he was paid on commission so that he earned, for a while, what seemed like a large amount of money.

They lived in a small third floor flat with one bedroom. Mary continued at the university but, as her pregnancy continued, she decided to take a year out. She never did go back to complete. And when Emily was born they both felt as if the unexpected pregnancy, that they had initially blamed on the cheap condoms handed out in the student's union, had been a godsend: Emily was a spring baby, small, blonde, healthy and beautiful.

The bedroom of the flat was too small for the cradle and so they moved their double bed into the living room. The kitchen off it was so small that the flat felt like a large bedsit.

The summer that year was warm and Botanic Gardens was only a small walk from where they lived. They didn't need a garden.

Often, there'd be loud singing in the street at night and sometimes brawls, but the noise kept neither Robert, Mary or Emily awake.

Each morning as they threw open their own windows and heard the latest song drift from across the street they felt part of the student dynamic, sharing a space that was alive and free from the drudgery of parents, even though they were now parents themselves. They never thought further than payday at the end of the week and what treats they might afford. The rent was low and there always seemed to be plenty of disposable cash. They never thought, at that carefree time, of owning their own car, or their own home. They lived in the present.

Robert heard a muffled shout from the kitchen. He switched off the shower, wondering how long he'd stood

100

under it. When he got out he combed his hair in his usual side parting, pulled on a pair of jeans and went downstairs.

'Look,' said Mary pointing to the kitchen ceiling. 'You were in that bloody shower for ages and it's begun to leak. I thought you said you'd fixed the grout.'

'I had,' said Robert, scratching his head.

'Well, if you'd have fixed it Robert, it wouldn't be leaking.'

'I'll do it again over the weekend.'

'Properly this time?' she said.

'I'll do it,' he said, imitating a monster about to strangle her. Mary wasn't amused.

'And the tree house?' she said. 'You promised Peter.'

'Yes, and the tree house,' he said.

The phone rang. Robert picked it up; it was Alexander on the other end wanting to know whether he was going out that night for a drink.

'Aye,' whispered Robert, 'but I'll have to talk Mary round.'

Mary stood in the doorway as Robert replaced the receiver.

'I don't mind,' she said, 'if you go out with Alexander for a drink. You've worked all week. Don't pay any attention to me.'

'I won't go if you don't want me to,' he said.

'Go,' she said, 'but Robert, please start on the tree house before you head out. Peter's waited long enough.'

Robert began to work that morning on Peter's new den. He built a rectangular box on the ground with a roof and a hole in the front for Peter to climb through. He built the frame, but couldn't lift it, so he rang Alexander who came immediately, and with his help hoisted the box on top of it

101

so that it was completed that afternoon. Robert had thought it would take longer to build.

Peter climbed up the ladders of the tree house and called to Samson to join him. Samson barked furiously from the garden below, getting up on his hind legs and placing his front paws on the bottom rung. 'Come on girl,' shouted Peter, trying to persuade Samson to climb. Samson took a few paces back and made an attempt to leap up, falling awkwardly back to the ground. 'Can't we do something?' said Peter.

'I could build a ramp,' said Robert.

Peter clapped his hands. The clapping excited Samson who made one last attempt to leap up the ladder, falling again awkwardly to the ground. She retreated to the back door of the house, lay down and sighed.

Peter expected his dad to build the ramp there and then, but when his father said that he'd have to buy more wood before he could build it, Peter felt disappointed. He climbed down the ladders and went to the back doorstep. 'It'll be alright girl,' said Peter, 'Dad promised me a tree house and there it is,' he said pointing to the tree house. Samson barked. 'And he's promised you a ramp to get up to it, but you'll have to wait like I did.'

His mum came out of the house and gave him a carrier bag full of coloured paints and stencils. Peter kissed Samson and told her to be a good girl. He climbed the ladder of the tree house and got lost for the remainder of the late afternoon and early evening stencilling and painting the walls of his new den.

When Emily got home from her dancing class she bartered for a new costume.

'Peter got the tree house,' she said. Robert and Mary soon gave in.

The two children were so unalike: Emily had blue eyes, Peter had brown; Emily had blonde hair, Peter's was dark; Emily was top of the class in school, academically, creatively and on the sports field, Peter lagged behind in almost everything he did. But Peter was a sensitive child and an affectionate child too; you could see this in the way he stroked and cared for Samson. You could see this in the way he got so upset at the slightest remark from the other kids, constantly coming up the path crying, because so and so had said this, or so and so had said that. Yet there was the other side of Peter too.

Robert put the remainder of his tools in the garage and went into the house. Mary handed him a cup of coffee and a letter. 'I'm sorry,' she said. Robert took the letter and read that there'd been 'another serious incident' in the classroom. Peter, the letter claimed, had 'drawn blood' from a boy with the sharp end of a compass. The letter invited them to a meeting.

'They'll be exaggerating as always,' said Robert after he had read the letter. 'Besides, I don't know what you're saying sorry for; it's not your fault.'

Mary was less convinced.

'It's not the first time,' she said, looking out the window at Peter who seemed content painting his new den.

'It'll be all of nothing,' said Robert, putting the letter back into the envelope.

Mary knew that she'd have to go to the meeting alone. She would have liked Robert's support and dreaded having to face the teacher and the educational psychologist alone.

In the evening she felt tired and was glad when her own friends rang to say that the Anne Summer's party had been cancelled.

Robert went out with Alexander and his mates as usual. She was glad to have the house to herself, and after she bathed Peter and Emily and put them to bed, she picked up the book she'd been trying to find time to read. It was after midnight when she woke up on the settee. Robert was due home soon so she made herself a hot cup of cocoa and went to bed, but she couldn't sleep and so switched on the side lamp to read a little more.

The front bedroom was bigger than the back room but the back of the house was private. The fir trees blocked off an industrial complex that lay behind them and there were no other over-looking houses, despite being in the middle of a housing estate. It was the privacy of this back bedroom that had been one of the attractions Mary felt towards the house when they'd bought it, that and the price: for a three-bedroomed semi-detached house, with garden back and front it'd been a bargain.

Yet it was, she remembered, a bit of a culture shock; they'd moved from the heart of student land to the outskirts of suburbia, and for the first while Mary could not sleep at night because it was too quiet.

The house felt quiet tonight, as it had felt when she'd moved in, though it was windy outside; the kind of night her father used to tell her when the banshee was abroad and the black horse-drawn carriage ready and waiting to take the living into another realm.

As a child she'd half-believed in the banshee, as other children believe in Santa Claus. The wind seemed to rise and the letterbox downstairs clanged intermittently.

104

Robert was later than usual. Mary got out of bed and made another cup of cocoa. She opened the Venetian blinds in the living room and sat on Robert's burgundy wing chair. It was after two and he was still not home.

At two thirty a taxi pulled up outside the door. Mary heard the key fumble in the front door lock. She came downstairs to greet him, expecting that he'd been unable to hail a taxi earlier, but he was red in the face and unusually drunk.

'Sorry love,' he said. 'I didn't realise how late it'd got.'

He put his hand around her waist, drawing her in closer, but she leant backwards away from his drunken breath.

'You've had me worried sick,' she said.

'Ach don't be like that, sure I'm never this late.'

'Exactly! Why do you think I got so worried?'

Robert smiled, 'Afraid I'd turn into a pumpkin or something.'

'Don't be so stupid Robert,' she said, pushing him away from her. 'It's not funny.'

She climbed the pine wooden staircase and checked on Peter and Emily, tucking their downy quilts around their sleeping angled bodies before climbing into her own bed. She was glad Robert was home and fell fast asleep as soon as her head touched the feather pillow.

Robert made a cup of tea and paced the downstairs of the house. He lit a cigarette and sat on the wingchair but he could not settle, so he rose and retrieved the yellow and black screwdriver from underneath the kitchen sink, determined to repair the letterbox: he poked at it, unscrewed the screws, tightened them but only managed, it seemed, to increase the gap so that the letterbox clanged and the wind continued to whistle through.

105

He gave up and went back to his chair, lifted a cushion to put behind his head and lit up another Marlborough Light. Eventually he fell asleep and woke about five in the morning feeling cold and disoriented. He clambered upstairs, still a little unsteady on his feet, and climbed into bed.

He slept badly and blamed Mary's mood when he got home as the cause of it. It felt to him unreasonable that for the sake of an hour on a Saturday night and a couple of drinks more than usual she should have been so upset. If I was a bad husband, he thought, or if I didn't earn money to keep the house and all of us together, she'd have something to complain about.

His irritability was heightened when on taking a shower he spotted a second lank shiny dirty-grey hair. He plucked it out as he had the first and was throwing it with disgust into the waste bin when Mary called from the kitchen.

'Can't even take a shower in peace,' he muttered under his breath. She called again.

'Can you get Peter?' she said.

'What's up?'

'He's stuck in the tree house,' she shouted up. 'Says he can't get down.'

'He's probably having you on.'

'Can you get him or not?' Robert took a deep breath. He wasn't the only one, it seemed, who was feeling irritable.

'Sometimes I wonder,' she said when he came downstairs and through to the kitchen, 'what's wrong with him. He can do things and then he can't. He's been up

106

and down that ladder non-stop since yesterday and now suddenly he's stuck.'

'Maybe he got caught on something,' Robert said.

'No Robert, it's just Peter being Peter. Half the time I think he lives in another world.'

'Maybe he does,' Robert said, half smiling. 'Are you still angry with me?'

'I wasn't angry,' she said, 'I was just tired.'

He bent over her small frame and put his hand gently around her waist, depositing a kiss on her left cheek.

'Peter,' he yelled, opening the back door. 'If I've to come and get you.' Peter emerged from the side of the garage holding a jam jar full of grass and weeds. 'So you managed to get down after all.'

'Look,' said Peter, 'a beetle.'

'Magic,' said Robert. 'Now go and wash your hands for breakfast.'

Monday, as always, came too soon. At noon, precisely, Robert hastened to the elevator to leave the office block. He held his lunchbox under his arm like a newspaper and walked to the wooden bench at the front of The City Hall and sat down. It was habit with him to spend lunchtime, when the rain held off, on one of the many benches, but he had his favourite and was glad it was empty.

A rainbow hovered in the sky as two old ladies walked past, linking arms. They wore flowery dresses, wrinkled tights and flat black brogue-like shoes. He could have sworn that the peach, orange and light cream pattern on the taller lady's dress was the exact same pattern, perhaps even the exact style of dress that his grandmother had often worn.

He wished that like his grandmother and grandfather before him he could be content with his life. He had a beautiful wife, two beautiful children and a home set in leafy suburbia. He didn't want for anything and unlike his grandfather who worked as a road digger he did not come home from the day smelling of asphalt and exhaustion. But he was fed up filing, computerizing and distributing paperwork that he didn't give a toss about. Desk jobs, he knew, bored holes in the mind as surely as his grandfather had drilled holes into the ground.

He watched the two old ladies pass out of sight. They had seemed part of a lost generation. He looked up at the clock above the old Robinson and Cleaver's building and breathed a heavy sigh, resealed the lid of his Tupperware box and headed back to the office, checking the time on his Gucci watch when he got to the door; he'd bought the watch shortly after he'd got married, when he'd won a sum of money in the Littlewoods Pools.

He was on time. Just. He liked it that way. He climbed the staircase to the third floor taking his seat in the open plan office.

The hour for lunch was flexible, but Robert took his early so that as he returned most of the other office workers were only beginning theirs. He lifted the files on his desk and logged onto the computer as Kenny intrusively leant towards him, feigning a whisper. Kenny's clique hung in the doorway.

'The boys reckon that you're having a mad affair.' Robert looked up blankly. 'We're putting bets on.'

'I'm busy,' said Robert opening the first file.

'Well are you or aren't you?' Kenny said.

'Yes,' said Robert.

'I knew it,' said Kenny, raising an indiscreet thumbs-up to the clique that still lingered in the doorway. ''Cause you've sat in that chair over lunch all these years and now you always go out and,' he continued, leaning closer into Robert, disrupting the files on the desk, 'if you don't mind me saying so, you've smartened your act up a little, new hairstyle despite,' he leant closer over the top of the desk, hovering parasitically close to Robert's head, 'the little bit of grey. If you don't mind me saying that.'

'With Madonna,' said Robert. 'She flies in every lunchtime just to share my sandwiches. We'd corned beef today and half a cup of coffee each.'

'So you're not,' said Kenny, jangling the coins in his beige Chinos.

'I love my wife,' said Robert narrowing his eyes.

Kenny slid off the desk, feigned a yawn and stretched out the words, 'Boring.'

Robert could hear monies change hands in the foyer.

There was a time when he'd have stood up and punched Kenny or anyone like him in the face. It was hard to stomach the fact that when Kenny had started in the office – a seemingly shy boy lacking confidence, Robert had taken him in, showed him the ropes, befriended him.

109

Chapter 9

Alexander never wanted to be a barman, but he resigned himself to the need to make some money when Tommy offered him a full-time job. He held onto his plans to open his own second hand bookstore, though he saw that collecting old library books had been a stupid idea: it would take too much time; besides, he couldn't drive and how was he meant to carry the books without a car.

The years he'd spent on building sites in London seemed to him a waste. After ten years of being a general dogsbody, he had with one misplaced foot lost his balance and free fallen to the ground. He only cracked a couple of ribs. It was a miracle, the hospital said, that he was alive, and so he'd returned home not a rich man but a poor and injured one. Elsie called him The Prodigal Son; the ribs soon mended, but his pride took longer to mend, was still mending.

He took the job at the bar and worked as many shifts as he could, giving half his income to Elsie. She took her housekeeping from it and put the remainder in a savings account. 'It'll go towards getting a bathroom,' she said. With working nights he spent very little of what he earned and was saving his own money. In the past he'd always been careless with it – spending without thought or care for the lean days, but that had all changed: he had a goal, something to save for.

Elsie was glad that Alexander had settled into a job, but she missed his company and in the evenings the house seemed cold and empty. In the mornings he was also out of the house, attending a business course in the college. Alexander told her that most of those on the course were considerably younger, but that it didn't matter because he knew he was going to make a success of himself and that the course was teaching him about accounts and how to set up his own business.

'What business?' she asked.

'Not until it happens,' he said. 'Then you'll believe.'

'You mean I'm not allowed to know?'

'I don't want to spoil it,' he said.

Elsie was baffled. She wished that she could believe in him more than she did and was afraid that this was another one of his hair-brained schemes. He could see her disbelief and it hurt him; simultaneously it made him more determined to succeed.

As the months wore on and Alexander continued to work in The Rock and continued to attend his business course she began to wonder had she underestimated his commitment.

Increasingly, Elsie felt less capable of managing the house. Even mundane tasks such as cleaning out the fireplace seemed to drain her. She slept longer at night, rising not at her usual six-thirty but later, so that instead of attending early morning mass she often went to the church in the afternoon to light a candle and sit for a while.

111

She thought of Rosie more often and of God: they lived in a dimension she could never truly understand, but they would recognize each other nonetheless, when the time came. She thought of her mother too, and what she must have endured to have lost a child so young. Having Alexander had allowed her to think more clearly; had allowed her to forgive.

Her mother had kept a picture of Rosie in the wooden dresser in her bedroom.

Elsie remembered opening the door one night and watching her mother as she took the picture out to look at it. Her mother's face was reflected in the three-tiered hinged mirror on the dressing table; she lifted the picture to her lips and kissed it, sighing as she uttered Rosie's name repeatedly. Elsie had wanted to go to her mother and comfort her, but she hung back, torn between wanting to take away her mother's pain and knowing that she could not.

She remembered feeling jealous too. Rosie was loved, would always be loved. But just as she felt this pang of jealousy she saw her mother's face become suddenly twisted and distorted; it pulled out and upwards and sideways from her so that it looked not like her face at all but as though some demon had possessed it. Elsie turned and fled from the doorway.

Her mother slipped the photograph back into the drawer and descended the staircase. 'You should not watch people unawares,' she said. Her tone was cold and unforgiving.

It was only as the years went by that Elsie had forgiven her mother for not being able to show affection after Rosie died. Yes, she'd envied her dead sister, knowing that at night her mother's kisses were reserved.

Chapter 10

Robert closed his umbrella, secured the silver button around it and draped it over the side of the wooden bench. The black handle gently swayed as he unpacked his lunch. He looked in at the white pan bread and used his thumb to lift off the top layer of the sandwich; the lettuce, tomato and scallions stared limply back at him.

He was wrapped snugly in his long black overcoat and a grey woollen scarf that Mary had knit for him. It was March but the trees that lined the perimeter of the town hall were so drenched that they seemed to suffer their own brand of sadness. As he ate, a woman, wrapped in a navy overcoat with a collar she'd buttoned around the neck tightly and long shiny black leather boots, sat beside him. She was having difficulty taking off her left glove and resorted to gripping the fingertips with her teeth; the glove slid off to reveal long manicured nails coated in an off-white gloss. An unusual alluring silver bracelet hung on her wrist. She withdrew a packet of cigarettes and offered one to him.

'Given up,' he said as he closed the lid of the plastic Tupperware box.

'Yes,' she said as she fumbled for a lighter in the bottom of her handbag.

From the one syllable she'd uttered he could tell that she was foreign. 'Let me,' he said, offering her a light. Despite several attempts the wind blew the flame out. He was about to pass the lighter for her to try when she leaned towards him and cupped her hands around his to protect the flame; it held and she inhaled and sighed. 'Where are you from?' he said.

'Hungary,' she replied. The rain stopped and a gap appeared in the sky where the sun broke through. Robert looked up at the clock and stood up to leave.

'Back to work?' she said, looking up at him as he unbuttoned his overcoat.

He was taller than she'd thought. She traced the outline of his body: six foot, perhaps, dark hair, large but competent hands, protruding vein on the left hand, office suit that sat well on his obviously trim body. She found him attractive, typically Irish yes, but attractive. It was only as he turned to go that she saw the wedding ring on his left hand.

'Take care,' he said. He'd taken a few steps away from the bench when he felt a gentle tap on his right shoulder.

'Your lunch-box,' she said, handing it to him.

'Thanks,' he said, taking the box awkwardly. 'Perhaps I'll see you again.'

'I doubt it. I leave on Monday.'

'Back to Hungary?' he asked.

'Yes,' she replied.

'Take care,' he said for a second time.

She watched him as he made his way down the high street until his outline faded and was lost among the shoppers. Despite being married, he had seemed to her a strangely solitary person.

On Saturday Robert rang Alexander to arrange a night out but he pleaded poverty. Robert said he'd stand him a few drinks, but Alexander argued that he couldn't get the night off work anyway, even if he did have the money to go out.

'If you can't get one night off to go out with your best mate,' Robert said, 'then you're not much of a mate.'

'Easy on,' said Alexander, feeling cornered and obliged. 'I'll try.'

'We haven't been out in ages,' Robert said, less annoyed than plaintive this time.

'I know.'

'Then don't try to get the night off, get the night off.'

'Right.' said Alexander. 'And I'm not really skint,' he added.

'Why'd you say that then?'

'Because I'm saving.'

'For what?'

'I just am, that's all. Now stop asking me questions. I'll get the night off.'

'Great. Meet you at The Crown Bar, seven o'clock.'

'Hold your horses,' said Alexander before covering the mobile handset. He called to Tommy at the end of the bar. 'How's about a night off?' he said.

'It's Saturday,' said Tommy. 'How long have you been working here?'

'Five months,' said Alexander

'You know how many Saturday nights I've worked in the last ten years?'

Alexander shook his head.

116

'All of them,' said Tommy.

'No chance then.'

'No chance.'

Tommy's nephew was sitting at the end of the bar. He was twenty-one and eager to make a few pounds before returning to University. He seized on the opportunity. 'I'll do it,' he called out, toppling sideways on his stool and saving himself with his left foot. Tommy looked at his nephew and back at Alexander. 'I guess it's your lucky day,' he grunted.

Alexander lifted his hand from the mobile. 'Seven,' he said to Robert.

****

Robert arrived early at The Crown Bar and sat on a barstool. He ordered two pints of Carlsberg that the barman, dressed in a white shirt, black waistcoat and tie, poured and set down on the granite topped Alter bar. 'You must be thirsty,' the barman said. Robert laughed.

'My mate's always a bit late.'

'But he always turns up?' said the barman.

'Yes. Always.'

'You're lucky to have a mate like that. Sometimes I see people waiting. Often. And the disappointment.' The barman shook his head and looked at Robert as though waiting for an answer.

'I suppose I am lucky,' answered Robert. 'I never really thought about it.'

'No?'

'No, we don't, do we?'

'What?'

'Think about our luck.'

This time the barman laughed mildly, nostalgically, as he picked up a glass and a white polishing cloth.

The Crown was unusually empty for a Saturday night; Robert had been in it many times before but he had never really taken the time to look at it.

'It was decorated,' the barman said, 'in 1885 by poor Italian craftsmen who worked mainly on local churches.' Robert nodded. He knew it was a listed building; his eyes wandered from the vigorous woodcarvings to the ornate mirrors, brocaded walls and even to the floor that was smartly laid in a myriad of mosaic tiles. Vivid amber-stained glass and carmine painted shells proliferated. There were even drawings of fairies.

'What's with the fairies?' he asked the barman who was polishing an already polished glass.

'Bored workmen, I guess,' he said.

Alexander arrived just after seven, propping one foot on the heated foot rail.

Robert moved the pint he'd pre-ordered and set it in front of him.

'Cheers,' said Alexander, lifting the beer, 'it's good to be out.'

They clanked their glasses and propped an elbow each on top of the Alter bar.

Gradually, the pub filled up with a mixed crowd of young and old, some solitary, some in groups, until the gentle din rose and deepened so that the mosaic tiles were lost underfoot and the alcohol consumed a pendulum twin to the noise. Robert and Alexander were themselves on their fifth round of drinks.

118

At intervals Robert left the bar to have a cigarette. He'd stopped smoking on Monday but it was always the way: as soon as he'd have a pint in his hand he'd crave for one and give in. Perhaps he could become a social smoker.

The doors of the pub were open and led onto Great Victoria Street. He brought his pint with him. Those outside, mostly smokers, were flanked by a riot of polychromatic tiles and decorative windows that made up the exterior facade of the building. The breeze scuttling down millionaire's row, as the street was known, was a welcome palliative. Robert lifted his arm and wiped his forehead with his sleeve. He hadn't realised how hot it was inside.

He inhaled the Marlborough Light with his head tilted back, drawing slowly and at great length. 'It was,' as Alexander had said, 'good to be out.' The smoke circlets he playfully blew floated and evaporated into the cool night air.

He had just blown another smoke ring when he saw the Hungarian woman he had met on Friday. She was with a man who was tall, like Robert.

Robert stubbed out his cigarette and went back inside to join Alexander at the bar when he felt a light tap on his shoulder. He turned around. The Hungarian woman smiled at him and held out her hand.

'Maya,' she said. Robert looked over her shoulder, wondering where the man she had come into the bar with was.

'He's just a friend,' she said, as though reading his mind. 'They're with the others in one of the booths.'

'A leaving party,' Robert suggested.

'You remembered,' she said.

119

Alexander held out his hand, hoping for an introduction. She shook his hand politely and turned her attention straight back to Robert.

'Can I get you a drink?' Robert asked.

'Vodka,' she said, holding her smile steadily, 'will you join us?'

Alexander nudged Robert. 'She's a pick-up,' he whispered.

'Don't be daft,' said Robert. 'A bit of company will be good craic.'

'As long as you know what you're doing.'

'I'm not doing anything.'

'You sure about that?' said Alexander.

'Sure I'm sure. We met before that's all. She's leaving on Monday.'

'It's only Saturday.'

'For Christ's sake Alexander, I'm not going to sleep with her.'

Alexander apologised and they both entered the booth.

Maya had reserved a seat for Robert beside her, leaving Alexander to take a space at the other end of the booth. He tried to make an effort, but the girl beside him spoke little English and after a while she too turned her attention away from him. Robert was too far away to speak to, and Alexander felt uneasy sitting among strangers so that it was long before midnight when he wanted to go home, but he waited.

At midnight he looked at Robert and pointed at his watch. Robert shrugged and ordered another round of drinks, for Maya, himself and for Alexander. When the drinks arrived Alexander lifted his and went back into the

120

main bar.   At twelve-thirty he opened the door of the booth.

'I've ordered a taxi.'   Robert checked the time on his mobile.

'A bit early for me,' he said.

'Right,' said Alexander. 'I'll call you tomorrow.'

Alexander stood outside waiting for the taxi. But the street was busy and the taxi didn't come, so he started walking. It was only a mile and a half home to Rockdale Street. The walk would give him time to clear his head. He knew that it was none of his business what Robert got up to. He was married, yes, but it was none of his business.

****

Robert called a taxi much later. When he got home Mary was lying asleep on the settee. For a moment he felt a pang of regret. She lay huddled under a cream woollen blanket with her parted hair swept off her face. She didn't look her age, she never would, but he felt no passion for her. He drew the Venetian blinds and switched the lamp off. Clearly she had been waiting up for him. When she woke, she looked up at the clock and went to bed.

It was four in the morning. Robert looked around the house, at the photographs on the wall and sideboard and at his wedding picture. But they did not feel as though they belonged to him, or he to them. He could think only of Maya and their next meeting.

Chapter 11

The sun came through the curtains of Mary's bedroom early that morning. She got up, opened them and lingered at the window to watch the doves that had settled in the fir trees fly back and forth with twigs and dried grass in their mouths.

The garden below was sectioned into a play area for Peter and Emily, a lawn, and a separate vegetable patch. The play area had a sand pit and a swing; several toys were strewn on the lawn – a football, trampet and Emily's purple hula-hoop, for Robert had gone out the night before without tidying them away.

She had her own part of the garden that she'd marked off with latticed fencing. The children knew it was out of bounds. Mary had erected it herself shortly after they'd moved in. She planted clematis around it so that it was now grown and the vegetable garden private. Over the years she'd grown cabbage, parsnips, beetroot, rocket and potatoes; she'd tried to grow tomatoes several times and failed miserably.

As she was looking at the garden one of the doves flew out of the nest and gathering speed flew towards the window. At the last minute, seeming almost to brake, it flew upwards and over the roof. Mary stepped backwards, for its speed was closer in kin to that of a mourning dove than the collared dove she knew it to be: she really thought that it was going to hit the window. But its speed and sudden change of direction were so remarkable that she almost wanted to applaud. She lifted the binoculars that she kept on the window-ledge to watch it closely: it had a black and white collar band as she'd thought, and was eating berries that lay on the ground. As it flew back up to the flimsy platform of twigs it had built in the fir trees, above Peter's tree house, she heard its loud cooing song.

But turning back into the room she looked at the bedclothes; the sheets on Robert's side were unruffled. She pulled on her dressing gown and went downstairs to find him asleep on the wingchair, without as much as a cover around him, so she lifted the blanket from off the back of the settee and put it over him before going to the kitchen to fill the kettle up.

Mary opened the back door and stepped down into the garden. She could feel the dew on the grass through her pale blue cotton slippers and went back into the house to change into her garden shoes – they were lying at the back door, muddy from yesterday's digging. She poured a cup of coffee and went back out to the garden, stepping delicately through the furrowed soil to reach the back of the vegetable patch where she liked to sit on the white metal bench. She'd painted the bench herself, painted most of the house, for Robert was not good at painting. She sat down and sipped at the coffee, glad of the space that the garden afforded her; it was like another room, but a private one where she could think. Her coffee was just finished when a light drizzle began to fall and so she returned indoors. Meanwhile Robert had woken and was upstairs taking a shower.

'Good night out?' she said as she handed him a cup of coffee when he came down the stairs. Robert took the coffee but didn't answer. 'You look tired,' Mary said. 'Perhaps you should go back to bed.' She had promised herself in the garden that she would not complain about his late arrival home.

Robert lifted his mobile out of his pocket to check the time. Alexander had left a text message. 'Sorry,' the message said, 'for giving you grief last night. I guess I just wasn't in the mood.' The message made Robert feel guilty, for he had to meet Maya at two o'clock.

'Just Alexander,' he said to Mary. 'Wants to meet up at two to go and get the wood to build the decking.'

'Thought we were going to wait until next year,' said Mary.

'Changed my mind,' he said.

Mary nodded. She'd hoped to spend the day with him and the kids; it'd been ages since they'd had a proper family outing, but she didn't complain.

As the weeks passed and Robert began to go out more and to come home later, Mary knew that her marriage was in a rut, but when she found his wedding ring in his jacket pocket her worst fears felt confirmed. Even then, she did not want to believe that he was cheating on her, or that her marriage, like a badly put up tent on a windy night, had all but collapsed.

****

Alexander took one end of the Eglantine decking boards as Robert lifted the other. They pulled it to the side where a neat pile they had checked for knots and stacked separately rested.

'I was meant to get this a couple of weeks ago,' Robert said, 'but I told Mary they were out of stock. It was better waiting anyway,' he said, 'for they're cheaper now than they were even two weeks ago.'

'How many?' said Alexander, who was busy lifting and checking another board.

'Another four,' Robert said, taking out his pocket calculator to cost it. The total came to one hundred and forty-three pounds.

'That's a lot of money for a bit of decking,' said Alexander.

Robert scratched his head. 'We'll need ten of these,' he said holding the end of a plank and 'then maybe twelve of the smaller ones.' He sounded vague.

'You sure you know what you need?'

'Almost,' said Robert scratching his head for a second time. He bought timber treatment, nails and six large double hinges. When he got to the till the total came to over two hundred and seven pounds.

'It's as well you're getting the labour for nothing,' said Alexander.

'I don't think I could do it by myself.'

'Course you could.'

'You've always been better at practical things than me.' Alexander raised an eyebrow.

'Seriously,' said Robert, 'you have.'

'That's the first time I've heard that,' said Alexander.

'It's true,' said Robert.

'I'll die of the shock,' said Alexander, feigning a stumble backwards.

'I know I haven't admitted it before.'

'I'm helping you already. What are you buttering me up for?' said Alexander.

Robert tucked his receipt and card into his brown leather wallet and put it in the back pocket of his jeans. 'Better at being the joker too,' he said as he wheeled the industrial trolley through the double doors into the porch outside, leaving Alexander to mind it while he went to get the car and trailer. They loaded it up quickly, as old workmates do, lifting and manoeuvring without seeming to communicate at all.

It was only ten am. They hoped to work solidly for the remainder of the morning and afternoon and finish the job on Sunday.

'We'll have half of it done by teatime,' Robert said as Mary handed him a cup of tea and nodded. She looked at Alexander.

'Thanks,' she said. Alexander dipped his head forward and blushed. His embarrassment made Mary smile.

'Someday you'll find the right woman,' she said. 'Be good to her when you do,' she added as she turned her gaze back to Robert.

She continued to take cups of tea to both Robert and Alexander, but the effort Robert was putting into their home seemed to her an unforgivable hypocrisy. As the day wore on, she felt as though she would burst and break if she did not confront him. Instead, she took Peter and Emily to her mother's house.

Peter insisted on driving his plastic go-cart. He had outgrown it but somehow managed to squeeze into it, though his knees poked awkwardly out of the main frame. Emily put on her roller skates.

'Can we get ice-cream?' said Emily.

'You're ice-cream crazy,' said Mary.

'But can we?'

'If I have enough money with me.'

Samson pulled on the choke lead and Peter asked for a push as they began to walk up the hill. Emily was only too happy to oblige, pushing him faster than was necessary which caused his feet to jam awkwardly in the pedals.

'Do you have to do that?' Mary bawled. Peter began to cry. 'Get out of that bloody thing,' she said. 'I told you not to bring it.'

Emily stuck her tongue out at Peter. Samson sat on the ground, curling her tail tightly into her body and stared blankly up at her.

'Not another word,' their mother warned.

They continued their journey without speaking, but as they passed the newsagents at the bottom of her mother's street Mary withdrew her purse and handed each of them enough change to buy a large ice-cream. Emily ordered hundreds and thousands on the top of hers and Peter decided that he'd have hundreds and thousands on the top of his too.

Mary stayed later at her mother's house than she intended, for she fell asleep on the settee. When she got home she found a note from Robert to say that he'd gone out for the evening with Alexander. The note was written on lined notepaper, torn from the notebook she used for shopping lists; she did not want to touch it and left it lying where she'd found it, beside the kettle.

In the sitting room she picked up the telephone and flipped through the household address book. She ran her finger down through the addresses until she arrived at the

127

phone number of The Rock. 'I heard there was a band on tonight,' she said as a young man answered the phone.

'No band,' he said.

'I guess I got it wrong. Is Alexander working there tonight?' she asked.

'Some bird asking for you,' said Tommy's nephew as he handed the receiver to Alexander, but when he put the phone to his ear the line was dead.

It was the first time in the eleven years of her marriage that Mary had checked up on Robert. She wondered whether this affair was his first. The clichéd, lepers don't change their spots, once a liar always a liar came flying through her tunnelled mind and she wondered had she spent eleven years of her life in complete and stupid naivety.

But he had lied to her and the phone call had further proved her suspicions. She felt her stomach heave and ran upstairs to the bathroom where she knelt in front of the white toilet bowl and vomited. When she'd emptied her stomach, wiped the edges of the toilet bowl and flushed it, she felt dizzy and angry. It was time to confront him, but the following morning her resolve waned.

Perhaps, she reasoned, Alexander had been called in to work to cover someone else.

'A good night?' she said instead, as Robert came out of the shower.

'It was okay,' he said.

She made a fried breakfast of bacon, eggs and toasted soda bread.

The children came downstairs in their pyjamas and sat in front of the television. Mary went outside and into the vegetable garden with a cup of coffee and as she heard the

128

doves cooing in the fir trees she envied the simplicity of their lives.

Alexander arrived at eleven, hoping to get the decking finished. He blushed as Mary greeted him with a hug and sat him down at the kitchen table for a late breakfast.

She joined him and dared herself to ask him about his night out with Robert. But she didn't ask, for she was frightened that he would lie to her, she was frightened to face the truth.

When he'd finished the breakfast he thanked her politely and joined Robert outside.

'Did she ask you?' whispered Robert.

'No,' said Alexander.

'Nothing?'

Alexander had bent down to screw in a nail, but he stood up and stared at his friend whom he felt he no longer knew. 'I told you I'm not going to lie for you.'

'Sssh,' said Robert, looking up at the back of the house.

Mary lifted the plastic wash basket from the landing and held it in front of her as she descended the stairs; it was brimming over and heavy. She couldn't fathom where all the washing came from and wondered how they'd ever managed without a tumble dryer. She remembered her mother saying that in the old days you rarely washed woollen garments and if you did wash a jumper you would only do the underarms, rinse it, wring it and hang it out to dry. Were there more chores in the old days or was less done? For all that, she couldn't imagine standing washing clothes in the sink.

She emptied the wash basket onto the kitchen floor in front of the Zanussi washing machine and loaded up the children's school uniforms and a couple of pairs of

Robert's work trousers. It was a task she'd hitherto performed perfunctorily, but as her right hand delved into his trouser pockets she began to shake. She half-expected to find carelessly left evidence: a receipt for dinner, cinema tickets, the purchase of a gift she had never received, but the pockets were clean. Her right hand continued to shake so that she gripped it and held it with her left until the shaking subsided.

The decking was finished at teatime. They lifted the furniture Mary had assembled at the side of the house. There were four wooden chairs and a round table with a slate in the middle where the parasol would fit for they'd decided to wait until the following summer to buy one. Mary brought out a bottle of chilled Chablis and three wine glasses. Peter and Emily climbed up on the bench. She poured each of them a tall glass of Orangeade and slipped a whirling stripped straw into each glass.

'We'll have a party to celebrate next summer,' she said, and feigning joy at the completed work she topped up their glasses. But Alexander saw through the façade.

'She knows,' he said to Robert as he left.

Chapter 12

It had been fourteen years since Alexander had sat any kind of test. He had bad memories of his school examinations, of the preceding nerves and inevitable failure. It was with that same sense of doom that he got into the passenger seat of the Fiat Punto.

His driving instructor, a slim man with big hands, told him not to worry. He would pass, he was told. Alexander was not convinced.

The instructor drove carefully to the test centre where they went inside to wait their turn. A young girl, barely nineteen with sun-tanned skin and a confidence that Alexander envied, sat down beside him. The other would-be drivers were all under twenty-five years old. He felt a veteran, catching up on something he ought to have put behind him years back.

Eventually Alexander was called and proceeded to the car park. The examiner asked him to read the number plate of a car that was parked below the fencing, but he read the wrong number plate.

'The one behind it, further away,' the examiner said.

'Is it true,' Alexander asked as he secured his seatbelt.

'Is what true?'

'What they say about quotas?'

'Nonsense,' said the examiner. 'If you drive well you'll pass.'

Alexander switched on the ignition and checked the mirrors before signalling to take off. His three-point turn and hill-start went well. He hadn't made a mistake, as far as he knew, but on his return journey to the driving centre he hesitated as he manoeuvred out for a right turn at the traffic lights; the lights had turned green, but traffic was coming the other way so Alexander held back instead of moving forward.

'Move out,' the instructor said autocratically.

Alexander moved out and took the turn down Boucher Road, but out of the side of his eye he saw the examiner mark one of the boxes with an X. He parked the car in the test centre knowing that on the last leg he had failed.

The examiner proceeded to ask a series of questions on The Highway Code. Alexander knew it back to front. He had kept a copy behind the bar and had pestered punters, including Aiden, who couldn't see too well without his glasses and who never seemed to have them with him, to check his knowledge. But he knew that he'd already failed the test and believed that the examiner's questions were a waste of time, and so he answered them without hesitation and without nerves, wishing only that this prolonged charade were over.

When the instructor told him that he had passed he thought that he had misheard. 'You've passed,' the examiner repeated. Alexander nodded and thanked him without displaying any emotion.

132

'Now you've got wheels,' his own instructor said, 'your life begins anew.' Alexander got into the instructor's car and was driven back to The Falls Road.

He went into the garage at the top of St James's street where Jim the mechanic, dressed in oily navy overalls, came out onto the forecourt.

'That one,' said Alexander pointing at the Rover 200.

'What?' Jim said.

'Can you have it ready for me by teatime? I'll have to ring the insurance company.'

'Quickest sale I've ever had,' said Jim. Alexander's squashed emotion burst open and he threw his arms around Jim.

'I've passed,' he said. Jim stared at him. 'Passed my test,' said Alexander explaining.

'You mean you've never driven before?' said Jim.

'Nope, never. There are lots of things I've never had, but that's all about to change.'

'Good for you,' said Jim. 'I'll have it ready for you, throw in a valet too.'

'Great,' said Alexander, leaving the forecourt.

'How are you paying for it?' shouted Jim.

'Cash,' said Alexander. He walked proudly back to Rockdale Street to tell Elsie the news.

'We'll celebrate,' she said, offering to take him out for dinner.

'Tomorrow,' said Alexander. 'I want to take a wee run up to Robert's at teatime.'

Elsie nodded, 'Tomorrow then.'

'It's a date,' said Alexander. 'We'll go to the seaside. How's about it?'

'A trip to the supermarket would be grand.'

'Aye,' he said. 'We'll do a tour of the shopping malls, stop off for lunch in a country pub.'

'I don't drink,' said Elsie.

'Apart from the occasional sherry,' she added.

'Aye but it's never too late to start,' he said. She swiped at him with a blue and white chequered tea towel.

'You be careful,' she said, waving him off at teatime.

****

The Rover 200 pulled up slowly in front of Robert and Mary's house. The side lamp from the living room emitted a faint light through the blinds. Alexander unravelled the wrapper of an air freshener and attached it to the mirror; it surprised him when it gave off a genuine forest pine smell. He wiped the dashboard with a cloth and arranged the tapes he had taken from his bedroom neatly into the tape holder in front of the handbrake.

The car was inexpensive but it felt plush. It had electric windows and a sunroof. He felt singularly proud of his investment and his newfound independence. He could drive anywhere without having to wait on public transport. He could play his own music instead of having to listen to other people's mobile phone conversations. His business course would soon be finished and if he kept saving he could begin to look for premises.

He got out of the car and pressed the button on the keys to lock the doors, but he didn't trust the central locking and double-checked them manually before walking up the tarmac path to Robert and Mary's front door. He rapped but no one answered. He rapped a second time and still no one answered, yet the light indicated that there was

134

someone in. He was about to give up when Mary came to the door.

'Robert's not in,' she said.

It was early, but she was wrapped up in her dressing gown. He could see that she'd been crying. 'What's wrong?' he said.

'You'd better come in,' she said, standing aside and closing the front door behind him. She led him into the living room and went to the kitchen to make tea. The television was on but the volume was turned off and the children were in bed.

Mary returned with two cups of tea on a tray and some biscuits. She heaped a shovel of coal onto the fire and sat down on the settee, fastening the belt of her dressing gown. 'I don't know what to say,' she said looking at him. Alexander looked down at the varnished wooden floorboards, following the pattern of grain with his eye. He didn't know what to say either. 'You knew,' she said.

Alexander nodded.

'There's no need to look like that. I don't blame you.' Alexander lifted his eyes from the floor. 'For how long?' she asked.

'It's not for me to tell,' he said.

'No,' she said. Alexander nodded, raising the cup to his lips; it tasted bitter. 'I forgot to put sugar in it.'

He followed her into the kitchen. 'The decking looks nice,' he said.

She shrugged, 'Not much point really. I guess it'll go up for sale.'

'That bad.'

'I won't stand by him Alexander. He's made his bed.'

135

She broke down into tears and leant towards him. He put his arm around her, feeling the warmth of her against his chest. He could smell her body odour; it was sweet, pungent, almost child-like.

'He's a fool,' Alexander said, wiping her fallen hair to the side. He looked down at her as she placed both hands on his chest, gripping his shirt angrily so that the blue worsted fabric creased and sagged. He could feel his own body grow suddenly hot and flushed. Still she leant into him. He bent his head towards her and though she looked puzzled she did not move away from him. He moved closer, finding at last her tear-ridden lips: luscious, soft, tender.

She undid the buttons of his shirt and ran her hands along his bare chest, feeling his closeness to her, feeling his desire. It had been so long since she had felt wanted. He undid the strap of her dressing gown and pushed the gown gently from her shoulders so that it fell onto the floor. She held onto him and pulled him into her as she felt his passion and his longing, and for a moment when he was inside her she felt that she might love him, but as her head leaned upon his shoulder and tilted to look up at him, her eyes sought Robert's face. She pulled away from him, picked up her fallen gown and placed it around her, tying the belt securely in a double knot. 'You must go,' she said.

He looked at her again with love and with longing, but she felt overwhelmed for it was circumstances beyond them that had brought them together and not themselves alone; and she felt pity, for herself and for Alexander and she turned away from him. She had never felt such passion, such longing, not even on her wedding night, but it was not enough.

136

Alexander remonstrated, placing a hand on her right shoulder where she stood with her back frozen against him. 'Go,' she said a second time, fearing to look at him, but turning nonetheless, with pity in her eyes.

Her look of pity drew him back to his early days in the orphanage when he had lined up with the other children in front of would-be mothers and fathers, to be chosen for adoption or for a home visit, or not chosen at all. Alexander withdrew his hand and left.

As he walked along the path a solitary tear fell from his left eye and trickled along his cheek so that, as he opened the car door, it cut bitterly across his lip; it was as though his own hurt had seeped back into him because it had nowhere else to go.

He got into the Rover 200 and switched on the ignition. But as he turned the car into Rockdale Street he saw the eyes of the Virgin Mary stare down at him. But they were more than the Virgin's eyes: they were the eyes of Doctor T.J. Eckleburg looking at the valley of ashes he felt himself to be; they were the eyes of the sisters in the orphanage who looked at him with contempt and condemned without apology; they were the eyes behind the door of Rockdale Street; they were Elsie's eyes.

In the early hours of the morning Elsie found Alexander drunk and cold as he lay huddled on the front door steps.

Chapter 13

It was Friday night and The Rock was busy, but Alexander felt as though he was not busy enough; he wanted to work, not think, for his head hurt. There was so much mess and he'd no one to blame for it but himself. If Tommy found out that he'd slept with Mary, he might even lose his job. It wasn't just a mess, it was a fucking mess.

He took two aspirin and decided to rearrange the coolers; it would keep him busy, keep him from having time to think. He could shift between ten and twenty bottles in between pouring pints, if he was quick. He had one cooler cleared and cleaned before the first hour of his shift was over.

'You'll be getting promoted if you keep that up,' said Tommy. Alexander polished the glass door and closed it.

'Is the pay any better?' he said.

'Nope, but think of the status. Head Barman,' said Tommy, drawing the letters broadly in the air with his thumbs and index fingers.

'Think I'll just stay a low-grade barman if you don't mind,' said Alexander.

'But wouldn't you want to take over, as manager some day?

'Manager?' said Alexander rolling his eyes.

'Aye,' said Tommy, 'you heard right. I'm thinking long-term, into the future.'

'What?'

'The pub will be left to Robert of course, but he's no interest in it, never has. He'll be needing someone to run the place after I go.'

'Excuse me,' said Alexander as he got up from the floor.

'Where are you going?' said Tommy.

'The Guinness needs changed,'

'Right, but...'

'Unless you want me to leave your customers standing?'

'But you'll think about it?'

'Later,' said Alexander as he scratched the stubble on the side of his face, 'I'll talk to you about it later.'

Alexander went to change the Guinness, wishing that he smoked so that he could go outside and get a breath of air. His head hurt more than ever; he couldn't believe that of all the days and nights he'd worked in the bar, Tommy had chosen this one to dangle 'manager' in front of his eyes. A week ago he'd have jumped at the opportunity, but he knew that he couldn't tie his lot in with Robert's future; the present was precarious enough. He changed the barrel of Guinness and went back into the main bar.

'Three Guinness and a G&T coming up,' he said to Aiden. 'I'll bring it down to you when it's ready.'

'Saw Elsie today,' said Aidan. 'At mass. She was looking a bit peaky on it.'

Alexander hadn't seen Elsie today at all, for he'd been avoiding her since the night she'd found him on the doorstep. Aiden lingered at the bar.

139

'I'll bring it down to you,' Alexander repeated.

'You'll need to be taking care of her. She's a bit like myself, not getting any younger.'

'And how's...'

Alexander was about to ask after Aiden's wife, but he'd forgotten that she'd passed on earlier that year, so that the unfinished sentence hung painfully in the air. He knew that Aiden had heard it, as though it had been spoken.

'You'll bring it down then,' said Aiden, dropping his head forward so as not to have to look at Alexander.

'I'm sorry,' said Alexander as he put the settled Guinness onto the table. 'This one's on me.'

'Don't be daft,' said Aiden, holding out a twenty pound note. His hand shook as he held it, tremors that affected him only after his wife's death, tremors that were pronounced. 'We all make mistakes,' said Aiden forgivingly. 'I do the same thing myself sometimes in the house. I forget she's gone and I turn and I say something.' Aiden's eyes glazed over and he bit the side of his lip and made a smacking noise. 'We're all a bit daft on it sometimes. Here,' he said, holding out the twenty. No hard feelings.'

Alexander put his hand over Aiden's, folding the twenty back into his palm.

'On me,' he said. He went back to the bar, wrote out an IOU and placed it in the till.

'What's this?' asked Tommy, pulling out the IOU.

'I'll explain later,' said Alexander as he nodded to Aiden and his friends. Tommy sighed and scratched his head.

'You'll never make any money if you keep giving it away.'

140

'Aye,' said Alexander, 'maybe I won't.'

He looked up at the clock. It was only after ten and the bar had a late license. He was thinking (something he'd tried not to do) that it was going to be a long night when his mobile rang.

'It's Robert,' said Robert. 'Just a quick call to remind you about the match at Casement tomorrow.'

'I'd forgotten,' said Alexander.

'I've loads to tell you,' said Robert. 'The kids are looking forward to seeing you.'

Hearing Robert's voice made Alexander feel nauseous.

'Are you still there?' said Robert.

'I don't know that I can make it,' said Alexander.

'These tickets are gold dust. Course you can make it. Twelve, usual spot.'

'But...' said Alexander, but Robert had already rung off.

At the end of the shift Tommy handed Alexander his wages. He paid for the IOU and for a pint for both of them. 'I didn't know what else to do,' he explained, 'Aiden's a good bloke.'

'Nothing else you could have done,' said Tommy, accepting the apology while he poured them both another pint. 'I meant what I said about moving up, managing the bar. I'm not getting any younger myself and I know that you haven't been here long and you've a bit to learn, but now that you're helping me with the accounts.'

'It's not for me Tommy,' said Alexander.

'But I thought...' said Tommy, 'you'd jump at the chance.'

'It's a good offer and I appreciate it. But I've my own things that I want to do. Get my own place.'

141

'Robert wouldn't bother you.'

Alexander shook his head.

'I'd leave it in the will that that's the way I want it.'

'Yes, I mean no. He wouldn't. But it wouldn't work.'

'Course it'd work,' said Tommy. 'You're just being pig-headed. Is it because Robert would own it?'

'It's just not for me,' said Alexander. 'I'd be happy to continue doing the accounts. Help out too, but manage the place. No.'

'I just don't want the place to change hands and Alexander, well, you're practically family.' Alexander shuffled his feet. 'I don't want to force it on you,' said Tommy. 'But for God's sake Alexander, Robert and you are like brothers and you've always got on. What could go wrong?'

'Leave it Tommy,' said Alexander. 'I appreciate it, I really do, but it's like I said, it's not for me.'

'Right, right,' said Tommy, 'I get the message.' He stood up and walked behind the bar. 'I don't know that you would be any good at it anyway.'

'Jesus Tommy, there's no need to be like that.'

'Have you paid for that half bottle of whiskey?'

'Course I've paid for it.'

'Right then,' said Tommy. 'It's time to lock up.'

Alexander got his coat and left. He felt sick. As he turned into Rockdale Street he saw the statue of the Virgin Mary staring at him. He lifted the half bottle of whiskey out of his pocket and took a swig of it before climbing up onto the rock.

He took the child's route to the top where the Virgin sat, his large feet barely fitting into the edge of the footprints left by generations of small children. Footprint sunk on

142

footprint, so that through time the indentations had become monuments etched into the earth of those who had played there.

There were two routes to the top, a lower one for the younger children, and a tougher, higher climb. They were rites of passage, not just for those who lived in Rockdale Street, but for the children in neighbouring streets too.

As a child when he could find no-one to play with he would sometimes go and sit on the rock. Someone always turned up, nearly always.

And even as a child he sometimes imagined the form and shape and laughter of other children on other days, of other children before he himself was born, for Rosie had played here too. He saw Elsie look at the rock sometimes, remembering.

Alexander took the bottle of whiskey out of his pocket and took another swig, offering a swill to the lifeless three-foot figure beside him.

'Don't drink?' he said and laughed. 'The first shall be last,' he said, taking another swig, 'and the last shall be first.' He could see his breath in front of him and pulled up the collar of his coat. The blue paint on the statue was chipped in places so that it looked worn and uncared for.

'Don't you get lonely?' he said to the Virgin, offering her another drink. She declined. 'I'll have this one for you,' he volunteered, 'for it's cold tonight.' He pulled his collar up and took another swig. The bottle was almost empty.

'Now,' he said, striking up a full conversation with the statue. 'This business of miracles. Do they really happen?' The statue didn't answer. ''Cause if they do really happen, I have quite a few I'd like you to perform.'

143

'First,' said Alexander as he pulled and unravelled an imaginary scroll from his pocket, 'there's Aiden. He'd quite like his wife back. And then there's Mrs. Cullen – she'd love it to be 1942 and shacked up with her new husband. They could have a kid, and live happily ever after. And Tommy, well, he'd like to live forever and keep his goddam bar, and then there's Mary, yes Mary, she's got your name. She'd quite like her husband to be faithful. And Elsie, well, she doesn't want much, has never asked for much, but isn't it time she stopped having to scrimp and bloody well scrape for everything? A goddam bathroom, that's all she wants. That's not too much to ask, is it? She'd love it too. My God she'd love it.'

Alexander drained the last of the whiskey.

'And as for me,' he said, 'I don't want fuck all. Not a fucking thing,' he said, as he stood up and grabbed the Virgin, determined to shift her, but she was screwed into the rock.

He clambered in his drunken stupor off the rock, took off his shoes and tiptoed down the street with his shoes in his hand before pulling the key through the letterbox. He went quietly into the house and opened the cupboard under the stairs where the gas meter and tools were kept, but he couldn't find the right tool.

His head felt heavy and the tiredness gripped him, but he remained resolved to finish the job he'd started. After that, he couldn't remember very much except that when he woke in the morning the statue of the Virgin Mary was manning the inside of his bedroom door.

Alexander didn't know how he was going to get the statue back onto the rock without anyone knowing that

144

he'd stolen her. He needed a bloody miracle. Meanwhile, he cleared the junk from the bottom of the wardrobe and stuffed her into it.

'Someone stole the statue,' said Elsie when he came downstairs.

'No,' said Alexander. 'I was up early this morning. Going for a pee and I saw a couple of guys taking her for some restoration work.'

'You sure?' said Elsie. 'What was the name of the firm?'

'Don't know,' said Alexander, 'but I'll find out for you.' He could feel himself sweat.

Alexander left the house and drove straight to Hamilton's, the local graveyard sculptor. 'Can you do it?' he asked.

'Bring her in,' said the sculptor. 'We can do it, but it'll cost you. Repair work is almost as expensive as buying new. It's the detail, getting the right match, smoothing over the chips.'

'Yes,' said Alexander, checking his watch, 'But you can do it?'

'A hundred up front and the rest when it's ready.' Alexander gasped.

'I told you it was expensive. Do you want it fixed or not? It's all the same to me.'

'Yes,' said Alexander, 'how long will it take?'

'Bring her in first and we'll have a look.'

Alexander nodded.

He drove home, covered the statue with a sheet and put the Virgin into the back of his car.

'Her finger's broken,' said the sculptor, 'and the heel's chipped. Bit of paintwork. Not too bad. She'll be ready by Wednesday.' Alexander gave him the hundred quid; he didn't have the time or the energy to barter. He just wanted the statue fixed and back on the rock, for he didn't want Elsie to be upset. 'It's just a statue,' she'd said in the past, but he knew that she liked it. It made her feel safe, she'd said.

He drove home, left the car in Rockdale Street and gathered himself together as best he could, for he still had to face Robert. They hadn't met since the night he'd slept with Mary. Had she told him what had happened? He couldn't remember making arrangements to go to the hurling match and he wondered was Robert's phone call a ruse.

Chapter 14

Alexander walked past the railings of The Falls Park and on past the walls of the cemetery. Pedestrians thronged the pavement and a mother wheeling a double buggy came towards him so that he had to step onto the road; it too was jammed with traffic forcing him to manoeuvre between parked cars to make headway. He'd only a short way to go before he reached Casement Park.

The hurling match, for many, was a family outing but nevertheless Alexander encountered a crowd of teenagers hanging around the exterior walls, holding beer cans and cider bottles. They were unlikely to get through the turnstiles, even if they had a ticket. Alexander walked around them and saw Robert standing in one of the queues to get into the grounds. His arm was raised above the crowd, and he was shouting to grab Alexander's attention.

If the meeting at Casement was a ruse Robert wouldn't have brought the children, so Alexander strained to see them. It was only as he got closer that he saw Peter.

Mary hadn't told him after all, and Alexander considered, perhaps for the first time, that what had happened between them would remain hidden.

147

Yet as they queued to get into the park Alexander felt unwell.

The crowds continued to irk him so that he began to feel claustrophobic and slightly out of breath. He wiped his forehead with his sleeve, for he was sweating profusely, though it wasn't that warm. Perhaps it was just the crowds, perhaps a little anxiety. It would soon pass.

'Where's Emily?' said Alexander, and as if on cue Emily skated towards them eating an ice-cream. She reached for Alexander's hand; he took it and held it gratefully.

'We thought we'd lose you in the crowds,' she said.

Once through the turnstile and seated the match soon kicked off, and Emily, who wasn't all that interested in hurling, sat contentedly munching her way through a full bag of wine gums and a litre of coke. For a while it felt like old times. The terraces cheered for their home team Antrim, rising from their seats in excited synchronicity to applaud a point over the bar or to jeer at foul play from their opponents Offaly. But as half time approached the rain began to fall.

'Lucky we got tickets under the roofed terrace,' said Robert.

Alexander nodded and pulled out a fiver for Emily to go and get more sweets.

'We're back together,' said Robert emphatically as soon as the children left.

Alexander nodded but kept his eyes focussed on the pitch in front of him. He knew Mary would take Robert back, despite what she'd said, but he hadn't wanted to hear it.

148

'I've been meaning to ring you and tell you, but what with finishing with Maya and making it up to Mary there hasn't been much time.'

'How did she take it?' said Alexander, still unable to look Robert in the face. But Robert didn't notice, and kept on talking.

'Maya was grand about it. She said she knew it couldn't last because I was married.'

'I meant Mary,' said Alexander, without bothering to cover up his annoyance. 'How did Mary take it?'

'Oh, right. I think she was just glad that we were back on track. You know I'd forgotten how beautiful she is and I don't know how that happened. I was such a fool. But it's better now.'

'Better?'

'The love bit. Better than it's ever been.' Alexander felt his stomach heave as though he was about to throw up. 'Are you all right?' said Robert.

'No, I don't feel well.' He excused himself and retreated behind the terrace where he stuck his fingers down his throat and retched.

But he hadn't eaten all day and puked only bile. He wiped his mouth with the palm of his hand and returned to where Robert sat.

'You still don't look well,' said Robert.

'No,' said Alexander, feeling sick again. 'It's probably just indigestion. I'll go and get a can of coke.' He left, returning soon after, shook the can up and down and opened it to release all the gas before drinking it.

'That should cure it,' said Robert. Alexander nodded as Emily and Peter returned. 'Got enough sweets there?' said their father.

'I won't be sick,' promised Emily.

'Ssh,' whispered Robert. 'Alexander's feeling a wee bit ill.'

The match was long over before the final whistle. Offaly streaked ahead and when the end came the sky darkened so that the rain broke and a funereal mood of black umbrellas rose above the defeated home team. When they got outside Alexander put his hand up to his throat. It felt raw. A chip van was parked at the side of the road, but the greasy smell of fish and chips emanating from it made Alexander's stomach churn.

'It's as though what happened didn't happen,' continued Robert. 'As though it was a bad dream.'

'I don't care,' said Alexander.

'What?'

'You don't deserve her.'

'I thought you'd be glad,' said Robert, surprised by Alexander's abrupt and judgemental tone.

'I am,' said Alexander, hearing his outspoken lie.

Robert put his arm around Alexander's shoulder.

'You'll meet someone one of these days and then you'll understand what I'm talking about.'

'Understand?' questioned Alexander.

'Yes. But you know mate, you could do a wee bit to help yourself.'

'What do you mean?'

'Image. You could lose those glasses for a start. For Christ sake, you don't even need to wear glasses; your eyesight's perfect.'

Alexander took off his glasses and looked at them, as though for the first time. 'I love these glasses,' he said as Robert snatched them.

150

'Come get them,' said Robert, holding the glasses above his head.

Alexander wasn't amused, 'Give me the glasses,' he demanded, but Robert only laughed. 'Give me the goddam glasses,' he repeated.

'What do you want to bloody well look at the world through a window for?' said Robert as he continued to hold the glasses above his head.

Alexander couldn't reach up high enough to regain them and his anger swelled. He stepped back and rushed at Robert, bulldog fashion, knocking him to the ground. But Robert's jovial mood remained undisturbed.

Alexander had fallen over too, but as he lay on the ground Robert still held the glasses away from him, so he stuck his foot right into the middle of Robert's knee and leapt at them.

'Christ mate,' said Robert, sitting up. 'You could have busted my knee. We're not teenagers anymore either, for you to be charging at me like that.'

He rolled up his trousers to inspect the damage. 'That's going to bruise,' he said as he heard a crunch on the asphalt.

'There,' said Alexander. 'No more glasses.'

'You didn't need to do that,' said Robert as he got up from the ground. 'I said lose them, not break them.'

'Just about the same thing, isn't it?' replied Alexander, looking down at the glasses regretfully.

'What the hell's got into you?'

'Nothing,' said Alexander.

'Something's bloody well got into you.'

'Like what?'

'Like you're a different person.'

151

'Different!' said Alexander, and began to laugh. Robert scowled. 'You've known me a long time Robert but you don't know everything. Nobody knows someone completely; it's what makes life so goddam sad, and even if you did know me completely or I you for that matter maybe we wouldn't be standing here, maybe we wouldn't be mates at all.'

'I'm sorry,' said Robert. 'I didn't know the glasses meant that much to you.'

'The glasses,' exclaimed Alexander. 'You think this is about the bloody glasses?'

'I said I'm sorry.'

'Don't fucking patronise me. I'm not your fucking wife.'

'What's that meant to mean?'

Peter looked up at them both.

'Walk ahead son,' said Robert.

'A few birthday treats, a bit of the old Robert charm and you think your marriage has hit some sort of paradise. Get real.'

Peter had taken a couple of steps forward but hesitated before turning around to go back. 'Go on Peter,' said his father encouragingly, 'catch up with Emily. There,' he said pointing to Emily who was skating ahead of them. 'Do you see her?' Peter nodded and followed Emily, though every few steps he looked over his shoulder to ensure that his father was still in sight.

Robert turned around so that he stood in front of Alexander, barring the way.

'You've no fucking right to pass judgement,' he said.

'No, and you've no fucking right either. So keep your goddam opinions to yourself. The Mr Almighty, Mr Robert McMurray, isn't so bloody godly anymore.'

'Yes,' said Robert, 'I fucked up.'

'And you can fuck off as well.'

Alexander turned and walked back into the crowd, disappearing gradually from Robert's confused but angry gaze. He pushed his way through the crowd; it walked against him and he felt dizzy as though he'd drunk too much alcohol, even though today he hadn't touched a drop.

His mouth was parched and his brain hurt with images of Mary, on the night he had been with her, and on the night, described so vividly during the hurling match, that she and Robert were reconciled. His heart and mind and body felt like a pinball in the thronging endless mob that surrounded and jostled against him.

He grasped at his throat; it felt as though it would close over so that he could hardly breathe. He pushed harder through the crowd with flaying arms in order to break free of them so that he could breathe again. The crowd jeered as he stumbled and then someone gripped his wrist, grinding him to a halt. Still he couldn't breathe. He clenched his right hand, ready to land a punch in order to break free of his assailant, but as he turned and looked he saw that it was a pensioner who gripped him.

'Are you alright?' the old man said in a broken and frail voice. He stood a foot smaller in height. Alexander unclenched his fist and dropped his head forward.

'I'm sorry,' said Alexander as the tension in his body released so that he felt he might collapse onto the ground.

153

'You don't look too good son,' the old man said as he held onto Alexander's arm and led him through the mob to the nearest steps.

He helped him to sit down and told him to rest, but Alexander still felt as though he couldn't breathe. The old man momentarily left him, returning with a bottle of water.

'Drink,' the old man said. 'You've had a shock. At first I thought you were drunk.' Alexander nodded. 'But you're not drunk,' the old man stated, leaning closer into him.

'I better go,' said Alexander, stretching up to the black iron railing to get up.

The old man's strong but veined and purple hand gently fell on Alexander's arm. 'A wee while yet,' he said.

Alexander sunk back onto the concrete steps, took another sip of water and coughed. He raised a hand to his mouth to cover it.

'Polite too,' the old man said, withdrawing a clean white handkerchief from his side pocket. 'Here,' he said as he unravelled the ironed folds. 'Was someone chasing you?' the man said. Alexander shook his head. 'None of my business I suppose. But the way you were pushing.' Alexander looked up at the old man repentantly. 'Never mind,' he said. 'No harm done.'

The old man looked down at Alexander whose slim, chiselled features, Roman nose and freckled skin reminded him of a friend.

'Are you a sailor?' the old man said.

'Bookseller,' said Alexander, his breath gradually returning, 'or soon will be.'

'Aye,' said the old man. 'It's just that you remind me of someone.'

154

The old man sat down beside him. 'We'd some fun in those days, me and the friend that you remind me of.

We were both sailors, Jimmy and I. At least I was for a while. Travelled the world together when we were young. You look like him. In fact the more I look at you,' he said, turning his head and weighing the dimensions of Alexander's face more closely, 'the more you look like him. What's your surname?' Alexander shook his head. The old man grunted. 'I see,' he said. 'I was just being friendly.'

'I'm sorry,' said Alexander. 'It's just that I don't know what my surname originally was. I was left in the home, y'see.' The old man grunted again.

'What happened to him? Your mate,' said Alexander.

'Fishing accident. Off the coast of Newfoundland. I'd stopped the sailing long before. It must have been about twenty years ago. They said he fell overboard.'

'And did he?'

'I've my doubts. He was always getting into bother. Had a bit of a bad temper. He was the kindest bloke you'd ever meet too.'

'Aye, the kindest,' the old man said. 'Would've left himself with nothing in order to help someone out if they were stuck. Fond of the women, too fond of the drink. Never married. Bachelor boy he called himself. But by God, you're the spitting image of him. Do you think?' said the old man... but he didn't finish his question.

Alexander drank the last of the water and got up. He reached a hand out to the old man in order to help him up off the step.

'You alright now?' the old man asked.

'Better,' said Alexander, trying to smile.

'I didn't mean to interfere.'

'You helped me,' said Alexander, holding out his hand. The old man shook it, wrapping his left hand around the handshake.

'You be good,' the old man said, 'and take care of yourself.'

The crowds leaving the hurling match had all but disassembled. Alexander walked with his hands set deep into his pockets, contemplating the grey and dirty tarmac spat with used gum that would relieve his shame and his guilt and his self-pity only if it swallowed him whole.

As he walked on he thought of Elsie – the one constant in his life. Her face came before him slowly, usurping his hurt and his rejection and his self-pity.

If he thought about it properly, he was one of the lucky people, for there were many in life who were truly alone: without friend, without family, without love. His eyes gradually lifted from their downcast stasis and moved to take in the air and breathe easy with the sky, wide and open above him.

As he past St. John's the church bell chimed. It seemed a good omen. Perhaps all was not lost. He had fallen out with Robert before and they'd always made up. Why not now? Mary had not told him and there was no need for him to know.

He reached Rockdale Street, pulled the key on the long string through the letterbox and opened the front door, glancing sideways at the empty space on the rock at the top of the street. It would be less than a week before Hamilton's put it back where it belonged. But the street felt eerie, even to Alexander who did not believe in God, for its absence.

156

When Alexander entered the house the scullery door was wide open despite the cold that drifted through from the late autumn day; the fire in the living room was unlit, the house smelt of bleach and the yard had been scrubbed. A plain fresh white loaf, as yet unopened, lay on the drainer beside the sink. Elsie was in the small back room.

She had folded out the old darkly stained wooden table and laid newspaper on top of it. The newspaper was strewn with matching china cups and saucers.

The china had a gold leaf trim and a floral, predominantly dark red pattern. It had belonged to her father and mother, and had made its way to the city by horse and cart in a box laden with straw. It had been a wedding gift, and despite the intervening years remained in perfect condition. Elsie took it from the cabinet to wash it at least once a year, for it wasn't practical to use it from day to day; she did use it for special occasions though, if a priest called or she had something to celebrate, or when there had been funerals.

'Can I help?' Alexander said when he saw Elsie washing the china, but she shook her head.

Alexander went into the scullery and as he was filling up the kettle Elsie came through with a basin of dirty hot water. She pushed past him without speaking and threw the water out into the yard. It splashed over the walls and trickled down into the sunken drain.

'Out of my way,' she said, as she lifted the kettle and refilled the basin. In her haste the hot water spilled onto her worn and bleached-stained apron. Alexander lifted the kettle and refilled it. 'Is that all you can do?' she said. 'Drink tea.'

Alexander said nothing.

'You'd be better getting yourself a job.'

'I have a job,' Alexander answered. 'In the pub.'

'You call that a job.' she said.

Alexander could feel his head spin. He lifted his hand and cupped the edge of the sink to support himself. His head became dizzy as it had earlier when the thronging mob outside Casement had closed in upon him. He felt, like then, a tightening around his throat and a failure to breathe.

Elsie shouted to him from the back room where the china lay sparkling and polished on the table. He moved from the sink, supporting himself by the frame of the scullery door as the dizziness intensified. He hadn't had an asthma attack in years, but it was the self-same constriction he felt and with that panic and fear.

She kept shouting at him, but he couldn't hear her properly, about not having a job, about being a waste of space, a waste of time and effort.

It was only a few steps between the scullery and the door of the back room, Alexander moved towards it, laying his hands against the frame of the door to support himself.

He saw Elsie kneeling on the ground in front of the open door of the china cabinet, lifting the plates and cups from the table to put them back into the cabinet. 'What have I done?' he said.

'Done?' she screeched at him, jumping up from the floor and pointing her finger at him. 'You stole the statue.'

'I didn't,' he said.

'A liar too,' she screamed.

'Sssh,' he said. 'The neighbours will hear.'

158

'The whole bloody world can hear for all I care. Lily saw you. She said if it'd been anything else she wouldn't have said a word but no, she said that it was the statue and that you bundled it into the back of your car.'

'No,' said Alexander.

'You calling Lily a liar?'

'No.'

Alexander reached into his pocket, took out the receipt he'd kept and handed it to her.

'It got broken. I didn't want you to know so I took it to get it fixed.'

'You did what?' said Elsie, taking a step back from her confrontational stance.

'See,' said Alexander pointing at the receipt that Elsie held.

'Get me my glasses,' she said, trying to read the receipt. 'What'd it cost?'

'Two hundred.'

'And who paid for it?'

'I did,' he said.

'You bloody fool. It wasn't your responsibility. If it was broken by vandals it didn't mean...' But mid-sentence the truth dawned on her. 'You broke it,' she said. She pushed him away from the door, went into the living room and sat down on the settee. She crumpled the receipt in her hand and began to cry. 'How could you?' she said. 'How could you have done that?'

Alexander looked at Elsie's fallen and grieving posture. He wanted to go to her and hold her; he wanted to make it better, but he couldn't make it better. Her tears soon gave way to anger so that she clenched her left hand.

159

'Go to Lily,' she said, as she got up and pointed to the door. 'Tell her what you've told me. Show her the receipt too and hope to God that she hasn't told anyone else.' Elsie threw the receipt at Alexander's feet. He stooped to pick it up but as he bent over he fell forward and fainted onto the floor.

Chapter 15

Mary closed the diary and placed it at the back of the locker drawer. She descended the stairs and went into the garden to call the children and to send Emily's friend Leanne home, but as she began to open the door she overheard Emily.

'We adopted him,' said Emily.

Mary could see the children through the window and decided to leave the door ajar so that she could listen in on the rest of the children's conversation.

'Mum and Dad felt sorry for him,' continued Emily. 'But you'd have guessed that because we don't look alike at all.'

Leanne nodded.

'See,' said Emily persuasively. 'My hair is blonde while his is black. His is straight and mine is...'

'Beautiful,' interjected her admiring friend.

'Gee, thanks Leanne. Yours too.'

Leanne smiled and swayed from side to side. Emily gave her a quick hug and shouted for Peter, but he was up in the tree house and did not answer.

'Peter,' she called again but again he did not answer. She began to call him as you might call to a cat or a dog. 'Here Peter Peter,' she said.

Peter peeked his head out from the tree house.

'I'm not going,' he said. 'I don't like that man.'

'I don't want to go either but we have to go. It's your fault anyway.'

'It's not,' said Peter.

'It is,' said Emily. 'And you know I'm not allowed to say why.' Peter muttered something inaudible as he climbed down the ladder. 'He can't even speak properly,' said Emily as she poked him on the back with her finger. 'Ask him,' she said.

'Ask him what?' said Leanne. 'Tell Leanne that you're not really my brother.'

'No,' Peter answered.

Emily rolled her eyes. Leanne nodded, but she felt a little sorry for Peter whose face had become red and puffed out as though he was about to cry.

'I've got the car started,' said Robert as he came through the open front door, 'I think it needs a new battery.'

Mary was standing in the kitchen, still listening to Emily and Leanne's conversation.

'Have you called the children?' he said.

'Ssh,' she said, putting her fingers up to her lips. Robert walked up the hallway and into the kitchen so that he stood behind her.

'She's vicious with him,' said Mary in a low whisper.

'What happened?' he said.

'Nothing, just the way she speaks to him.'

'Don't be daft,' he said, 'it's just children. It's the way they are.' Robert opened the back door. 'Get your coats,' he said to Emily and Peter.

162

'I'll call you later,' said Emily as she waved goodbye to Leanne.

'What coat?' said Robert as he stood looking at the overfull rack of coats hanging under the open staircase.

'That one,' she said pointing towards her red coat. Robert lifted it and helped her to button it up.

'Can I have a scooter for my Christmas present?' she asked. 'Leanne says she's getting one.'

'We'll have to wait to see what Santa brings.'

'You know that Santa doesn't really exist,' said Emily, 'so can I have a scooter or not?'

'We'll see,' said her father.

Can I?' said Emily, turning around to her mother.

'You'll have to wait and see what Santa brings,' said her mother as she helped Peter to zip up his blue woollen fleece.

'Have you the letter?' she asked Robert.

'Yes,' he replied, checking his coat pocket, but he couldn't find it.

'Jesus Robert. It was just a bloody letter. You'd think you'd be able to hold onto a bloody letter for five minutes without losing it.'

'I have it. I know I have it,' he said, checking through his pockets once again. Mary went into the kitchen to look for it.

'Damn it Robert,' she said. 'We'll be late. You must have set it down somewhere.'

'Found it,' he said. 'It was on the floor underneath Peter's blue and red tricycle.'

'And how'd it get there?' she said, shaking her head from side to side. Robert shrugged. Emily and Peter looked up at their mum's angry countenance. 'Let's go,' she said. 'We'll be late.'

'We'll get ice-cream afterwards,' said Robert.

Emily took her father's hand and squeezed it as Mary stooped to pick Peter up. 'Take your thumb out of your mouth,' she said.

****

On the way to the hospital the gentle motion of the car rocked the children to sleep. Robert pulled into the carpark and took a parking ticket, complaining about having to pay.

'Who's sick?' said Emily waking.

'No-one,' replied her mother.

'Oh,' said Emily, rubbing her eyes, 'I'd forgotten.' She nudged Peter to waken him up.

'We won't be long,' said Robert. Mary glared at him.

'And then where are we going? said Emily as she leant over the passenger seat.

'Are you okay?' said Robert to Mary.

'Yes,' she snapped. 'I wish you'd stop asking me that.'

'I'm just trying Mary,' he said.

'I know.' As he pulled the jack up she reached out her hand, placing it on top of his to give him a gentle squeeze. 'I know,' she repeated.

They got out of the car and walked towards the modernized wing of the Royal Victoria Hospital. Mary withdrew the letter from her handbag. 'Room 19, second floor,' she said nervously.

164

They entered the building and decided to take the lift. As the door was closing a man in a beige dressing gown jammed it back open and entered. 'Takes for ages for it to come back down again,' he said. He wore long stripped pyjamas that were freshly creased and his white chest hair stuck out from his top where it had been wrongly buttoned up.

'Why is he in his pyjamas?' said Emily out loud. The man laughed. 'What floor?' he asked before pressing the lift buttons. Mary could smell disinfectant. She didn't know whether the floor had just been cleaned or whether the smell came from the man's bandaged arm, but it made her feel nauseous.

It had been a year since their last appointment with the educational psychologist.

'I don't like it here,' said Emily. 'Will it be the same man? The one with the weird moustache.'

Mary told her that she'd too many opinions and that she must be quiet for a change as she stopped to double-check the room number on the card she held. It was the right door, at last.

Inside the room several toys lay on a multi-coloured rug making a play area at the far end. The room was brightly lit, glaringly so, but there were no windows and therefore no natural light. At one side of the room a large mirror stretched across the wall. It was only halfway through their first visit when Mary realised that there were people on the other side of it: doctors or nurses or psychologists, watching her. For though she had been unable to see them, the room was not fully soundproofed and she had heard one of them cough.

165

Peter and Emily immediately walked towards the toy area. Peter picked up a plastic truck, attached a trailer to it and began to run it manually along the small line of track that was laid out. Robert and Mary sat down at the long rectangular table; he reached under it to take Mary's hand but she refuted his comforting gesture, 'There'll be somebody watching,' she whispered as she looked at the mirror. A nurse came in and told them that the doctor was delayed but would be with them shortly.

Mary fixed her blouse. It was pulled at the front so that you could see her brassiere. It was the first time she had noticed her weight increasing. Soon, if she kept the baby, she would have to buy new clothes.

She looked at the mirror, hoping to see even an outline of a shape behind it, but she could see nothing. Emily left the play area and went over to sit beside her father. Peter followed her, though he climbed onto his mother's knee. Even the children had grown impatient.

Mary leant towards Robert and took his hand. 'I wish he'd hurry up,' she said. 'I feel like a caged animal in a zoo.' 'Me too,' he whispered.

The doctor came in and apologized for his lateness. He wore a pale grey suit and a plain navy tie. As the session continued Mary knew that she would forget about the mirror, but she was angry at having to wait, angry at the double sided mirror that had the year before fooled her, for a time.

There was always someone watching you – the CCTV in the shopping mall or on public streets, the speed camera on the motorway, the person in the car beside you at traffic lights.

Always eyes, watching.

166

Dr. Smyth had been in the hospital over thirty years. He was of average height and had a mouth full of gleaming white teeth. Despite this, when he spoke, his one gold tooth, a prominent front molar, seemed to draw all of your attention. He had white soft fleecy hair, marred by the occasional fleck of black. He leant towards Peter to tousle the top of his head, but Peter jerked away from him.

Robert got up from the chair and held out his hand. Dr. Smyth smiled congenially. 'No need to get up,' he said. Robert sank back into the chair. 'So how are we?' the doctor asked.

Mary and Robert turned to look at one another.

'Fine,' said Robert. Emily held firmly onto her father's hand and leaned into him as though for protection.

'Perhaps you both would like to play with the toys?' said Dr. Smyth to the children. Peter put his hands around his mother's neck as if to draw her closer to him.

'It's alright,' she said, taking his clinging arms away from her neck. 'Go back and play with the toys.'

Emily leaned closer into her father. 'I don't like him,' she whispered, but the doctor clearly overheard. Robert blushed.

'Go on,' he said, letting go of her hand. Emily sighed.

Dr. Smyth reassured Mary and Robert that it was all very natural for children to be a little strange with people they didn't know. 'If we could go and sit on the settee,' he added.

Mary and Robert got up and moved to the red cushioned settee that lay along the simulated living space. The settee was positioned in front of the multi-coloured rug. The doctor took a seat on the armchair and flicked over the first page of his clipboard.

167

Emily pulled Twister from the bottom of a pile of boxes of games and spread it on the floor.

'Will you play?' she said turning to her father. Robert looked at the doctor.

'You can if you like,' the doctor said. Robert shook his head.

Occasionally Dr. Smyth made a note on the clipboard with the silver Parker pen he withdrew from his inside jacket pocket. As soon as he made a note he put the pen back in the inner pocket, withdrawing it when necessary. The action irritated Robert. Why didn't he just hold it in his hand?

Emily tried to get Peter to play Twister with her but Peter ignored her and continued to run the toy truck up and around the lines of track. Emily folded up the Twister mat and tidied it back into the box. She ran her eyes along the boxes of games and withdrew Connect 4. She fixed the legs on the plastic frame and separated the coloured counters.

'Will you play?' she asked her father. Robert nodded and sat down on the rug beside her with his legs crossed beneath him. Dr. Smyth looked on as he continued to make the occasional note on the clipboard.

Halfway through the session Peter stopped playing with the truck and climbed up onto Mary's knee to huddle into her. Mary was glad that he had come to her, for she had become conscious once more of the mirror through which they were all being watched.

As she nursed him she wondered would he grow up to be normal. Would he be able to do things for himself? Would he be able to count, read, interact socially with others? She wanted to ask the doctor questions that she

168

couldn't ask in front of the children. She wanted answers, but nobody seemed capable of giving her any. At least Robert had agreed to have him assessed, for he'd refused for years to accept anything was wrong. 'You'll see,' he said, 'he'll come into his own someday.'

She remembered the time Peter threw a tantrum in the supermarket, screaming for no apparent reason and then running down one of the aisles, knocking food and tins deliberately off the shelves. He'd always had sporadic violent tantrums but Robert denied anything was wrong.

'Peter is Peter,' he said. 'He'll grow out of them.'

The session ended. Dr. Smyth rose and thanked them both for coming. He said goodbye to the children and showed them to the door.

'Bloody waste of time,' said Robert as they entered the lift.

'I expect they know what they're doing,' said Mary. When they got downstairs the children ran ahead of them towards the car park.

'I don't think they know a thing,' Robert continued. 'The doctor talked to Emily more than he did to Peter or to you or me for that matter.'

'I know,' she said. 'But they've seen kids like Peter before. They must have a system for assessing him.'

'What assessment?' said Robert. 'We've had no feedback whatsoever.'

'It was only our second meeting.'

'All they do is pry. What business is it of theirs to know how much time I spend at home? He practically accused me of being a bad father.'

'I don't think that's what he meant. Just that Peter needs more attention than the average kid.'

169

'Am I a bad father?' he said.

'No, Robert. It's just Peter, the way he is.'

'I don't think we should go back,' suggested Robert.

'Then how are we going to find out what's wrong with him?

'There's nothing bloody well wrong with him,' said Robert. 'He'll be alright. You'll see.'

'That's typical.'

'What?'

'Of you. Ignoring things. Thinking they'll just go away.'

'For Christ sake Mary, I'm here, aren't I? If I was ignoring it I wouldn't be.'

'In body,' she said.

'So you think I am a bad father? Is that what you're telling me?'

'This isn't about you. It's about Peter.'

'Well it doesn't sound like it,' he said. 'Let's just get the kids into the car and go.'

Emily got into the back seat and fixed her own seatbelt as Robert leaned over to attach Peter's for him. They'd planned to take the children to the park, but the rain had come down so they stopped at an ice-cream parlour before heading home.

The streetlight outside the house had blown out so that as they pulled into the driveway it was dark. Peter was still asleep in the back of the car, unlike Emily who automatically woke when the ignition was switched off. Robert lifted Peter as Mary opened the front door. He carried him upstairs, zipped off his fleece and gently took his elastic waisted jeans off before easing him into the bed. He went from there to Emily's room. Everything was pink

– the walls, the carpet, her quilt cover. Even her favourite china doll, Victoria, wore a pink brocaded dress. Victoria sat prominently on the dresser, amid a profusion of other dolls. Her hair was neatly plaited and hung down the bodice of her dress. When she had got her for Christmas the year before Emily had been tempted to call her Rapunzel.

'Are you happy?' said Robert, sitting down beside her on the bed.

Emily nodded. 'Victoria's happy too,' she said, lifting the doll from the dresser whose life-like Renaissance eyes opened and shut when it was moved.

'Don't play for long,' said Robert. 'I'll bring up some juice and biscuits.'

He heard Peter waken and crossed the pine-floored landing to his room.

It was smaller than Emily's room, but the furniture had been arranged to maximize the space; at the end of his bed was a raised built-in wardrobe; to the left of this a tall thin cupboard, also built-in, that stored Peter's toys. They were piled haphazardly on top of each other so that the cupboard barely closed.

But Peter was not looking for toys to play with, for he was rummaging in the freestanding chest of drawers.

'I want my pyjamas,' he said. Robert found a top and a bottom, though they didn't match. He held them up.

'I'll put them on myself,' said Peter.

Robert sat on the edge of the single bed, encouraging him in this newfound desire for independence. Peter pulled up the bottoms, but when he hauled the top over his head it got stuck. He started to scream, pulling at the pyjama top as his face got redder and redder. Robert

171

quickly undid the neckline buttons on the left side and lowered it over him.

'I'm sorry,' said Peter.

'You haven't done anything,' said Robert, tucking him in for a second time as he kissed Peter on the forehead. 'Goodnight son,' he said.

When he came downstairs Mary was pouring hot milk from the saucepan into two mugs. He leant against the frame of the doorway and as she handed him the cup she tried to smile. Robert took the cup gratefully.

'Shall we light the fire?' she said.

Robert immediately set to work. He loaded rolled newspaper and sticks onto the grate. Within a few minutes, the sticks caught and he placed logs on top of them. He sat back on the wingchair and lifted the remote control, but Mary asked him to keep the television off for a while. He acquiesced and put the remote on the side table as she sat down on the rug at his feet.

'Would you have left?' she said, as she took his hand.

'I thought you wanted to talk about Peter,' he said.

'I just wanted to talk, that's all. I need to talk,' she said. 'You owe me that at least.' Robert nodded. 'When you were with her, did you ever seriously consider leaving me and the kids?'

Robert let go of her hand and got up from the chair to put more logs onto the fire. He lifted the poker and prodded at the burning wood.

'I can't talk about this,' he said.

'We have to. I need to know whether you still think of her, whether you have any regrets.'

'I don't think of her,' said Robert.

'You always look at your feet when you lie,' she said.

172

'I don't.'

'You do, and I never told you this before but you blush too. The redness starts at the neck and works its way up.'

'I'm not lying,' he said, poking the fire and turning one of the logs over so that its red belly and blackened edge crackled.

'You're not telling me the truth either.'

'I loved you more,' he said, raising his voice. 'Isn't it enough that I loved you more and that I'm here with you now and with the kids?'

'Is it enough? That's what I need to know.' Her voice was calm and controlled.

'More than enough,' he said, putting the poker back into the compendium.

'And if it happened again?'

'It won't. I was a fool,' he said, stooping down to her on the floor. 'A stupid fool. I nearly threw everything away.' She put her hand up to his cheek and ran her fingers through his hair, caressing him. 'Puppy-dog eyes,' she said. He lay down on the rug beside her and rested his head on her lap. The fire blazed in the hearth and the quiet of the night and the shadows on the walls gave the room a restorative calm. She continued to caress the top of his head, sighing, hoping. They sat on in the quiet, comforting each other and wishing away the hurt that had been.

After a time Robert got up and cleared away the cups. 'Shall I put more wood on the fire?' he said. Mary nodded and followed him into the kitchen.

The wood was stacked outside the back door and covered over with a blue plastic sheet. As he fetched it, she filled the dishwasher and rinsed out a dirty cloth in the sink, draping it over the spout of the taps to dry. She boiled more milk and made another two cups of hot chocolate.

Once the fire was loaded, Robert came back into the kitchen. He watched Mary's gentle movements while admiring her slim and curvy physique. He went towards her and kissed her softly on the nape of the neck. She leant back into him, fighting back a tear. But she cast off her tearfulness and shooed him back into the sitting room, swiping at him jokingly with the tea towel.

'Go on, you big eejit,' she said, 'before that chocolate, like the last one, gets cold.'

Robert lifted the cups and retreated. She came and sat beside him. He lifted his arm and put it around her and they sat together, stroking and caressing one another in the shadow of the night. And for a time, it was once more quiet. But Mary broke the silence. She'd been building herself up to ask him all evening. 'Have you ever thought of having another child?' she said.

'I've never really thought about it,' he said. 'I know we always said that two was enough.'

'But if it did happen, would you be happy?'

'Are you?' he said, remembering the night of their reconciliation, for they hadn't used any protection.

'No,' she said.

Robert gave a sigh of relief.

'We don't need any more kids,' he said.

'No?'

'Another baby in nappies, crying at night, disturbing our sleep. And the cost doesn't bear thinking about.'

'I suppose,' she said.

174

'Maybe it's time I went and got the snip. What do you think?'

Mary looked towards the fire. If he didn't want another child then what was she going to do with the child inside her. She didn't want to disturb the happiness they'd re-established; she didn't want to lose him a second time. She couldn't take the risk.

Chapter 16

The following week Mary made plans to go to London. She had gone to visit her sister Eliza before, and though it was close to Christmas Robert did not object. He made light of the expense and immediately applied in work for overtime.

He needn't the extra money anyhow, for he needed to pay off the credit card whose mounting bill was becoming difficult to manage. The expense of the children's toys would have to be met with further debt; it seemed an unavoidable cycle. He did not tell Mary about his financial concerns for she had always left financial matters for him to manage: he gave her a set rate for the housekeeping each week and paid the bills himself separately.

When Mary discovered she was pregnant she had begun to save. She cut down on the grocery bills and other minor expenses, but despite her thrift she had only managed to gather just under two hundred pounds; the money was tucked away in a manila envelope at the back of her locker drawer, underneath the diary. The abortion and her overnight stay in London would cost six hundred.

Robert gave her two hundred pounds for the trip and booked her flight online; she still had a shortfall of two hundred pounds and although it was the last thing she wanted to do she'd had to go to her mother for a short-term loan to make up the deficit.

Robert believed that despite their difficulties his marriage was back on track. He drove her to the airport, happy for her to have a short holiday. When he said goodbye and tucked an extra fifty pounds into her pocket and kissed her, she feigned delight; once the foetus was gone they could get back to normal life, he would never have to know.

On arrival at Heathrow airport she took a taxi straight to the clinic and paid for the treatment up front. The nurse led her into a room and asked her to undress. It was a simple operation, they said, and she would be ready to leave that evening.

She sat on the bed in a white gown, open at the back, though tied. She hadn't rung her sister at all, nor had she booked into a hotel. She'd thought only about getting rid of the child that Robert didn't want, that she didn't want. Before long the nurse came back, pushing a wheelchair.

'I don't need that,' said Mary.

'It's for when you come back. You'll need to rest for a while afterwards,' said the nurse.

'You don't understand,' said Mary, 'I don't need it. I've changed my mind.'

The nurse didn't look surprised. 'Right,' she said. 'You're not the first to have a change of plan at the last minute.' Mary quickly changed into her clothes. 'You'll still have to pay,' said the nurse.

'All of it?' said Mary.

177

'Afraid so,' said the nurse.

Mary sighed.

When Mary left the clinic she roamed about the footways along The Thames River, watching the endless traffic – cruise liners, barges, pleasure boats, but there was no joy in her seeing; the river reminded her only of books by Dickens, rich in character and dark in their depiction of human life: the good struggling against the bad and the Little Nell's losing. She looked at the river's murky depths. How many had drowned there? How many had thrown themselves away?

Her head felt ready to crumble in its confusion. How had she come to be here? She felt she did not know herself at all, except that she felt without hope. And as she looked at the river, she understood that it was not courage that drew her towards its murky depths, but despair.

But she could not think like that, Peter and Emily needed her and hope would come again, if only she would wait.

And so she walked upstream towards Tower Bridge where the pleasure boats berthed. The sun was strong in the sky; she stopped at intervals, lifting her head up and closing her eyes, letting the sun's rays float towards her, letting it warm the shell of her and reconcile her to the child she carried.

As early evening approached she rang her sister. They met up in front of Parliament Buildings, went for dinner and afterwards took the tube back to her sister's house. She did not have to tell her sister why she had come, for her sister guessed; but neither did she tell her that she had not gone through with it. 'I'll be leaving tomorrow,' she said instead. 'I want to get home, see Robert, see the kids.'

When she got to Belfast International she phoned Robert's mobile, but there was no answer so she took the bus into the city centre and went for a coffee in Castlecourt shopping mall.

The shop windows effulged with Christmas decorations: establishing a mood distant from her own, for she didn't know whether or not she'd made the right choice. In some ways it would have been easier to have gone though with the abortion, but if Robert found out that she'd even thought about abortion, he'd never forgive her.

She took the bus and picked the children up from school. She had bought them both a present – not in London, as they supposed, but in Castlecourt.

When Robert got home from work she told him that her and Eliza had had an argument. He did not question her further nor comment on the money she'd wasted on the trip.

In the month of November and early December Robert worked late at the office almost every evening. He took the extra paperwork home with him, but he complained that Emily and Peter interrupted him and soon decided that he would have to stay late at the office to get his work done.

Mary still didn't tell him about the pregnancy, though he'd noticed that she'd put on weight.

She was alone more often than she would have liked and when Robert did get home he was often too tired to make conversation or to play with the children, who would, anyhow, be in bed an hour or so after he returned.

She tried to stay strong, for they had two children with carefully prepared Christmas lists and it was her job to give them the best Christmas they could have. Emily had written Peter's list for him because he had not yet learnt how to write. The list she prepared for him was short: a Scaletrix for his main toy, a selection box and some picture books; pyjamas to wear on Christmas Eve and a surprise because she couldn't think what a boy might actually want for Christmas.

Her own list was somewhat longer.

She wanted an x-box with the latest games. She wrote down the names of five favourites but suggested that three would do because she didn't want to seem greedy. She also wanted a mobile phone, though she knew that her mother and father didn't want her to have one, so she created a list of justifications: my friends have one; in case I get lost; in case I am late so that I can ring home; everyone has one.

She wanted a new outfit for Barbie. In this too she added justifications. She wanted a surprise too and made several suggestions – a camera (although if she got, she said, a really good mobile then it might have a camera), a new pair of roller skates, pink preferably, and a cd or two: either Britney's latest one or one from the new boy band.

Emily wrote the lists in gold and silver pens and decorated them. She was happy with Peter's list, but she changed her mind about her own list and decided to rewrite it. When she'd completed it for the second time she presented it to her mother. 'Will you pass this on to Santa for me?' she said as she giggled. Her mother took the list and sat down in the living room in front of the fire to read it. Emily sat beside her, leaning in.

'Are you sure that's all?' her mother asked. Emily scratched her head with one of the silver pens.

'I think so,' she said.

180

'Wouldn't one big surprise do?' Emily smiled and said of course but that it was Christmas and therefore important to make a list, a long list, to make sure that you got something you really wanted.

'That's very wise of you,' her mother said as she hugged her. 'I'll put this where Santa will find it,' she added, winking. Emily tried to wink back, but she hadn't quite mastered the art, and so she closed both eyes and held them shut before re-opening them. 'Are you going to help me set the table for dinner?' her mother said.

Emily loved setting the table. It was one of her favourite chores. She did it with care and precision so that it was both neat and ornate. When she'd finished she ran into the hallway and opened her schoolbag. 'I forgot,' she said. She'd drawn a picture and handed it to her mother.

'I'll put it up with the others,' her mother said.

The noticeboard in the kitchen had grown in size. It had started as eight corked tiles that Mary attached to the wall. One of Emily's first drawings still hung there – indecipherable splotches of paint that according to Emily was a ballerina, a stage and an audience. Her drawings were colourful – yellows and pinks and purples, girly colours, and her talent had developed quickly so that she could draw portraits and landscapes with considerable skill for her age. As the children had brought more and more pictures home from school, Mary had added further corked tiles so that the top half of one of the kitchen walls was almost completely covered; but Peter's drawings showed little development from his early years so that the contrast between his and Emily's was stark.

When Robert got home Emily ran to him.

'I've made my list,' she said. 'You should see what I'm getting for Christmas.'

Robert looked up at Mary who half-smiled and shrugged her shoulders.

'Let me see,' he said.

'Oh, I can't,' she said. 'The list's gone off to Santa land. But maybe Mummy will let you see it.' Then she hugged him around the waist and squeezed her head into his thigh. 'It'll be great,' she said. 'Can we put the tree up?'

Robert was tired but Emily was right, it was time to put up the Christmas tree. They had left it late this year.

Robert climbed into the attic and retrieved the shabby dusty box. It was the same tree they'd bought for their first Christmas in the house, when Emily was only two years old. He lifted the box of trinkets and handed it to her as he stood on the ladders. Emily felt excited. She ran into the living room and tipped the box of decorations onto the floor while Robert and Mary put up the tree. Emily began to decorate it and even Peter in a rare moment of participation lifted a figurine from the pile of trinkets on the floor and handed it to his mother to put onto the tree.

'Here,' he said pointing to a branch. 'Put it here.'

Robert arranged the lights, though he had to change the fuse before they would work and a few bulbs too. When the tree finally lit up Emily clapped, enraptured by the lights, though she'd seen them before.

'It's pretty,' she said. 'It's always pretty.'

As the tree began to take shape Mary wondered whether things would sort out in the end. She would have to tell Robert about the child, but not yet, not until Christmas was through. The children were not even finished their school term yet and Peter had got into more bother: he'd destroyed a boy's painting.

When the school rang to ask her to come and withdraw Peter from class she had had to go alone. She was used to this, for invariably Robert was at work when school meetings took place.

The school had also sent her an invitation to Emily's nativity play.

She asked Robert to take the time off work, but he said the office was busy and that he couldn't. The following week she went alone to the nativity, feeling the extra weight she carried, feeling tired.

At night she refuted Robert's advances because she was afraid that he would know in her nakedness that she was pregnant. She was also worried about the amount of time he seemed to be spending at the office, and when she confronted him and was told that the office had a backlog of case studies she did not know whether to believe him or not; it wouldn't be the first time he had lied to her. And so she hid her pregnancy from friends, from neighbours, from her mother and from Robert, and she relied instead upon the confessional diary.

****

Robert knew that she kept a diary. He respected her privacy, but as the weeks moved slowly forward and her taciturnity increased he began to wonder about her true feelings. Perhaps she had not forgiven him. He was tempted to read it, but he rejected this as an unforgivable violation.

183

As the weeks passed it seemed to take him longer to get through the same amount of work. Initially he believed that the case studies had become more complicated, but he soon realised that he was simply over-tired. There didn't seem to be any time in the day and the extra money he made was a pittance; it would never clear the credit card. But the money was less important to him than his disintegrating relationship. Mary would not let him touch her.

It was late January and Mary was out at her mother's house. The drawer of the locker was not fully closed. Robert lay on the bed, exhausted from his day's work and tired of feeling that he didn't have a life beyond the office; he looked out at the fir trees and the night sky – powerfully luminous though there were only a sprinkling of stars visible. He held the diary in his hand, hesitate to open it but wanting to nonetheless; but he put it back in the drawer, quickly taking it out again. He needed to know what she was thinking; he needed to fix his marriage.

The first half of the diary was full of mundane events and occasional notes or reminders of things to do, even minor details such as mending a button on a coat or jacket were listed. It had further lists of goals Mary had set herself: to exercise more, lose a little weight, to spend less on the housekeeping and save a little. She also had a list of last year's resolutions, some achieved and ticked, some not and therefore stroked out.

Robert turned the pages of the diary. It had several entries relating to books Mary had read; there were summaries or notes or simple quotes that had struck a chord with her and that she'd annotated in the margin, 'commit to memory'. Robert sighed as he read these,

184

regretting that the opportunity to finish her studies had never been realised. On one occasion, years before, she had filled in an application but had not posted it. 'It's been so long,' she said. 'I'm not sure whether I'd be able to study anymore. And when would I find the time?' It was just after Peter was born. He remembered the difficult time she'd had with him during pregnancy and the post-natal depression she'd suffered afterwards. It had been a difficult time for all of them.

There were ticks in the diary too, ringed S's and a drawn smile beside these, commemorating special days or birthdays or outings. Robert laughed when he saw the tick and double capital S beside the night when they'd got back together.

'SS, the diary said, again in the margin, 'Smile plus Sex.' And two faces drawn beside it.

He was smiling at the badly drawn faces when he heard a key sound in the lock downstairs. Robert hastily stuffed the diary back into the drawer of the locker. He went downstairs, but there was no one at the door. He poured a cup of tea, feeling his heart palpitate, when the phone rang causing him to jump.

It was Mary.

'It'll be after ten before I'm home,' she said. Robert looked at the clock. It was only nine-thirty.

'And how is she?' said Robert

'Fine,' said Mary.

'Do you want me to pick you up?'

'No,' she said. 'I've the taxi booked. Have to go,' she said, ringing off.

Robert lifted the tea and went back upstairs. The night sky remained clear and luminous, but it was strange for the house to be so quiet. He realised that he had never spent a night alone in any house throughout his entire life. He lifted the diary out.

As he read on his face began to twist and contort. He moved to the edge of the bed and rubbed his temples, not wanting to believe the words so clearly written in black and white.

He read on, flipping back over the pages as though by re-reading them he might erase what they said. His face reddened in anger and with the book held nervously in his hand he began to pace the floor. Finally he closed the book and hurled it across the room.

'But she didn't,' he argued with himself. 'She didn't do it.'

But he could not quell his anger. The veins on his neck seemed to enlarge and pulsate, and every sinew of his body gathered into a wild intemperate fusion so that as the front door opened Mary heard the bedside lamp break into smithereens.

He descended the staircase with his fists clenched, stopping in front of her. 'You bitch,' he said.

Mary pulled the children into her, 'Go up to your room,' she said to Emily, 'bring Peter with you.' Emily started to cry. 'It'll be alright,' said her mother. 'You'll see, it'll be alright.'

'What's the matter Robert?' she said calmly, masking her fear while she kept one eye on the children as they walked up the staircase.

He lifted his arm high above her and smashed the back of his palm against the side of her face so that she fell to the ground.

'Are you mad?' she screamed, looking up.

'If you weren't pregnant I'd kick the living daylights out of you. Get up,' he said.

'What? So that you can hit me again?'

'Hit you?' he laughed shrilly. 'That's funny,' he said, 'really funny.'

'What's funny Robert?'

'You'd have killed it,' he yelled, bending his face in all of its violence towards her.

'Killed what?' she said.

He put his hands forcefully around her upper arms and raised her up off the floor. He began to shake her.

'Why?' he screamed. She did not answer him. He continued to shake her until his voice gradually lost its violence and its loudness so that the why turned into a murmur of abandon. He stopped shaking her and sat down on the floor beside her, cupping his head with his hands. 'Why?' he said.

'I was afraid.'

'Of what?'

'That you'd leave.'

'You didn't want our baby,' he said.

'I didn't do it. I didn't go through with it. Here,' she said, pulling up her jumper and holding her belly out to him. 'Our child is still here.'

'I have to get out,' said Robert, pulling at his tie.

'Leave?' she said.

'Just out of here. I can't think. My head's swimming.'

'You can't leave Robert. You have two children.'

'Three,' he said. 'Three children.' He opened the front door and gasped at the air. 'I can't stay,' he said.

'Forgive me,' she said.

'I hit you.'

'Sssh,' said Mary taking both his hands in hers. 'It was a slap, that's all.'

'I hit you,' he said.

Chapter 17

Hamilton's rang to say that the statue had two hairline cracks and was not, after all, worth mending. 'Can you make another one? An identical one?' said Alexander. 'Cost you,' said the sculptor. They agreed a price, though Alexander knew that he was being ripped off.

'At least you made up for it,' said Elsie when the statue was replaced the following week. It was her way of saying that she had forgiven him.

In the weeks and months that followed Alexander attended his business classes with stronger commitment. He continued to work long shifts at the bar and spent as little as possible and saved as much as he could. His savings alongside his thrift gradually mounted so that within six months he had begun to look for premises for the second-hand bookstore.

It was not as easy as he had anticipated. The right location was problematic in itself. He viewed several areas, initially intent on setting up in the University district, but he soon learnt that premises there were inordinately expensive. He came therefore to search closer to home. It made economic sense and perhaps would also reach a market that was not inundated, but he had to find the right building.

The estate agents, for there had been a lull in the market, had several premises to let. None of them suited. 'There's still the old doctor's surgery,' they suggested.

The surgery was on the floor of a three-storeyed terraced building on the front of the road. But even as he climbed the steps Alexander knew that it was not what he was looking for. It had been empty a long time and when the estate agent opened the door a puff of dust seemed to float out of it as though the vault of a tomb had just been opened.

The sickly yellow walls were marred with the imprint of sticky fingers and the red plastic chairs were scratched and worn.

Alexander remembered being in the surgery as a child, surrounded by people who looked either fed-up with waiting, or genuinely worried. He heard the gruff phlegm of heavy smoker's coughing, but most of all he saw poverty – the torn lining of a coat, hastily pulled over as the coat fell open; the shoe laid flatly on the floor to conceal the cardboard that had been inserted to stop the rain from soaking through its wore sole.

'It's like a walk back in time in there,' said Alexander. 'Why's it never been touched?'

'There was a legal battle over rights of ownership,' said the estate agent. 'The doctor's father had apparently sold the premises – a gambling debt, but it had never been called in 'cause the paperwork was lost. Anyhow, the doctor that was there, the one that retired, thought he did own it until the paperwork was found.

'And who'd it fall to?' said Alexander.

'Dickensian that one, eaten up with legal bills.'

'And now?'

'Bought over. Cheaply. I can tell that you're not impressed.'

'It doesn't suit,' said Alexander.

The estate agent set the alarm at the end of the drafty hallway, pulled the heavy door closed and locked up. 'Give us a call if you change your mind,' he said as he got into his car.

Alexander sat down despondently on the steps.

'Are you sick?' shouted Tommy from the pavement.

'Funny,' said Alexander getting up.

'You're on tonight aren't you?'

'At five,' said Alexander.

'Still not found premises?'

'Nope.'

'Just as well,' said Tommy. 'I know a good barman when I've got one and I don't like the thought of losing you. See you later, got things to do, business to attend to.'

Lucky him, thought Alexander, tucking his hands into his hooded jacket as he descended the steps where he kicked a polystyrene box that lay on the pavement, but its discarded contents, a curry, spilled out and spat up over the bottom of his trousers. Alexander stared at the mess in disbelief.

****

Elsie had missed early morning mass that day for she'd woken later than usual, feeling dizzy. It was still dark outside, but a stream of moonlight shone across the

191

landing and slipped through the slightly ajar bedroom door, creating a dusky twilight vision.

It was in this half-light that she threw back the bedcovers: layers of blankets with a crisp white cotton sheet underneath, folded tidily over the top. She eased herself out of bed, pulled her long winter nightie down, for it had a habit of pulling up during the night, and dangled her feet off the bed.

She looked at the clock and was annoyed with herself for not waking earlier. She sighed and reached her hand down to her stomach. No, she thought, rubbing it gently, I'm not well.

In the half-light she looked about the room, remembering her father and mother and sisters, remembering the life that the house had once known.

A large black and white framed photograph of Rosie in her first holy communion dress hung over the right hand door of the wardrobe; it was the same photograph her mother had ritually looked at at night, holding it to her breast and kissing it.

When her mother too passed away Elsie had felt so empty inside, and angry too. There was so little left to remind her of her family: photographs and trinkets only. She had had to clear out her mother's belongings. It had taken time for her to be able to do that, but when she found the picture of Rosie it had returned troubled memories and she'd set it aside, though safe, in an empty shoebox. It was months before she returned to the box, lifting the picture and kissing it as her mother before her had kissed it: with aching nostalgia and with love.

Elsie's eyes adjusted to the light so that she could see the now framed photograph clearly. She looked so happy in the photograph, but Elsie sighed again at the thought of how Rosie had suffered.

She crossed the landing and ran her finger along the sill of the window, checking for dust, before turning to descend the stairs when she heard a noise in the bedroom. As she looked back the door seemed to move as though someone within the bedroom had pulled it towards them.

'Is that you Rosie?' she said as she moved back along the landing. She stopped halfway across where a floorboard beneath her creaked. 'Daft,' she said to herself. 'I'm just being daft.' She pulled on her dressing gown, feeling suddenly cold, and went downstairs.

In the scullery she struck a match to light the gas stove but none came on.

'Bloody nuisance,' she said as she loaded the gas meter under the stairs with a fifty pence piece, turned the handle, waited for it to drop and repeated the procedure. Back in the scullery she put a single boiled egg in a small saucepan and popped some toast under the grill. Afterwards, she threw open the yard door and lifted the black plastic coal bucket to fill it up.

The toast was ready when she returned from the yard. She liked it done on one side and immediately spread it with thick creaming's of butter. She poured the hot water from the kettle into the teapot and put it on the stove to stew. 'God,' she said to herself, 'you make a good cup of tea,' as she drank it back and smacked her lips. 'Proper tea mind, not those bloody teabags the world and its wife uses,' she said out loud.

She sliced the top off the boiled egg, lifted the Saxo saltcellar and sprinkled salt onto it, eating the egg where she stood. Once she'd finished she went into the living room and stooped down to set the fire and to light it, but the nausea returned and she leant back against the settee.

Alexander had got up that morning later than Elsie. When he came downstairs he saw her lying on the settee with a blanket pulled around her. The yard door was wide open and the fire in the grate set, but unlit. He had rushed to shut the door, expecting as he pulled it shut, for the door needed shaved, that the noise would wake her, but Elsie didn't stir. Even as he lit the fire, making unavoidable scraping noises with the shovel, she continued to sleep, and to snore, though gently. He knew she was getting old and he wanted to look after her, but if he couldn't find premises then his hard work over the last lot of months was a waste of time. He'd never had any money, not real money, and his personal history harped in his ear and shouted failure.

****

Disgusted, Alexander wiped the spilled curry with a tissue, managing to remove most of it; there were a few stains left that he could have got away with, but the trousers, he realised, stunk of curry and he would have to go home to change.

When he got into the house Elsie was asleep on the settee as she had been that morning, but at least the fire was lit. He went upstairs and came back down wearing a clean white shirt. Elsie had heard him come in and woken up.

'Have you seen my other black trousers?' he said.

'They're in the wash. What's wrong with those ones?' said Elsie, nodding at the pair in his hand. He held them out to her. 'How'd you bloody well manage to do that?'

194

'Don't ask,' he said. Elsie took the trousers and washed out the curry stains at the bottom of the legs. She set up the ironing board and steamed the bottom of them until they were almost dry. 'Thanks Elsie,' he said, bending down to kiss her forehead.

'Go on,' she said, swiping at his bare legs. 'Get them covered up. It's winter in case you hadn't noticed.' He pulled on his trousers and buckled the belt. 'Any luck with the premises?' she said. Alexander looked at her despondently. 'Something'll turn up, you'll see,' she said.

Despite the encouragement, Alexander knew that she still didn't believe he would make a go of it. He knew too that she didn't love him any less for his failure, probably wouldn't love him any more if he succeeded, but he wanted her to believe in him.

He looked up at the ticking clock. It was only four-thirty and he didn't usually leave until quarter to five but he grabbed his coat, 'Tommy wants me in early,' he said.

When he arrived at The Rock Tommy's nephew was behind the bar. 'Aren't you meant to be at university?' said Alexander.

'I left,' Tommy's nephew grunted.

'Right,' said Alexander looking around the bar.

'Tommy said to give you this.' Alexander took the envelope and walked outside.

The steps at the back of the pub were loaded up with empty crates of beer bottles and empty barrels, mostly caged in. He didn't blame Tommy, family came first and if his nephew needed the job then he understood Tommy's preference.

But he thought of Elsie and what she'd say. He thought of her disappointment in him and set the unopened envelope down so that it dangled over the edge of an empty crate like a hangman's noose in its finality.

'You going to open that or what?' said Tommy as he leant against the open back door. Alexander looked up from the step.

'I understand,' he said. 'You're nephew comes first and you were good enough to give me work in the first place. After all, I'd no experience of bar work.'

'No, that's true,' said Tommy. 'But you took to it well.' Alexander nodded. 'I hope that's alright,' said Tommy, inviting Alexander to open the envelope.

'It'll have to be,' said Alexander, snatching at the envelope to open it. He expected to find his wages and perhaps a few extra quid in the envelope, but the only thing in it was a single piece of paper with an address on it.

'What's this?' he said, holding out the piece of paper. Tommy laughed.

'You bloody fool,' Tommy said.

'What?'

'I'm not dismissing you. My nephew's crap at this job and never will be any good. I told you this morning that I didn't want to lose you. But you might find this address useful to you.'

'How so?' said Alexander.

'Jesus Alexander, you can be a bit thick sometimes. It's premises. Cheap too.' Alexander reread the address.

'Here,' said Tommy dangling a set of keys in front of him. 'You've one hour, my time, to go and have a look. If you're happy with it then we can agree terms and bob's your uncle.'

'You own it?' said Alexander.

'Aye,' said Tommy, 'but don't go letting anyone know. I've a few bits and bobs here and there. Nothing worth talking about to be honest.'

'Why?' Alexander said.

'I'm doing you a bloody favour Alexander. I like you, that's all the bloody reason any man needs for doing something decent. You work hard, you deserve a break. Anybody can see that.'

'The real reason,' said Alexander, unconvinced by Tommy's sudden transformation to Mr Benevolent.

'For Elsie,' Tommy said. 'I gave her a promise once, long time ago, that I'd look out for you as a father might. You can ask her if that's true. I'm not trying to pull any punches.'

'How much?' Alexander asked.

'Nothing,' said Tommy.

'That's not good business,' said Alexander.

'Sometimes when you get older, nearer the grave as it were, the type of business you go chasing is a different kind. In other words it stops being about money.'

'I'll give you a fair rent,' said Alexander.

'A fair rent then,' said Tommy, shaking his hand.

Alexander began cleaning out his new premises the following day. He looked at the dusty and shabby interior and saw possibility – a metamorphosis not just of the décor but of his own life.

He did not tell Elsie, for he wanted the interior to be completely set up before, blind-folded he imagined, he would lead her there and surprise her. He couldn't wait to see the look of incredulity on her face as she surveyed the result of his labour and he ached too to see her turn and look at him, finally, with belief.

It was with this vision of her face that he woke daily at the crack of dawn. On the first day, as he opened the premises, he thought he heard shuffling under the floorboards. The electricity board had not yet turned the supply on and so it was by torchlight that he laid traps for the vermin and blocked up gaps in the walls and floorboards. He ripped out the old fittings and rang the council for the delivery of a skip. He changed from his overalls, leaving them at the shop and went home to change into his black trousers and shirt before starting his evening shift at The Rock.

The following day he drove to the local builder's yard and loaded up the back of the car with the material needed for plastering. He wasn't a plasterer but he had worked in London on a building site and felt capable of the work.

The trick, he knew, was all in the preparation: of making small amounts, mixing it vigorously so that it ran off the trowel smoothly and applying it as soon as possible before the mix thickened. He'd need plenty of water and bought a hose, running it from the small galley kitchen in the back of the premises to the front room. If the finish wasn't as smooth as necessary he could go over it with a light sander.

He worked every day with an urgency and adrenalin that he'd never felt before, at least about work. It was hope that drove him. At last, he had hope.

On one of the days when he was plastering he had accidentally messed up his own clothes and had had to go home to change. Although the dusty white residue was only on part of his clothing he knew that Elsie didn't miss a trick and would spot it. He hoped that she would be out, but she wasn't out and made immediate comment. 'Are you moonlighting?' she said. He told her that he was helping a mate, and at the end of the week he gave her an extra forty quid housekeeping. He always gave her extra money if he earned extra and so she expected it and was grateful; she ordered a couple of extra bags of coal, and put the rest away in her savings.

It took a week to plaster the interior. He left the heating on both night and day to help it to dry out. It would take a week at the earliest before he could paint it. It couldn't dry quick enough for he was already running up bills.

As the plaster dried he busied himself with designing the interior fittings. He kept the design simple for he intended to do the work himself, but he didn't have the tools. He paid a trip to the local D.I.Y. store and costed the necessary equipment but the total sum seemed too large and he wondered would greater economy be found in employing fitters.

He rang around to get quotes but on the third estimate he knew that he'd have to return to his original plan of doing the work himself.

He mentioned, in passing, his latest dilemma to Tommy's nephew. The following day Tommy gave him the name of a shop-fitter. Alexander felt a little uncomfortable with this further help from Tommy but what could he do? He needed the shop fitted and he needed all the help he could get.

Jimmy, the fitter, was a tall lanky fellow. Tommy said he wasn't the most reliable of blokes but that when he did a job he did it well. Alexander rang him and arranged to pick him up each day. On the first morning he had to wait in the car, for when Jimmy finally answered the door he wasn't even dressed.

Still, he was cheap and by the end of the second week they'd shelved the interior. Alexander paid him and thought it was the last he'd see of him, but the next day Jimmy turned up with four box loads of books. 'What'll you give me for them?' he said, scratching his unshaved wispy stubble. Alexander rummaged through the boxes. They were mostly brand new. 'Where'd you get them?'

'If you don't want them,' said Jimmy, stooping to pick up the books.

Alexander put a hand on his arm. 'I didn't say I didn't want them.'

'How much?' Jimmy said, curtly this time.

'How much do you want for them?'

'Twenty quid a box and there's more where that came from if you want them.' Alexander nodded. 'No questions asked?'

'None,' said Alexander. 'You'll take forty?

Jimmy grunted and held out his hand.

There were just the walls to paint, the flyers to hand out and he was ready to open. With the addition of the unforeseen boxes of books from Jimmy and the stock he had himself accumulated from auctions and house clearances over the last lot of months the shop was almost ready.

On the business course he had designed a webpage where books could be ordered, and had invested in a computer so that he could conduct business onsite. His catalogue needed updating, but he could do this during the day when the premises were open.

200

It'd been a month since Tommy handed the keys to Alexander. He'd worked harder than he'd ever worked in his life – during the day fixing the premises coupled with six nights a week behind the bar. He was exhausted and couldn't remember a time in his life when he'd felt so tired, but adrenalin kept him going.

There was just the grand opening to arrange. He wished that Robert could be there to see it happening, but it'd been months since they were in contact and he didn't know whether or not he'd come even if he were invited. He missed him, but Robert and Mary had their own lives to get on with and now he had his.

Besides, it was Elsie that mattered most. Alexander couldn't wait to see her face as he led her down Rockdale Street and into his new shop.

There was just the name to think of. He went over ideas in his head and scribbled them down on a loose scrap of paper as a list:

Second Hand Bookstore

The Good Book Store

Take a Second to Read

Turn The Page

But nothing seemed right. He even thought of The Second Chance as a name. He preferred this name to all of his other ideas but when he reflected on it he felt that it sounded too much like a shabby charity store. He painted the interior and stocked the shelves, but still couldn't come up with a good name.

He asked the local postman to distribute flyers, again wishing until the opening night to maintain his anonymity, but the postman refused: 'More than my jobs worth,' he said. He thought of asking Jimmy, but figured that even if he agreed to distribute them the flyers would end up en masse behind the doors of a handful of houses. Perhaps he could send them out after the opening night. The shop's location was fairly prominent and word would spread quickly anyhow but he sent out invitations by mail for the opening night, to people he knew.

He bought in some supplies of wine and at the last minute purchased a couple of boxes of beer. He was serving the locals after all and how often in the local pub did they ask for wine?

He organised refreshments via the local bakery: sandwiches, sausage rolls, cakes and bought in paper plates. He set up the coffee machine and mugs, buying the most expensive brand. He could resort later to cheaper brands. The shop was ready.

It was the night before the opening. Alexander switched off the lights and set the alarm. He had used Elsie's birthdate – the one no one knew. He'd managed to come up with a name that he liked and the shop front was sorted. He'd called in professionals to put the name up because he wanted it done right and though he was anxious about the shop's future success he knew in his gut that it would succeed.

He locked up and walked up past the sleep-filled houses of Rockdale Street.

It was three a.m. and so quiet that he felt he could almost hear his excited heartbeat, but the quiet and the calm and the silent order of the night soothed him.

Before entering the house he even turned to look up at the statue of the Virgin Mary and smile. 'All's well,' he said as he tipped his hat to her. He tiptoed up the stairs and undressed quietly, holding the belt of his trousers so

202

that the buckle would not clink, then slipped in underneath the covers. He pulled the quilt close into him and chuckled inside as he imagined the following day.

****

Of late he was used to being up earlier than Elsie and slipping out of the house before she was even awake. He was glad that she had taken to going to the later mass for he'd always thought, though it had been habit with her, the six-thirty mass was too early. It suited those who needed to go to work, but it made the day too long for her. This morning, however, it was eight o'clock before he woke. Elsie would have been up and out before him.

He went into the scullery and boiled up an egg and popped some toast in the toaster. He threw open the yard door and cleaned out the ashes from the fire, emptying them into the metal bin in the yard. He set the fire but didn't light it.

When Elsie returned from church he would take her out for the day. She'd been wanting to visit the new shopping mall. 'Next week,' he'd kept saying. It'd made him feel mean not to honour his promise to her, but things had kept cropping up; there'd been the burst pipe in his new premises that had caused their first arrangement to be put off, and when they arranged to go out for the second time Tommy had asked him to do an extra shift during the day. After that, Elsie hadn't mentioned it.

After breakfast Alexander took the car down to the local garage, vacuumed the interior and ran it through a hot wash.

Elsie had mentioned that she wanted a new rug for the living room, but he wanted to get her a new coat too and whatever else she wanted and for this he'd kept money aside. The lining was torn on the coat she usually wore though she had other good coats in the wardrobe that she kept for special occasions or wore on Sundays when she'd had her hair washed and set.

Alexander looked up at the clock. It was nine o'clock and she would be home from mass soon. It would be hard not to tell her about the shop when they went out but he was determined that it would remain a complete surprise.

Curious about his constant absence, and perhaps too because she missed his company, she had confronted him, 'What are you up to?' she said. He had shrugged it off, laughed and said he was just making a few extra quid. 'Better not be anything dodgy,' she said, casting him an admonishing glance, 'or you can find somewhere else to live.'

'Nothing dodgy.'

'Why the secrecy then?' she said.

'No secrecy. I'm helping some mates do a bit of work. That's all. Cash in hand.'

'Are you sure?' she said, scrutinising his response. He nodded, knowing that she hadn't believed him. After all, he hadn't a good track record and that wasn't her fault.

He looked at the clock again. It was nearly ten o'clock and still Elsie hadn't returned from mass. Alexander went across to Lily's, but Lily had not seen her that morning either.

'What mass were you at?' Alexander said. 'The later one,' said Lily. Alexander scratched his head as he tried to think where Elsie might be, for if he didn't catch up with her soon his plans for the day would be completely foiled. If only he hadn't slept in that morning then he'd have caught her going out.

204

He lifted his coat and went down to the newsagents where Elsie sometimes helped out behind the counter, but the owner, who lived above the shop, a single, elderly lady, had not seen Elsie that day either. She was a woman of few words. 'No,' she said, as she turned to the next customer for business as usual. Alexander left the shop but lingered outside it, scratching at his uneven stubble. Time was wearing on. Where else could she be? He went to the post-office. But no, she hadn't been there either. He ran his hand along the side of his cheek and decided to go home and shave.

As he turned into Rockdale Street he saw ambulance men lift a stretcher out of the back of their vehicle. It was only as he walked further up, when he saw Lily with her hands in the air, pointing at the upstairs bedroom of Elsie's home, that he realised Elsie had never left her bedroom that morning at all.

Chapter 18

The playground in the park had swings, a slide, monkey bars and a basketball pitch, but the basketball net had long since been torn off by vandals. The swings were broken and the asphalt torn up in patches where small fires had burnt.

The park was a night-time haunt for local teenagers. In the mornings the debris from their carousing: broken bottles, empty beer cans and the occasional used condom or needle could also be found.

The entrance to the playground was narrow and hedged along both sides; it ran like an alleyway between two sets of semi-detached houses. The residents had erected tall fences in their back gardens and left hedges to overgrow so as to barricade themselves away from the nuisance behind them. They wanted the council to demolish what was left of the playground. Instead, every few years, the council made minor repairs and as the locals expected, it was torn up within a matter of months.

The overgrowth of brush was so dense that the entrance Mary took each morning, after she left the children off at school, was almost hidden. She had to follow the path past the playground before reaching the open field beyond it where a leisure centre on the other side of the field, closer to the road, was situated; to the side of it were caged-in pitches that were used for five a side football, hockey and basketball. A wooded walkway, also hidden, lay at the far side of the field; it was lined on one side by large elder trees.

On Saturday and Sunday afternoon the field was often used for football matches, but on weekday mornings it was empty.

Three identical rusting metal benches were bolted to the ground on the pathway. Out of habit Mary sat on the third bench; it was further down, set into the northeast corner, but the trees behind it provided some protection from the wind that could on this hilly site cut fiercely through you.

It was five months since Robert had struck her. It was only a slap, but her face had swollen and the next morning as she looked in the mirror a purple bruise had begun to form.

He'd stayed in the house that night but the next morning he packed a small bag of belongings and told her that he was temporarily moving out. She begged him not to go.

'I won't go far,' he said.

'You can't leave.'

'I'll come every day.'

'Don't go,' she said.

He raised his hand up and she jerked instinctively, involuntarily, away from him, yet he was only stretching up for his coat.

'I have to,' he said.

207

She stepped towards him and he touched the side of her bruised cheek. She leaned into the palm of his hand, tilting her head to one side so that it came to rest against his chest.

'I'm sorry,' he said. She put her finger against his lips and told him that she loved him.

'Stay,' she pleaded.

He lifted the blue and white holdall off the floor. 'I'll come tomorrow. I'm not leaving you Mary.'

'You mean you need time,' she said with sudden anger as he opened the front door.

'No, we both do.'

Robert came to the house every evening so that Emily and Peter, at first, did not realise that he no longer lived with them. In the morning when he was not there she told them that he had started work early and had already left.

Sometimes he would collect them from school and at other times he was there to bathe them on Saturdays, and at night to read them a bedtime story. They had been living separately two months before Emily's suspicions were aroused. She woke up in the middle of the night feeling ill and left her own room to go into her mother and father's bedroom. 'Where's Daddy?' she said.

Mary was too tired to make up an excuse. She told Emily to get into bed beside her, went downstairs and brought up a glass of milk. When she returned, Emily was asleep. Mary checked Emily's temperature which seemed to be normal and lifted Emily, while she remained asleep, back into her own bed.

In the morning Mary thought that Emily had forgotten about her night-time wander. But a week later, over

208

dinner, Emily looked up at her father. 'Why do you not live with us anymore?' she said.

Robert looked towards Mary. 'I do.'

'No you don't,' answered Emily.

'What makes you think that?'

'In the morning you are never here,' she said, 'and your pillowcase is always clean.' Mary remained silent. 'I've checked,' Emily asserted. 'There's no smelly socks in the laundry basket either and there's none of your clothes there.'

'You're imagining things Emily,' said Mary.

'No, I'm not.'

'Now you're being cheeky,' said Robert.

'I'm not,' said Emily, jumping up from the table and flaying her arms in a defiant tantrum. 'Even Peter knows you don't live here anymore. Don't you Peter?' said Emily. Peter continued to smooth the top of the pie he'd made by combining his fish fingers, vegetables and potatoes into one mass. 'Peter,' she yelled.

'Stop it Emily,' said Mary.

'No,' she said, stamping her foot on the pine floor.

'Go to your room,' said Robert.

'No.'

Robert got up from the table, lifted Emily and carried her upstairs to her bedroom, closing the door tightly behind him. Emily opened the door. 'Get in,' said Robert.

'No,' shouted Emily. 'You can't make me.'

'Oh, can't I?' said Robert.

He lifted her up and put her on the bed. He closed the bedroom door and lifted a chair from the bathroom to barricade it.

'What did you do?' said Mary when he returned downstairs.

'Nothing,' he said. 'I just locked her in her room.'

'I'll go up to her,' said Mary, slowly rising.

'No,' said Robert. 'She's got to learn.'

'Yes, but it's not her fault.'

Peter had stopped playing with the pie. 'Are you finished?' Mary asked. Peter nodded. She lifted the plate and told him to go into the living room to watch television. Peter gladly left the table and Robert closed the dining room doors so that Peter could not hear them.

'She knows,' he said. Mary nodded. 'Perhaps I could stay over some nights?'

'Maybe, ' she said, but there was no enthusiasm in her voice.

As the pregnancy developed Robert stayed more often, though he slept on the settee. Mary refused to talk about the baby, insisting that they keep the knowledge of it between themselves until the right time came.

She managed to hide the child from the world underneath loose clothing, and dieted to keep her weight as low as possible.

On the park bench in the mornings she would sometimes push and pull at her wedding ring, trying to understand exactly how her marriage had gone so wrong. She reflected on the months before his adultery and tried to pinpoint events or times when she could have been more loving or caring.

She knew that the child inside her was healthy, for sometimes she could feel it kick, and she hoped that as the pregnancy wore on she would begin to feel differently

210

towards it; she hoped that when it was born she might love it as she loved her other two children.

Chapter 19

The doors of the ambulance closed. Alexander got into his car and followed, but he lost sight of the ambulance at the top of Broadway when it hurtled through red traffic lights.

He drove to the Royal Victoria Hospital, parked the car opposite the hospital in the grounds of the Dominican Convent and rushed into the admissions reception.

'It's not our intake day,' said the receptionist. Alexander rushed back outside and over to the car. 'You're lucky you weren't clamped,' said the car park attendant gruffly. 'This isn't a public car park.' Alexander didn't have the time to explain. He didn't care to either. 'Fuck off,' he said instead.

He climbed into the car, drove down the lower Falls, cut across the outskirts of the city centre and took a left up the Antrim Road. He couldn't find a car parking space outside The Mater and parked on a double yellow, reaching hurriedly into the glove compartment so as to put a sign on the dashboard. Having found the paper and pen at the bottom of the junk-filled compartment he began to write, but the ink was faulty and wouldn't flow. He flung the pen against the passenger dashboard, opened the driver's door and went into the grounds of the hospital.

212

When he got to the door he stalled and breathed in heavily. He didn't know what he was rushing to meet. He had been in such haste to follow that he hadn't contemplated the worst. Was Elsie alive or dead? As he pushed open the double doors he heard a young woman in her early twenties begin to scream, and then to cry, and then to gently sob as her friends and relatives tried to console her. At that moment the building did not feel like a hospital that mended the sick, but like a huge morgue whose death toll waited in hospital beds. Was it circumstance or accident or just sheer bloody bad luck that swept people away from life and breath and disposed of them as casually as autumn leaves? 'It's a fucking mess,' he said. 'A fucking mess.'

He pulled himself together, he had to for there was no-one to lend support, and gave admissions Elsie's name.

'Next of kin?' the nurse said before telling him what ward she had been taken to.

He took the elevator. There was no one else in it but it stopped, as if by phantom, at the second floor; the door opened onto an empty hallway and closed with mind-frustrating slowness before the lift ascended to the third floor. Alexander stalled when he got out of the lift and inhaled deeply, for his breath was palpitating and he could hear his own heart pound against his chest.

He faced a corridor with two doors leading off it. There were no nurses or people within sight. The low ceiling made the corridor feel narrow and the low energy lighting gave it a sinister aura. He could feel the weight of his brain; it felt as though it was moving from side to side, suspended on light threads that might, any second, snap. He looked for directions and opened the door on the left,

213

but even as he entered he was faced with another corridor that made his walk feel like a labyrinthine nightmare. He followed the arrow and turned a further corner where a larger than expected foyer contained two desks pushed back to back.

The light emanating from the computers was brighter than that in the room itself. He walked closer, towards the nurses, and tried to speak. A choked, half-whispered name rose to his lips as his glazed eyes caught the attention of the smaller, younger nurse. She looked up from the computer screen, pulled out a pocket watch and checked the time. 'Ward 319?' she said, pointing to the arrow on the wall before turning back to face the computer screen.

The light inside the ward was bright. Alexander tightened his eyes while his vision adjusted. There was only one bed space occupied: an elderly woman who sat on a low chair, struggling to reach up to the wheeled-in bench upon which her dinner was laid. The curtains around the bed opposite her were drawn.

The elderly woman was trying to dislodge a piece of food that was stuck between her teeth. Her carious mouth was open as she scratched at the food-filled gap with her fingernail.

She lifted her fork and pushed it forward repetitively, urging Alexander to go through, beyond the drawn curtains. Alexander took a deep breath before sliding his hand between the curtains. He saw Elsie lying on the bed.

She lay so still. He walked around the side of the bed where her arm draped over the side and reached out to take her hand.

'You'd think you'd seen a ghost,' she said popping her eyes open. Alexander looked at her with slowly shifting

214

sadness. 'You big eejit,' she said, 'I had a wee fall, that's all. Here,' she said holding out her arm, 'help me to sit up.'

After he'd propped up the pillows behind her he leant his tall bony frame towards her and hugged her gently. 'A proper hug,' she said. Alexander laughed, nervously, and squeezed her a little tighter. 'That's better,' she said.

'When did you fall?' he said.

'Early,' she said, 'when I was going to bed. I felt a little faint and then I swooned. I can't remember anything else.'

'You lay on the floor all night?'

'It's not your fault,' she said. 'What time's the opening?'

'What opening?' he said.

'The bookstore! I'm not as daft as I look,' she said as she giggled into a paper hanky.

'Who told you?' he said.

'A wee fairy. But you haven't answered me. What time?'

'I'll postpone it.'

'You will not. Business is business and the sooner you're up and running the sooner you can buy me that rug I'm chasing after.'

'I'll buy you more than a rug,' he said.

Lily rushed back into the ward. 'I've phoned Tommy,' she said. 'He's bringing the things you'll need.'

Chapter 20

When Tommy entered Elsie's bedroom and switched the light on the sparseness of the room shocked him. There was no locker beside the bed, no alarm clock and no lamp. There were no personal effects or books and the floor, apart from a small rug at the side of the bed, was wooden and bare. He looked up at the naked bulb that glared and down at the bedclothes that lay pulled back on one side.

He moved across the room to open the heavy dark curtains and looked out onto the street and at his own house across the way. It was higher on this side.

The dormer window had been left ajar and so he tried to close it, but it refused to budge. He leant his weight down onto the upper frame and pushed again. There did not seem to be any obstacles blocking it, no chipped wood or excess paint, but it remained stubborn.

After the chip-pan fire he'd helped Elsie to redecorate. He'd repaired the plumbing on several different occasions, fitting a washer or unplugging a drain. He'd helped to move furniture and to lay carpet and linoleum, but he had never been upstairs in her bedroom.

He counted on his fingers the things that he needed to get: a dress, shoes, tights, underwear. There was

216

something else, he was sure there was something else, but he couldn't think what it was. He turned back into the room and opened the double doors of the wardrobe. The iron hangers clinked on the metal rail as he pushed several coats to one side. Some were covered in shop cellophane and looked as though they'd never been worn. Only two dresses hung in the wardrobe. He lifted both out and looked at them. The first had a navy and white floral pattern, the other, he decided, was more like a summer frock so he put it back in the wardrobe. If there were only two frocks then where were her clothes?

It wasn't a man's job to be poking around a woman's belongings and he wished that Lily hadn't asked him to get Elsie's clothes. But what could he do? Lily was at the hospital and there hadn't been anyone else to do it.

He draped the navy dress across his left arm and closed the wardrobe doors. Now that there was proper daylight in the room he saw that the furniture all matched. It was beautiful wood. It wasn't oak or mahogany but it was solid. Oregon, he thought, Oregon Pine.

He ran his hand along the grain once more. The wardrobe, like the chest of drawers, fitted perfectly into the alcove in which it was set, as though it had been tailor-made. He ran his hand for a second time along the heavy smooth wax finish as he glanced back at the room. It no longer irked him as it had when he had entered, there was even, he realised, something refreshing about its Spartan interior, for his own bedroom, in contrast, was annoyingly full of clutter.

But he did not want to intrude any further. Reluctantly he opened the first drawer where he found, without having to rummage through it, a pair of tights still in its packaging.

217

The second drawer was full of bedlinen; it was white, ironed and carefully arranged, with sheets on one side and pillowcases on the other. The next drawer was also full of bedlinen.

As he searched for underwear in the third drawer an envelope drew his attention. It leant against one side of the drawer, prominent in its solitary state. Its reappearance felt ghostly. Tommy took a heavy, laboured breath.

He lifted the letter out of the drawer with difficulty, for it was wedged into the dovetail join of the heavy wood where the glue had over time partially split. He had to coax it to come out. He held it in his hand to look at it, and stepped backwards to sit on the edge of the bed.

The envelope had yellowed. He held it gently, as though it might break or tear or disintegrate in front of him. He noticed too how old his own veined and purple hands had become; for the letter was from a distant past when both he and it were young.

He wanted to open it and read it. What harm? Hadn't he written it himself? He glanced at the door, stood up and closed it from the inside.

He sat back on the bed and turned the letter over in his hand. It was so long ago, but he remembered as though it were yesterday when he had travelled, solely for the purchase of that paper, to the city centre, selecting its colour with care and choosing this single envelope above the others because of its quality. He remembered too how costly it was. It was the only letter that he'd ever written, posting it first class before waiting, anxiously, for a reply.

Tommy opened the envelope and withdrew the letter inside. Before he'd unfolded it a page fell out and slipped

218

onto the floor. He stooped over as he sat on the edge of the bed, lifted the single folded sheet and pushed it back amongst the other pages. I've no right to read it, he said out loud, looking up at the closed door. It's the past and should remain there and so he slid the letter back into the wedge of the drawer where he'd found it.

He was glad that he had been able to resist reading it; took momentarily some gratification from the rightness of putting it back, but he knew that it was not right or wrong that had stopped him. He was, in truth, too frightened to read it, for he did not want to remember the silence that had followed its reception.

But the memories came anyhow, for finding the letter, accidentally as he had done, had been like meeting a friend or foe that he hadn't seen in over forty years. It made his mind alert and nostalgic.

He remembered the days, weeks and even months of waiting for an answer.

He remembered imagining that he saw Elsie in the street or boarding a Trolleybus or standing at a shop counter. Sightings that he believed were Elsie, until as the weeks wore on he understood were part yearning, part madness – the heart and the mind playing tricks. But even in his reasoning the sightings continued.

Months went by, and still he saw her, knowing too that she was in England and that it was his hope that he saw; his heart's desire that he imagined; knowing that none of what he saw was real. But the silence was real and her absence too real.

He closed the drawer slowly, methodically, and looked around the monastic room. Here is where she had lived, alone. He could understand if she'd met someone else, he could have understood that, but to have thrown him over and chosen to be alone instead, this he had not understood, could not now understand. He left the bedroom and returned downstairs.

After he'd carefully put the clothes that he had gathered into a white plastic carrier bag, trying not to crease them, and collected a pair of shoes that lay in front of the settee downstairs, he closed the front door tightly behind him and drove to the hospital.

Lily greeted him at the entrance. 'She's alright,' Lily said.

Tommy wore his long dark grey over-coat. He was tall. He wore a crisp white shirt and a dark indistinct tie that was tied in a neither too large nor too small knot. He looked like a family man, a man who was loved and respected and full of self-control, but Elsie's fall had shocked him.

'I am still in love with her,' he thought.

When Lily assured him that Elsie would live to see another day he found it difficult to retain his composure. He drew Lily to him so that his face was behind her and his anguish momentarily concealed, but he could feel his body shake.

The heart, he realised, is as dark as the mind.

He returned home from the hospital, entered the kitchen, boiled the kettle and sat down to read The Irish News, but he could not concentrate, and the words blurred into each other.

He turned to the sports pages and looked at the pictures and at the captions underneath.

Antrim was doing well in the hurling. They might even reach the final. There was a time when he thought he'd

220

make it onto the Antrim team himself, but an overreach and a late and careless hoist of his hurling stick into the air had left him unprotected. The heavy metal rimmed stick crashed against his arm. He'd been unlucky. Doubly so, for the stick belonged to a member of his own team.

If his arm had broken then it would have mended better, but it was fractured in three places; he give it a few months to mend as best it would and felt good as he picked up a hurling stick once more, but in his first match he realised that every clash caused the arm to hurt and that he had to give up the hurling altogether. Even now, in the cold, it gave him gyp.

He ran his index finger along the fibular bone of his left arm, feeling for the mini humped back bridges that the triple fracture had left.

Lily arrived home. He watched her as she hung her coat on the rail in the hallway, and took her apron from the hook on the back of the kitchen door, tying it around her waist. She was still a good-looking woman.

She felt the outside of the pot of tea. It was lukewarm. 'Make another. Shall I?' she said. Tommy nodded. 'What a day,' she said as she emptied the teabags into the rubbish bin.

'Aye,' he said.

'You're quiet.'

'Aye,' he repeated.

'Bit of a shock Tommy. Lily's the same age as me. It goes to show you.'

'What?' he said, looking up from the newspaper.

'You're not with it at all. It's just an expression.'

Tommy folded the newspaper and laid it on the chair beside him. Lily poured the hot water into the teapot.

221

'That'll be better,' she said, covering it with a tea-cosy. She sat down beside him. 'We haven't even made a will,' she said.

Tommy raised his eyes and looked at her. 'No need,' he said. 'It'll all be left to Robert.'

'But he doesn't want the bar. He's never had an interest in that kind of work.'

'It's a pity of him,' said Tommy. 'He'd make a better living than working in that bloody office. One of the suits. Pah.'

'That's enough,' said Lily.

'Well he would.'

'You're right,' she said, leaning her elbows on the table and putting her hands up to her face, 'But we've all got to make our own way.'

'You look tired Lily,' he said.

'I am.' She reached across the table and put her hand on top of his. 'I'll make a bite to eat,' she said, 'and then we'll head down to the opening.'

'Alexander's going ahead?'

'He is. And guess what?'

'What?'

'Hasn't Elsie gone and discharged herself. That's what she wanted the clothes for. She was thinking of the shop opening even as she was lying on the stretcher in the back of the ambulance.'

'For God sake.'

'I know,' said Lily. 'But that's Elsie for you. Never knew how to think of herself. She's at home now. Came back with me and Alexander.'

'He's a good lad that Alexander but he needs to do more for her.'

'What? Like Robert does for us?'

'Robert's his own family,' said Tommy. 'Alexander's only himself to look after.'

'I suppose,' said Lily, 'but we never see Robert these days. He visits once, maybe twice a month. We never see the kids either and it's not as if they lived a million miles away.'

Tommy lifted the newspaper off the chair and opened it, but he could feel Lily looking at him, waiting for an answer.

'He'll come to us when he needs us,' he said.

'I hope you're right but I've a feeling something's wrong.'

'With Robert?'

'Yes and no. I don't know.'

'He's a grown man. He can look after himself.'

'I'm his mother. Am I not allowed to worry about him?'

'Of course you are,' said Tommy, 'but you look tired Lily and there's only so much worry before...'

'What?'

'Nothing,' he said. 'What time is the opening at?'

'Six.'

'Do you mind if I give it a miss?'

'You can't,' said Lily, 'Alexander thinks you're coming. And besides I could be doing with a wee bit of support. Elsie's discharged herself. It doesn't mean she's well.'

'You think she could fall again?'

'Who knows?' said Lily. 'I hope not.'

****

223

Tommy had not been in the premises of the bookshop since he'd let it to Alexander and was astounded by its transformation. It looked new and potentially could have reaped a great deal more rental than he'd agreed, but at least he'd kept his promise to Elsie.

The main room of the bookshop was brightly lit. He mingled with the throng inside and lifted a glass of wine from the table. He hoped the evening would be over sooner rather than later.

'I'm glad you came,' said Alexander.

'Is Robert coming?' Tommy asked.

'I left a message for him,' said Alexander, 'but he hasn't got back.'

'Pity,' said Tommy. 'He'll call in no doubt. You think you'll be able to make it work?'

'What work?' said Alexander. He was still thinking about Robert.

'The shop,' said Tommy.

'I think so,' said Alexander. He put his hands up, inviting Tommy to look around.

'Aye, I've looked. You've made a good job of it,' said Tommy. 'Elsie will be pleased.'

'It didn't cost much,' said Alexander. 'I did most of the work myself.' Tommy nodded.

'As long as you know what you're doing.'

Elsie and Lily arrived.

They'd both made an effort. Lily was wearing a new dress and the pearl necklace she donned on special occasions. Elsie had changed from the navy and white dress to a grey suit. She wore black patent shoes and dangled a black bag on the end of one arm. Underneath the suit she wore a white brocaded blouse.

224

Tommy watched as Alexander went to greet her, taking her by the arm and leading her to an armchair beside the computer. Elsie refused the chair. He pointed to the bookshelves and began explaining how it would work. Despite the throng of people Tommy was close enough to overhear their conversation.

'I like a good book myself,' she said. 'Do I get special rates?' she asked laughingly.

'I've a wee surprise for you,' he said.

'You bought me a book?' said Elsie holding her side in a kind of nervous laughter. She didn't much like surprises.

'It's not a book,' he said.

'What then?'

'A surprise.' She scowled.

'You'll like it,' he reassured.

Tommy wondered what the surprise was.

Later, when Alexander popped open a bottle of champagne to mark the opening, he brought his would-be customers outside. He had covered up the name of the shop with a sheet. A cheer rose as the crowd stood merrily in the street drinking champagne. Alexander took one end of the sheet and Elsie took the other.

'One, two, three,' he said. 'Pull.' They both pulled, but the sheet did not shift. 'Bloody hell,' said Alexander. 'I'll just be a minute.'

He ran inside and came out with the stepladders. He mounted the ladders. 'Are you ready?' he said. Elsie rolled her big blue eyes and raised her eyebrows. 'You are, right then. One,' said Alexander. 'Two, three,' the crowd said.

Alexander was still on top of the stepladders, but as the sheet fell to the ground he turned his head quickly to see

225

Elsie's face light up. He'd named the shop after her. 'Elsie's Bookstore,' it read. 'The Second Chance' was written in smaller print underneath her name. He dismounted the ladder.

'Best day of my life,' she said, wiping a joyful tear from her eye.

'You like it?' he asked.

'I'm so proud of you,' she said, hugging him.

Tommy was glad that she was happy and he didn't want to spoil her evening or to spoil Alexander's evening for that matter, but the longer the night wore on, the less he was able to forget the letter. Why had she not replied? Towards the end of the evening Lily said she was heading home. She asked him to stay and to make sure Elsie got home safe.

'It's only round the corner,' he said. 'Alexander will be there to bring her home.'

'He'll have to tidy up,' said Lily. 'I never ask you to do much.'

Shortly after Lily left, Elsie realised that she was more tired than she thought. Tommy took her arm as they walked outside. Elsie stopped to look at the signboard.

'I'd never have believed it,' she said. 'Imagine having my name above the door.' Tommy smiled.

The streetlight illumined the side of her face. She looked prettier than he'd ever seen her. The rain started to fall, lightly tapping against the pavement. He put up his umbrella, careful to tilt it down over her side.

They walked in comfortable silence so that it felt like the old days, when they'd gone out to the movies or to a dance and he'd had the privilege of walking her home. But Tommy knew that this might be his only chance of asking her why she hadn't written back. At the corner he stopped, let go of her arm that he'd held as a sister or a friend might, and put his hand around her waist, softly and tenderly as a lover might.

'Don't Tommy,' she said.

'I have to ask you.'

'You're married. There's Lily to think of.'

'It's just a question,' he said. 'I want to ask you a question.'

'Just that?' she said.

'Yes,' he said.

'Go on.'

He looked away from her and at the ground and at everything and nothing and breathed in heavily. 'Tonight would be good,' she said, trying to make a joke to ease the tension that had come between them. He lifted his face up and focused all of his attention upon her, placing his hand lightly on the side of her arm.

'Why didn't you write back?' he asked. His voice was stern and solemn and broken. It was an old man's voice.

'I did,' she said.

'You didn't,' he answered, raising his voice.

'Sssh,' she said looking up at the bedrooms of the terraced houses.

'I got nothing. Months and months of waiting for an answer. And nothing.'

'I didn't know,' she said. 'I waited too. Months and months, but then it was too late.'

'Why?' he asked. 'Why too late?'

'It was Tommy. I can't explain. It was just too late. You'd moved on.'

'That's not true.'

'It *was* true. Anyhow, we shouldn't be talking like this. It's disloyal.'

'To whom?' he said.

'To Lily,' she retorted. 'Now drop it.' ,

'But...'

'I won't have it Tommy,' she said angrily. 'I simply won't have it. Now be the gentleman that you've always been and walk me home properly.' He pulled her into him.

'Kiss me,' he said. But as his lips momentarily came to rest on hers, urging the return of all that he felt, she dropped her head to the side away from him, away from all the tenderness and love he offered, to shed a solitary stoic tear. She reached up and placed her hands on his still broad shoulders.

'No Tommy,' she said plaintively. 'We can't do this. I've kissed you and I shouldn't have.'

'I've missed you,' he said, taking her hands in his.

'Stop it.'

'I can't help what I feel.'

'No,' she said. 'But you can help what you do.' She refused the shade of his umbrella as they walked up the remainder of the street and strode two paces ahead. When she got to her front door Tommy was behind her like a shadow.

She pulled the key through the letterbox, but instead of placing the key in the Yale lock she turned to him.

'It won't happen again,' she whispered.

'But...'

'It wasn't just a fall Tommy.' She let the key drop. 'I'm dying,' she said.

She put the tips of her fingers up to his trembling lips. 'Ssh now. It's been good. For both of us.'

228

'It could have been better.'

'No.'

'It could have been.'

'You forget. Lily's my best friend. Always was, always will be. It couldn't have been any different. You'll look after her when I'm gone?'

'I always have,' he said. 'But it's you Elsie, I wanted to look after you.'

'You did Tommy.'

She lifted the key that dangled on the long worn string, placed it in the lock and opened the door. He stood back and watched as she pushed the door from the inside so that the lock closed quietly over.

Chapter 21

Robert propped the pillows up behind Mary and laid the breakfast tray on her lap before moving to the window and drawing the curtains. The fir trees had grown at least two metres since they'd moved in. They were taller than the house.

'The baby is due soon,' he said. 'You must let me help you.'

Mary looked down at the breakfast tray.

'I can't,' she said.

'Not even some tea?' he asked. She lifted the tea and placed it on the bedside locker. 'We've got to let someone know about the baby,' he said. 'I think my mother knows. She commented on your weight. I said you'd take it off as quickly.'

'And what did she say?'

'Nothing.'

'Your mother never says nothing,' said Mary, fixing the pillow behind her.

'She asked directly. I didn't answer her but I didn't lie either.'

'Does she know?'

'I think so.'

'Great.'

'I don't understand why it has to be such a secret anyway. You haven't even been for a check-up.'

'Damn it Robert, I told you I didn't want anyone to know, not until it's born.'

'Until the baby's born,' he said.

'Don't get smart with me about semantics.'

'About what?

'Nothing.'

'Anyway, I'm not trying to be smart. I'm just trying, that's all. We've Emily and Peter and another child about to come into the world and I'm still sleeping on the settee. Relegated.'

'Can't you talk about anything but football?'

'Jesus! I can't say anything but you light on it.'

'That's not true,' she snapped.

'Fuck,' he said, lifting his hand up to his hair as though he might tear a clump of it off.

'No,' she said. 'You fuck off.'

'I've told you. I'm not leaving. You can treat me whatever way you bloody well like, but I'm not leaving. I did wrong Mary but for how long do you want to punish me?'

'Poor Robert,' she taunted. 'Can't go, can't stay.'

He tried to ignore her incitement. 'Emily's on a school trip today and Peter's off. Do you want me to stay off work to look after him?'

'He'll be fine. He'll play in his room without bothering me too much.'

'And Mary,' said Robert, lifting the tray. 'I'm sleeping in my own bed tonight.'

When his father left, Peter played in his bedroom with a Matchbox fire engine. He imagined the fireman, like Gulliver in Lilliput, peeing over the whole town to put out the unquenchable flames. His mother had read the story to him. It was one of his favourites.

He also talked to his imaginary friend, out loud because there was no one in the room, for he'd grown old enough to know that he was too old to have an imaginary friend and must therefore hide him.

When Gulliver finished putting out the fire, Peter delved into the inbuilt toy cupboard to find something to play with. He hauled the contents out so that a heap of toys gathered on the floor at the foot of the bed until he finally found The Lone Ranger and Tonto lying at the bottom.

Peter stuffed the pile of toys back into the wardrobe to create a space on the floor where The Lone Ranger and Tonto could wage a battle; he had to lean his body against the door to close it.

The battle commenced.

'Hi-yo, Silver! Away!' shouted The Lone Ranger as he mounted his stallion.

The Lone Ranger was masked and armed with holstered pistols; he had donned his best cavalry suit: blue with a yellow stripe.

Silver reared up on his hind legs, threatening to vanquish its enemy by squashing him underfoot, but the Lone Ranger saw that Tonto had no weapons and so he pulled the reins of the wild horse, but it was difficult to control; it kicked with its hind legs and reared up on its front legs so that The Lone Ranger almost toppled off.

232

He grabbed the reins, trying desperately to get the horse under control; its feet finally fell within inches of the passive Indian. From his pocket, the Lone Ranger withdrew a white handkerchief and waved it about. He dismounted and sat (Peter twisted the legs of the doll into a sitting posture) beside Tonto. A truce was made and a friendship begun.

In order to celebrate the truce, Peter sneaked into Emily's bedroom and borrowed her tea-set. He began to lay out a Wild West feast. There was roasted pig on a spit, sausages and beans and a tankard of beer for each of them. Peter coloured-in a piece of blank paper with a large Crayola crayon. He tore strips from the red paper and bundled them together to create a huge log fire. Tonto even shared his peace pipe, improvised with a hair clip that he also found in Emily's room.

After their meal Peter manoeuvred the legs and arms of both dolls so that they could lie straight out in front of the fire with their arms behind their heads. He'd seen real cowboys do that in films. To imitate the dark of the night he clambered up on the bed and closed the curtains.

But it was not night-time and he wondered why his mother was still in bed sleeping. He left the two contented dolls with their log-fire and the moon gently rising and went into his mother's bedroom. He climbed up beside her and stroked her hair, hoping that she would waken. He had barely begun when she woke, and reaching her hand under the bedclothes felt the wet sheet beneath her. 'Get my watch Peter,' she said.

Peter walked to the dresser in the far corner of the room and brought the watch over to the bed. He held it out for

233

her to take when a huge pain surged through her lower abdomen.

'What's wrong mummy?' he said.

'Go to your room,' she ordered.

Peter had become used to his mother wanting to be alone and promptly returned to his own room. He jumped up on his bed, re-opened the curtains, and knelt on the floor in front of Tonto and the Lone Ranger.

He flicked the log-fire repetitively with his middle finger so that the logs rolled and fell to the side. But still the dolls lay sleeping. He picked the Lone Ranger up and using the doll's head he battered the tea-set so that the so carefully created scene was destroyed.

'Stupid dolls,' he said as he stood up and kicked them. He went to his bed and sat on the edge of it, rocking back and forth.

Mary tried to get out of bed but a further pain, vicious in its attack, surged through her.

'Peter,' she called, but there was no reply. 'For Christ's sake Peter,' she said. Still he did not come. He continued to rock back and forth, plugging his ears with his fingertips to block out his mother's cries.

Eventually he fell asleep.

Mary continued in labour. She tried to get out of bed but could not. Intermittently, she lost consciousness. When she woke, she called to Peter for help. She tried to push the baby out from her, vociferated foul abuse, at Robert, at God, and she cursed the baby that was in her. Finally, miraculously, she gave birth, losing consciousness soon after. And when she woke she called to Peter. This time he came, but when he saw the blood on the bed he began to wail.

234

'It's okay,' she said. 'No-one's hurt, but I need you to get something for me.' He raised his eyes to look at her. 'Will you get me the scissors in the kitchen? she asked. 'They're in the cupboard under the sink. Can you do that for your mummy?'

Not comprehending the blood or the need for scissors; baffled too by his mother's request, for he was not allowed to play with anything sharp, Peter walked down the stairs and opened the cupboard drawer.

The scissors were in the tightly sealed first aid box. She had told him to bring the box. He lifted it but to his surprise he was able to prise the lid off; his eyes gleamed as he reached into the box where the shiny scissors lay.

He saw a newspaper sitting on the draining board beside the kettle and snipped at it, first once, then twice, then five, six times. The 'snip' noise each time excited him and made him smile. Again he heard his mother's voice.

'Peter,' she urged. 'Quickly.'

He left the hacked newspaper and brought the scissors upstairs, but when he entered the bedroom he saw the baby and the blood and began once more to cry.

'Now go to the bathroom Peter and get me a wet towel.' He shook his head. 'Do you understand?' she said.

Peter nodded and walked to the bathroom.

He lifted up the towel that was draped over the edge of the bath and turned the tap on. He pulled his hand away from the hot water, switched the tap off and ran the cold water tap so that the towel was saturated; it dripped onto the floor as he carried it across the landing. What was this thing, this baby that had hurt his mother so much? What was this thing that was covered in blood and so small that

235

it was almost not a baby at all. He saw it kick its tiny legs as it lay supine on the bed. It looked so ugly that it disgusted him.

Peter pushed his mother's arm, but once more Mary had lost consciousness. He looked at the baby and realised what the towel was for. It made him feel sick but he began to clean it. He wrapped the towel around it and started to rub it, harder and harder. The baby began to cry and still his mother slept.

He wrapped the towel tightly around the baby and looked at his sleeping mother and back to the baby and he blamed it for all the pain. He blamed it for the distance that had formed between his mother and himself; he blamed it and was jealous. Would this thing, this little bloodied thing try to take his place?

He lifted the baby, carrying it in his arms, downstairs and out into the garden where he climbed up to the tree house. Once there he took the white towel that was covered in blood off the baby and cast it over the edge so that it fell onto the grass. He then lay the baby down on its back on the floor of the tree house.

The baby continued to cry.

At first, Peter tried to console it by rubbing its belly. But it would not stop crying. His own head began to buzz so that he held it between his hands and rocked from side to side.

Still the baby cried and as the crying grew louder and louder Peter began to cry too. His head became heavy and sore and soon began to throb. His face flushed red but still the baby cried. 'Stop it,' he yelled. He jumped up on to his feet and began to stamp the floor. He nudged the baby with his right foot and threatened it.

'I'll hit you if you keep crying. Stop it. Stop it.' But the baby, lying naked in front of him would not stop crying.

Peter had tucked the scissors into his back pocket as he climbed the ladder and had laid them down on the floor beside the baby. He lifted them, trying to turn his attention away from the baby, but as he lifted them he cut his left arm so that a trickle of blood ran down and into the palm of his hand.

'See what you've done,' he yelled at the baby. And as he screamed, 'Stop it, stop it,' he thrust at the baby with the scissors, stabbing it once, then again and again and again.

Chapter 22

It was still light when Robert got home from work. He felt guilty about his behaviour that morning and was determined to make amends. He would continue to sleep on the settee if that was what Mary wanted or for as long as it took to make things better between them.

He turned the car a little too fast into the driveway and scrapped the left wing against one of the gateposts. He got out of the car and went to the passenger side to check the damage; the mauve paint had been taken right off. He ran his hand along the score; it was not that deep and yet had caused so much damage. He'd misjudged the distance by what? A millimetre? Perhaps not even that.

'Where are you?' he shouted, entering the house. Mary did not answer. He put the kettle on, made a cup of tea and moved into the living room to watch the television. He played with the remote, switching channels impatiently when the front door rapped.

'Thank God,' said Eddie from the house across the way when Robert answered the door. Emily was scoffing a chocolate-coated Magnum. 'I thought there'd never be anyone at home. This wee one's been with me since the school mini-bus dropped her off.' Emily smiled.

'Sorry,' said Robert. 'It's not Mary's fault. We just...well.'

'Aye, no worries.'

'She's had a ball by the looks of things,' said Robert.

'We watched High Street Musical,' said Emily and then we had orange juice and then...' She held up the remainder of her ice-cream.

'Go on into the house,' said her father.

'Oh daddy,' she said. 'I've had the best day ever. We got to see all these strange fish in the aquarium and then Miss Clarke and, I can't remember the name of the other teacher, took us to McDonalds. But guess what?'

'Go in,' said Robert.

'But daddy!' Robert bent down and picked Emily up. She put her sticky fingers on the side of his cheek and kissed him.

'It was good of you to look after her,' he said to Eddie.

'You know what Margie's like. A big kid herself. I think she enjoyed herself as much as Emily did.'

Robert laughed. 'It won't happen again,' he said.

'Never say never,' said Mr Poppins, rubbing his stubble so that you could hear it rasp. 'We never could have kids y'know. Tried but... ach...perhaps it was for the best.'

'How is she?' Robert asked.

'The cancer's in remission.'

'That's good.'

'Aye. Keep our fingers crossed,' he said as he turned to go.

'Bye Mister Poppins,' said Emily.

'Bye Emily,' he said, rubbing his beard.

'Where's mummy?' said Emily.

239

'Don't know.' He carried Emily into the front hall. 'We'll get those sticky fingers of yours cleaned first though, shall we? And then we'll try to find her.' Emily giggled.

****

The wooden staircase lay on the left side of the house directly facing the front door. Robert carried Emily on his right side. When he got to the top of the stairs he looked over Emily's shoulder and saw Mary lying on the bed. The white Laura Ashley quilt cover, a wedding gift, was smeared in blood. Instinctively Robert covered Emily's eyes and rushed her into the bathroom.

'What's wrong daddy?'

'Stay there,' he instructed and pulled the bathroom door shut behind her. He rushed into the bedroom. Mary was lying asleep or unconscious on the bed. He picked up the telephone and keyed in 999, but before he pushed the green button Mary woke.

She pulled back the bedclothes. 'Where is the baby?' she asked. It took a moment for Robert to register that she had given birth. He could only see the blood. 'Peter,' she said. 'Where's Peter?'

'I'm calling an ambulance.' Robert pressed the green button so that he could hear a voice on the other end, but Mary reached for the phone and snatched it from him. 'Find Peter. For Christ's sake, find Peter.' The baby was alive. Peter had taken the baby. 'Now,' she yelled.

Robert moved to the door. Emily came out of the bathroom. He grabbed her so that she wouldn't see the blood. 'Daddy,' she said. He picked her up and brought her to her bedroom. 'You have to stay here.'

'I heard mummy,' said Emily.

'You have to stay here. You have to be good.' Emily nodded. Robert shoved the chair on the landing up against Emily's bedroom door.

He moved down the stairs and opened the back door. A Terry towel covered in blood was lying in the garden. He looked up at the tree house where he saw Peter's white Reebok trainer sticking out of one side.

Robert climbed up the tree house ladder. It strained and creaked with his weight. He saw the baby and Peter lying on the ground, attached solely by a rivulet of blood that ran from the baby towards Peter's head; the rivulet stopped just before connecting.

Robert descended the ladder and retched. The vomit burst like a bullet, once, twice, three times, emptying the cartridge of his stomach so that all that was left was a despondent aching bile.

'Bury it,' said Mary as Robert sat on the edge of the bed weeping. 'Bury it,' she reiterated, 'Hide it.' Robert did not answer. 'We must. For Peter's sake, for Emily's, for ours. Go,' she said, shaking his all but frozen body.

Robert returned to the tree house and lifted Peter so that he carried him as you might a small baby. He walked slowly, somnambulantly, bringing the cradled child to his bedroom and laying him down on the bed before stroking a wisp of fallen hair away from Peter's forehead. Still Peter slept, and for this Robert was glad.

He returned to Mary and watched her stoop and strip the bed sheets.

'Is this the only way?' he said.

241

'Far from here,' she said. 'Bury it far from here.'

She gathered the sheets and threw them into the bath, running the cold water tap so that the blood seeped away from them. Still he lingered on the landing watching. She turned and yelled at him.

'Fix it,' she said, 'Lift it, bury it.'

He reached out his hands and moved towards her, but she stepped back from him so that her back jammed into the narrow space between the washbasin and the bathtub.

'Go,' she said.

The light was already fading when Robert got into the car. He felt no shock or horror as he drove but only numbness.

The clouds above descended and the rain fell heavily, turning at one point into thumping hailstones on the bonnet. Each narrow lane, each country road, to the left or to the right tempted him.

He had to find the right spot, but each time he saw what looked like a deserted zone a diesel truck, car, or tractor appeared.

He kept therefore driving straight, making his way steadily, without meaning to, into the busy and thriving Newcastle promenade.

In line with the traffic his car slowed to a stop and start five miles per hour. He watched teenagers pass with carryouts in hand and an old lady with buckled knees struggle to cope with a black umbrella that had turned inside out. He saw lovers walk hand in hand and kids eat ice-cream.

The Atlantic waves crashed against the reinforced rock-front that was built to try to protect what was left of the small and heavily polluted beach. Every available car parking pace seemed full. Yet he must stop. Must think. He pulled over onto a double yellow and got out of the car.

'You can't stop there,' said a stocky traffic warden as she waved her ticket booklet in front of him. 'Move,' she yelled, 'or I'll book you.' He pulled at his pale blue tie and unravelled it. It slipped off his neck and fell unto the asphalt as he was getting back into the car. 'Here,' the traffic warden said, holding up the tie as she peered through the driver window. Robert stared through her, turned the ignition on and drove forward. He took the next right and saw a signpost for Tullymore forest, but as he entered he saw that this too was over-crowded. He parked the car so that the driver's side was next to a hedgerow, opened the door and puked.

He didn't even have a shovel. What was he thinking? How could he bury it without a shovel?

'Fuck, fuck, oh Jesus, fuck,' he muttered, but there was no one to help him. He would have to drive home with the child still in the car.

He entered the house and saw Emily and Peter sitting at the table. Mary had cooked a dinner of mash potatoes and beef burgers. A wooden bowl full of salad sat in the centre of the table beside a heaped plate of cheddar cheese. Peter stretched over the table to scoop up a handful of grated cheese. The noise from cartoons on the television drifted through the double doors into the dining room.

'You're home,' said Mary. 'I'll get you a plate.'

Robert followed her into the kitchen. 'What are you doing Mary? You carry on as if nothing has happened.'

'Nothing has happened,' she said.

'You don't mean that.'

'I do.'

243

'No Mary.' He slammed the keys down onto the drainer. 'I can't do this.'

'Hasn't there been enough violence today?' she said.

'Jesus.'

She grabbed his shirt at the neck and pulled him into her so that their faces were inches apart.

'You listen Robert and listen good. Do you think they'll believe that a child did this? Do you think they'll believe that?

Robert shook his head.

'It's gone. You've buried it.'

'But...'

'And even if they did believe us. What would happen to Peter? To us?'

'We've got to phone the police,' he said, 'we've got to tell the truth.'

'Don't be so naïve. There's just survival. We've got to survive, to keep what we have.'

He leant back against the white tiles and slid slowly down onto the tiled floor. 'What have we Mary?' he said.

'Each other.' She released her grip. 'It'll be the way it was before.'

'And Peter?'

'He hasn't mentioned it.' Peter came into the kitchen and looked up at his mother and down at his father.

'Are you finished already?' his mother asked. Peter nodded. 'We have chocolate pudding for dessert. Do you want to watch it in front of the television?' She handed the bowl to him. 'Take it in with you,' she said.

'Jesus Christ,' said Robert, shaking his head.

'Enough,' scowled Mary.

'He hasn't said a word?'

244

'No.'

'And if he does?'

'He won't.'

'How do you know that?'

'Because even if he did remember, and I'm not sure he does, he won't say anything because he knows it'll get him into trouble.'

'You've it all worked out.'

'No...yes... survive...that's all, just survive.'

'I can't do this.'

'You said that; but you have to. For once in your life Robert you have to be there for me, for us, for your family. You promised Robert, even this morning when we were fighting you promised.' He closed his eyes. Mary took his hand. 'You're shaking. I'll run a hot bath for you.' He shook his head. 'What then?'

'Sleep,' he said. 'I need to sleep.'

'Go on then. Upstairs.' She bent down to help him to get up.

'No,' he muttered.

'Yes,' she said. 'Go. I'll bring up some tea.'

'Tea?'

'In a while.'

****

In the early hours of the morning Robert stole out of bed, lifted the spade from behind the lattice fencing and put it on the floor of the back seat of the car, covering it with a blanket. He wanted to bury the child before the light came up and drove therefore, in his panic, to a local walkway. There was dense undergrowth beside it; he would bury the

245

child there. It was still dark when he began to dig. He dug three foot, maybe more, when the dawn broke and rays of morning light began to filter in streaks through the trees and bracken. He put the child into the hole and filled it in. He gathered twigs and dirt from the surrounding terrain and spread them over the top of the soil, but as he drove home he knew that the grave was too shallow; he would have to go back.

Chapter 23

Jamie picked up a stick and cleaned it with the sleeve of his fleece. He reached back over his shoulder and threw it as far along the pathway as he could, but the misshapen stick twisted in the air and fell into the bracken.

'Fetch,' said Jamie to the Golden Labrador. The dog, who had retained its puppy nature despite being two years older than Jamie, wagged its tail and sprang forward with its front paws high in front of her before landing and laying its nose to the ground. 'Go girl,' said Jamie.

'She won't find it,' said his little sister.

'She'll find it. She's the best fetcher in the world. Aren't you girl?' he shouted to Gypsy as he followed the dog to the point where it had clambered off the pathway and down into the brush.

Jamie glanced back over his shoulder. His sister was picking blackberries and storing them one by one in the front patch pocket of her jeans.

'Mummy says you're not allowed to pick berries.'

'I'm not eating them,' she said. 'I'm feeding the butterfly.' She stroked the multi-coloured embroidered butterfly on the front of the pocket of her jeans. 'Still hungry?' she asked, feeding it another blackberry.

'Fetch,' shouted Jamie. He stooped down on the edge of the pathway and peered into the undergrowth, but he could not see where Gypsy was and so he crouched onto his hunkers and eased himself down the steep incline. When he got to the bottom he stood up and wiped his soiled hands in a single swipe on the front of his fleece.

'Here girl,' he called, stooping down once more. He saw Gypsy digging into the ground. 'You're not meant to bury it,' he said as he approached the dog. Gypsy kept furrowing into the ground. 'She's found something,' he shouted to his little sister who sat on the edge of the pathway watching.

'Treasure,' she said with a mischievous glint in her eye.

'What is it girl?' he asked as he tugged at the dog's floppy left ear. The dog ignored him and kept digging into the ground.

'We're going to be late,' shouted his sister from the edge of the pathway. Mummy's going to shout.'

Jamie picked up another stick and tried to tempt the dog with it. Gypsy fleetingly sniffed at the stick and went back to digging. A rain of dirt clods shot up and hit Jamie. 'That's enough Gypsy. Come on girl,' he said, but still the dog buried into the ground, kicking up dirt that its hind legs leapt over as its front legs dug. He placed his hands around the dog's body in an attempt to turn it and persuade it to come home, but as he did so he slipped on the wet soil so that his left hand fell into the soggy ground.

'We'll be really late,' shouted his sister just before she heard Jamie scream.

****

The police, when they came, closed up the pathway at both ends so that it became a ghostly place: an echo of the noise of children who had walked there and played there.

In the week that followed the story dominated the headlines: *Baby Found in a Black Bin Liner, Mutilated Child Discarded Like Rubbish, New-born Baby Murdered.* She was stabbed, the papers said, and suffered head injuries before she was buried in a shallow grave.

The police pleaded for the mother to contact them, but no one came forward. They engaged in a hitherto unprecedented voluntary DNA testing of ten thousand women, but still they could not find the mother or the murderer. Weeks went by, months went by and still they could not find a trail that would lead them to solve the crime.

The BBC programme Crimewatch revealed a new computer generated image of how the child would look, if it had lived.

Further leads, despite this highly emotional appeal, were not made.

The murder of the child hovered over the city like an untimely stain, for the city had moved forward and its long and troubled war was over; the economy was thriving and on the ground there was a rumour that the large furniture store IKEA might choose Belfast over Dublin city to set up one of its largest European outlets.

Tourism flourished. On the city streets the local population heard languages spoken that they could not identify, not French, German, Italian or Spanish, but what? they said indiscreetly, as they nudged each other.

The tourists were easy to identify: they snapped photographs prolifically, energetically; passers-by stood back so as not to get in the way. The locals were proud that people wanted to photograph *their* city; it was truly cosmopolitan, truly world class.

The hitherto filthy River Lagan was cleaned up and leafleted as a tourist attraction; small fishermen changed their trade, painted their boats in bright reds or yellows or other nursery colours, added seating, bought white trousers and a hat and raked in a fortune taking passengers a short way along the river.

The passengers saw the still partly run down Titanic Quarter: a rusted boat lay tilted along the quayside, but there was something ghostly and exciting about being in the same place the Titanic had been built, even if there wasn't a lot to see.

It took a while for the old boats to turn; they chugged and clucked and eventually managed to manoeuvre around. The captain of one boat said that the boat was top-heavy, whatever that meant; the tourists didn't argue, many of them thought that the old boat and the old captain were 'quaint', but those were mostly Americans.

The captain invited his passengers to look up at the hills on either side of the river. He began slowly, almost lyrically to name them. It was a magnificent view and well worth the trip, but because Belfast was built in a valley the panorama was often spoiled by cloud and then rain.

The new glass-fronted Waterfront Hall had an auditorium with a large seating capacity that attracted tenors and bands and orchestras to the city. The complex boasted a cinema, a W5 science forum and a multitude of eateries.

The Hilton, set behind it, was another of the city's new builds; it broke the skyline set by The Black Mountain, some said, by a single storey and stuck out, most agreed, like a sore thumb; but the city's town and country planners did not know what to do, they could ask for it to be fixed, but that was like asking the bride to slice off the icing on her wedding cake before the groom took her hand to cut the cake. The town and country planners kept quiet. It was The Hilton after all!

Even the locals became tourists and paid over the nose to see things they'd never wanted to see before: they visited the City Hall offices now that the banner 'Ulster Says No' had been quietly removed. The town hall was such an impressive building that its plans had been borrowed and a replica built some time before in Durban, South Africa.

People paid to see the underground water system that serviced the new weir: a labyrinthine run of claustrophobic passages with stone walls made more claustrophobic by teachers on school trips, with nothing at the end of it but a generator and a journey back along the increasingly suffocating dark passages; they even went out of town and paid to see the Tayto factory so as to take part in the celebration of local produce.

Sculptures were commissioned to celebrate the city's rich cultural history and the arts flourished. Even The Crown Bar (a true work of *Italian* craftsmanship) got a deep clean and plans were put in place to secure the foundations of the tilting Albert Clock.

A group of cultured citizens, artists, musicians, footballers and playwrights came up with the notion that

251

Belfast could win the much-coveted City of Culture Award.

A board was put together to formulate a bid, for the prize had done so much to regenerate Liverpool and would, if brought home, do the same for Belfast. The bid was, with some optimism, put forward. Meanwhile a playwright, who was not on the board, sent a script to The Lyric Theatre, but it was turned down, 'It's not the right time,' he was told. The play lamented the past instead of celebrating the future.

During this era of prosperity the Queen of England had sat down and written a very personal letter to the First Minister requesting the return of a chandelier she had 'leant' to Stormont Building many years before. The chandelier was quietly removed and posted on.

Nevertheless, the missing chandelier was noticeable.

'She's nervous,' said some, 'that's why she wanted her chandelier back.'

'Don't be daft,' said others, 'hasn't she had an Annus Horribilis; it's to replace the one that was destroyed in the fire; it's the least we can do for her.'

The economy was thriving and house prices rose. People felt rich and were happy to spend money. Home improvements, including extensions, were made on the smallest and the biggest of houses; front and back gardens were tended, fences built or freshly painted.

In the midst of this jubilancy the discovery of (some said) a mutilated child filled the people with horror; they thought that they'd put all that behind them – the murdering that is. But this! This was worse; this was a baby, a newborn baby at that.

Evil, pure evil.

252

Speculation as to the mother's mental health arose. Maybe she suffered severe post-natal depression, lost control and thrashed out. She needed help. *Help,* came the retort, *help with a friggin' life sentence.* Others argued that they'd need to bring back the death penalty for whoever did it, and gossip had it that a man was involved. Must have been.

Further leaks and gossip and speculation: of severed limbs and 'tampering' made people shutter. They did all they could to help the recently named PSNI with their investigations. But after a while, when the police still had not found the killer, or the mother, people became afraid to talk. *Careful,* the people said, *the police want someone for that,* and so mouths learned to whisper and finally to hush.

As Christmas approached and the city council spent a great deal of money on a Christmas tree imported from Germany, there were few who spared the child, or her murderer, a thought. It was too ghastly to remember. The past was the past and a pity of it. Besides, they had their own children to care for and to buy presents for. But the PSNI did not want people to forget, for they were determined that the infant's death would not be added to their long list of unsolved crimes.

Chapter 24

Alexander switched off the Calor gas, removed the rubber pipeline and brought the empty cylinder into the back hallway.

It was his first winter in the bookshop and the heater running at full blast had done no more than take the cold chill out of the air. He set the alarm and as he pulled the side door open he saw that the snow was coming down fast. There was already an inch or so lying on the ground.

'Hello.'

'Jesus,' said Alexander, 'you scared me.'

'Christ mate, sorry.' Robert kicked at the fallen snow underground. 'Been meaning to call,' he said, 'it must be a year or so since you opened.'

'Aye.'

'This the bookshop then.' Robert looked up at the sign. 'The Second Chance,' he read out loud.

Alexander shook his head and walked into the street so that he stood beside Robert in the falling snow. 'Oh,' he said, looking up, ' you can usually see it really well.'

'I can see there's something there but I can't read it.'

'Elsie's Bookstore,' said Alexander as he gently, nervously smiled.

Robert kicked at some more snow as Alexander put his hands in his pockets. They did not know what to say. The snow continued to fall making everything in the dark post-industrial street look starkly blankly white, as though its very canvass had sought and gained renewal.

'How is she?' said Robert, breaking the silence.

'You heard then.'

'Tommy told me.'

'Aye. Came as a shock Robert.'

Robert nodded and held his hands palm upwards at the silent falling snow. 'We used to love it when it snowed,' he said.

'We'll go in, shall we?' said Alexander. 'I'll give you a tour.'

'I'd like that,' said Robert.

Inside Alexander took a full cylinder of gas and reapplied the rubber tube before striking a match.

'No need for that,' said Robert. 'I'll not be stopping long.'

'It's bloody freezing though.'

Robert looked around the bookshop. There was a history section, a politics section, and different genres of fiction, including crime fiction, and sci-fi. Irish history was labelled separately: it took up an entire bookshelf from floor to ceiling.

'What way does it work then?' said Robert.

'Some buy and some don't. You can borrow a book for a quid as long as you return it within the week. Or you can take out membership for the year and borrow as much as you like. The advantage for members is that I'll buy in

255

stock that's requested. Others come in and simply buy, regularly too. Some sit for hours drinking tea and reading. Can't seem to get rid of them.'

'Pay for the privilege?'

'I own a bookstore Robert. I'm not a cutthroat businessman. Anyway, they can read as much as they want as long as they keep buying tea, or the occasional sandwich. And they pay to read whatever book they've borrowed too.'

'I didn't mean...'

'No. It's just, it's working that's all and it's the first goddamn thing that ever worked for me.'

'Elsie worked for you. I used to work for you, as a mate.'

'That's not what I meant.'

'I know.'

'Fucking thing,' said Alexander as he struggled to light the heater.

'I'm sorry,' said Robert.

Alexander gave up and threw the box of matches he held in his hand against the door. The matches hit the metal kick plate and tumbled out.

'Why did you come Robert? he shouted. 'After all these months. I tried to ring you and not a dickey bird. Nothing. Zilch.'

'I wanted to see you.'

'What for?' said Alexander.

'Because I heard about Elsie; because I wanted to.'

'You needn't have bothered.'

'If that's the way you feel then I'll...'

Robert got up, making his way to the inner door. He put his hand on the handle.

'It's fucking freezing,' Alexander shouted.

'What?'

'I said it's fucking freezing,' he repeated. Robert smiled and stooped down to lift the spilled matches, before turning back into the room where he bent down and managed to light the heater with his first strike.

'Beginner's luck,' said Alexander. Robert managed to laugh.

'The bookshop looks good,' said Robert as they sat warming themselves in front of the heater. 'Everything's so organised. To be honest Alexander, when Tommy told me what was happening I didn't think you'd make a go of it.'

'No-one did.'

'No-one?'

'Well, maybe Elsie, maybe her, even if it was just a bit. She was so proud when she saw her name above the door.'

'I'll bet. Still is, I'm sure.'

Alexander sighed. 'It'll not be long now Robert. They gave her three months to live after the last fall and it's been five already.'

'The doctor's know fuck all.'

'She's a fighter. That's why. Always was. Anyway, what about you?'

'So, so.'

'Umm. What about the kids? I bet they're all excited about Christmas.' Alexander got up suddenly and went into the back hallway. He rummaged for a minute among a pile of bags and finally got the one he wanted. 'Here,' he said handing the bag to Robert. 'Presents for the kids. There's a remote control car for Peter.'

'I see that,' said Robert looking into the bag.

'And I wasn't so sure about Emily, but I got her a make-up set; it's for kids and wipes off easily but if she doesn't like it...' Alexander took his brown leather wallet out from his back pocket. 'There,' he said, handing Robert the receipt. 'Wasn't cheap. You can change it for her if she doesn't like it.'

'She'll love it. They both will.' Robert closed the bag over. 'You won't be coming up then?'

'I wasn't invited.'

'You don't need an invite Alexander. Jesus, we've been like brothers since we were kids.' Robert began to shake, 'You don't need a bloody invite.'

'Right.'

'Bloody invite. Just 'cause we had an argument. I don't even know what we were arguing over. Something about your glasses.'

'It's forgotten.' Robert felt his left hand tremble and put his right on top of it to mask it.

'You don't look too clever,' said Alexander. He stood up and laid his hand on Robert's right shoulder. 'Jesus Robert, you're shaking.'

'It's nothing.'

'Can't be nothing.'

'It's just the cold. You said it was cold, didn't you?'

'Right.'

'You'll come up then? The kids have missed you.' Robert winced.

'Aye. I've missed them too but...'

'What?'

'Nothing.'

'No, say what you were going to.'

'Is Mary alright? Are you two alright?'

258

'So, so. Not really. I don't know.'

'Oh.'

'We'll get through it. We've come this far.'

'Aye.'

'You'll come over then? The kids would love to see you.' Alexander nodded and left Robert to the door.

'Here,' said Robert handing the bag of presents back to Alexander. 'You'll be able to bring them yourself.'

'Will I wear the Santa's outfit?' Alexander asked.

'If you like,' said Robert trying to manage a smile.

'Maybe not. They're getting a bit old for that.'

Robert nodded. At the door he pressed Alexander's arm. 'It was good to see you,' he said.

Alexander lingered at the door as he watched Robert walk down the street and turn the corner, leaving a trail of footsteps in the freshly fallen snow.

****

The front door of Elsie's was on the latch. Alexander pushed the door gently open and paused in the inner porch. He could hear light music and laughter inside. There was a jig playing on the radio and as he peeped through the stained glass inner door he saw that Lily and Elsie were dancing. It was hard to believe the doctor's prognosis.

'Would you stop trying to lead Lily Mahon.'

'I'm not.'

'You bloody well are.'

'Give over,' laughed Lily. Elsie dropped her hands stubbornly by her side. 'Right,' said Lily, 'You lead then.' Elsie pouted a smile. 'Hurry up,' said Lily switching position, 'or the bloody jig'll be over.' They moved slowly, yet managed to keep rhythm with the music.

'Stop,' said Elsie.

'What?'

'Ssh.' Lily lifted her hands up in exasperation.

'I heard something,' whispered Elsie as she reached for the poker that lay on the hearth.

Alexander pushed the door open. 'Sorry,' he said, 'it's only me.'

He entered and threw off his snow-covered coat onto the balustrade, turned and bowed chivalrously in front of Elsie. 'The next dance,' he suggested.

'You can't dance,' she said.

'Try me,' he offered as he held out his hand. Elsie turned up her face at him. 'Try me,' he insisted. A lighter, softer jig began to play on the radio. She took his hand.

'One, two, three, one, two, three...' repeated Elsie as their feet slowly then confidently moved in rhythm to the music so that midway through the song she'd stopped counting altogether. 'There now,' Elsie said as they finished. She moved towards the old grey radio and turned the volume down.

'He's turned out grand,' said Lily.

'I'll put the kettle on,' said Alexander, embarrassed by the small peck Elsie gave him on the side of the cheek.

'No,' said Elsie. 'There's a wee bottle of sherry in the cabinet in the back room. Get three glasses for us.'

'Should you be...'

'Quit your whish,' said Elsie. 'I'm bloody well tired of people fussing and mollycoddling me. You'd think...'

'What?' said Lily

'You'd think,' Elsie started to laugh, 'I was bloody well dying.'

'You bloody well are,' said Lily seeing the funny side of it.

'Are you getting those glasses or am I going to have to do it myself?' said Elsie.

Alexander returned with the glasses, poured out a small amount into each and held them up for Lily and Elsie to take. 'Away on with you,' said Elsie. 'Fill them up.' Alexander took the glasses back to the cabinet and filled the glasses up. 'And while you're at it,' she shouted to him, 'just bring the bottle in.'

'Jesus Elsie, you nearly took off my ear drums,' he said returning.

'Aye,' said Elsie grabbing the edge of the seat. 'Help me up,' she said. Alexander took her hand. She raised her glass. 'I can shout,' she said, 'and I can still dance, and I can have a wee drink too. What more could you ask for?'

'A toast,' intercepted Alexander.

'I can't get up,' said Lily trying to reach forward to clink her glass.

'Get up,' said Elsie.

'Jesus. I've sunk into the settee.'

'You're getting old Lily Mahon,' said Elsie giggling.

'Bloody cheek,' grumbled Lily affectionately.

Alexander put out his hand and helped Lily to stand.

'To Lily, the best friend I ever had,' said Elsie

'To Lily.' They clinked their glasses and drank.

'And to Alexander,' said Elsie. 'The best son a mother could ask for.'

'To Alexander.'

'And to Elsie,' said Lily. 'The best person...' Lily faltered, 'that ever lived.'

'I'm not dead yet.'

'No,' said Lily.

'Then quit that gurning.'

'I wasn't gurning,' said Lily as she used the cuff of her blue cardigan to wipe away a fallen tear.

'Am I getting a toast or not?'

'To Elsie.'

'Fill up those glasses Alexander,' Elsie said, 'or she'll have me started.'

Alexander wiped the lower part of his nose with the palm of his hand and sniffed. 'Did neither of you ever learn to use a bloody hanky?' Alexander and Lily laughed.

'One last toast,' said Elsie. 'To the future.'

'The future,' they chorused.

Chapter 25

The light from the morning sun came through the window of Elsie's bedroom at an angle so that the single drifting ray reached across the bottom of the wooden bed, crossing over Elsie's naked right foot that lay extended beyond the bedclothes. Her right palm was open but cupped as though in death, or in dying, she held a hand smaller than her own.

Her face was tilted forward and bore upon it the agony of a life going from it, of a life leaving. The muscles and skin were drawn downwards and the lines of age marked and plentiful. Her mouth lay open, testament to the incompletion of her last breath.

Alexander sat down beside her and lifted up her warm open hand. In the fixed gaze of her still so blue eyes he witnessed the faith she'd lived with, the faith that she'd died with: that her breath would be lifted up and taken on and that soon, when the agony ended, she would meet with those whom she loved – her mother, her father, her sisters, her brothers and with Rosie. With Rosie most of all. He breathed heavily and deeply and even as he loved her and was glad of her comfort, he felt jealous too. For he had no faith and she was gone from him, completely and forever.

He said her name aloud, willing with all of his heart for the life to come back into her. He called to her, repeating her name over and over as his own breath heaved and sighed and choked up within him. He stood up from the bed, careful not to let go of her hand and kissed her forehead and her cheeks, wishing all the while that she could take some of his breath, take all of it and live again.

He let go of her hand, not wanting to, and moved to the other side of the bed. He took off his shoes and eased himself up onto the bed beside her. He placed his arm around her shoulders, moving her carefully so as not to hurt her so that her head rested on his swollen heaving chest. 'It's all right now,' he said. 'There'll be no more pain,' and he rubbed her arms and her hands to keep her warm.

The morning sunray moved slowly across the room as he held her, marking time that would, defiantly, move on. If only he could hold her here. It was only a few weeks since they had danced together, when he had hoped, perhaps believed, that she would stay with him for much longer than the doctor's thought. She had laughed, they had danced, they had drunk, in Elsie's words, to the future. He had raised his glass to this? To hold her dead in his arms? He baulked at his own stupidity.

How could so much life be so suddenly gone?

And so he held her, even as the morning sun faded, and even as he knew that he would have to leave her, so as to tell Lily, he did not want to go, for he did not want her to be alone.

****

264

'He was meant to be here,' said Tommy as Lily undid his black tie and remade it.

'He'll be here,' said Lily.

'You'd think he could be on time. But no, Robert thinks that bloody funerals will wait for him.'

'That's better,' said Lily, fixing the collar of Tommy's starched white shirt.

Tommy looked up at the clock. 'If he's not here within the next five minutes...'

'He'll be here,' said Lily.

'Jesus Lily, go out to him,' said Tommy as he looked through the window at Alexander. 'He's been pacing up and down since the hearse arrived. You'd think he was bloody well anxious to bury her.'

'That's enough,' snapped Lily. 'You know as well as I do that he's falling apart inside.'

'Go out to him then.'

Lily lifted a hanky out of her pocket. 'I can't cope with you being like this,' she said, blowing her nose.

'Like what?'

'As though you're the only one who cared about her.'

'I just wanted Robert to be on time. You'd think he could do that,' Tommy said evasively.

'I loved her too,' said Lily as she took her coat from off the banister rail and went outside.

Tommy finished buffing his already polished black shoes, checked that his tie was straight and followed.

'There's no-one to go into the second car,' said Alexander.

'It's not far,' said Lily, 'most people prefer to walk.'

'You're right. I shouldn't have ordered two. I just wanted it all done properly.'

265

'It is,' reassured Lily.

She patted invisible dust from his shoulders. 'It will be.'

'Who will carry her?' asked Alexander, looking around.

'It's all been sorted Alexander. Tommy has it sorted.' Alexander nodded.

'It was so quick,' he said.

'She'd longer than they thought she'd have.'

'Not long enough,' he argued. 'Do you think it'll rain? I don't want it to rain.'

Lily looked up at the black clouds overhead. 'It'll be alright. We'll give her a good send off. That's all we can do.' She put her arm around his shoulder. 'She's in a better place,' she said.

'I'll never forgive him for this,' whispered Tommy to Lily when he got outside.

'God knows what's happened,' said Lily. 'Maybe he'll make it to the graveyard.'

'We're one short,' muttered Tommy, as a man with a white beard stepped forward to volunteer to carry the coffin.

Tommy had never seen him before but nodded to accept.

They lifted the coffin above them, putting the tallest men at the front to guard against the coffin sliding forward, for the gradient of the street was set against them. One of the official pallbearers walked at the front with his hand on the coffin.

They had turned right at the bottom of the street onto The Falls Road when the sky cracked open. The official hearse carriers wanted the bearers to load the coffin into the hearse.

'No,' said Alexander. 'We're going to walk her further.'

Five men changed hands and they walked a little further.

'We have to stop,' said one of the pallbearers. 'It's getting slippy.'

'No,' said Alexander refusing to let go. Tommy came up beside him.

'We've given her a good walk Alexander.' He put his hands around Alexander's shoulders. 'Let her go son, with dignity.'

The coffin was lifted and put into the back of the hearse. Lily and Tommy and Alexander got into one of the cars; the other was used by elderly neighbours, including Mrs. Cullen who had somehow managed to leave the house.

'She's only a young thing,' said Mrs. Cullen in the back of the car.

'I remember her as a kid, running around the streets. God, I was in my early twenties, during the war when my Albert was away. Smiley, he called her back then. 'Here comes Smiley,' he'd say.

'It goes to show you,' she said, snapping her false teeth into place. 'When our time's up it's up. No arguing with that.'

'You and her were close,' said Maisie, leaning forward.

'Good to me she was,' said Mrs. Cullen.

'And does she own that house of hers?' asked Maisie. 'And has she made a will?'

'Always the gossip Maisie Hunter.'

'But...'

'She'll have left nothing to you, you can rest assured of that,' added Mrs. Cullen as she pulled out her hearing aid and clucked her false teeth.

267

****

Robert had taken the day off work in order to be at Elsie's funeral. Whatever their differences he knew that Alexander would need him and he hoped that he would be able to be strong enough to support him. He put the children's lunch-boxes in their school bags and drove them both to school. Peter got out of the back seat and walked towards the front door of the school without saying goodbye, but Emily stood up and reached over to him. She kissed him on the cheek and told him that she loved him.

As he returned home he hoped that Mary would be up and dressed, but the mail lay uncollected on the wooden floor of the hallway. It had become habit with her to sleep on in the mornings. He went upstairs and nudged her awake.

'What time is it?' she asked.

'We need to make a move,' he said. She looked at the clock, uncomprehending. 'Elsie's funeral,' he said.

'Do I need to go?' she asked. Robert nodded. 'Alexander'll expect you.'

Mary got out of bed and went to the bathroom. She rinsed her face with cold water and took a clean towel from the hot-press, holding it against her half-woken eyes.

'It's at ten,' he said trying to hurry her.

She opened the bathroom door and lifted her clothes off the landing balustrade; she'd laid them out the night before. She knew she didn't suit black. It was a dress she'd bought for her father's funeral.

Robert lifted the mail and as she came down the stairs he handed it to her, retaining the one envelope that had no

268

addressee on it. He opened the blank envelope and withdrew the Christmas card inside.

'Just bills,' she said, shuffling through the mail.

Robert held out the card that was inside the envelope. She took it from him. It was a pink and white Christmas card addressed to 'Baby Clare' – the name the police had given to her child.

Mary walked into the living room and sat down on the edge of the settee. It was the first time she had spoken since the day Robert had buried it. 'It would be her second Christmas,' she said.

'Don't.'

'Look,' she said, pointing at the Christmas tree. 'We carry on as if nothing has happened.'

'You do,' he said. Mary shook her head.

'I went to the police.'

'When?'

'That week. I wanted them to know. I wanted somebody to know and then after, when those children found it, I went again. The second time I went in and up to the desk. I had to wait. The desk sergeant was on the telephone. When he finally hung up I made an excuse, said I'd forgotten the parking ticket and left.'

'You went without telling me?'

'Yes.'

'You had no right to do that.'

'You wouldn't talk, wouldn't say anything. Nothing.'

'There's nothing to say.'

'They'll find out Mary. It's only a matter of time.'

'No. Not now. At first I thought they would too. I thought we'd just have to wait but it's been too long. If they knew anything, then they wouldn't be doing this.'

'What?'

'Sending out wild cards.'

Robert sat down on the burgundy wingchair. 'But we know.'

'Yes.'

'What was it like?' she asked. 'When you found her in the tree house. What did Peter do to her?'

'Jesus!'

'I've a right to know.'

'Maybe you should have asked me at the time, when I needed someone to talk to, instead of shutting me out.'

'I had to. I had to pretend.'

Robert laughed eerily. 'Oh,' he said. 'It wasn't pretend; it was real, too real. The blood was real. He'd stabbed her Mary, not once, no, not Peter, once wasn't enough, he'd stabbed her three, four times, maybe more. Like he'd gone crazy.' Robert got up and imitated holding a pair of scissors. 'Like this,' he said, stabbing at the air around him. 'And this,' he said stabbing the air again.

'Stop it,' Mary screamed at him.

'I can't stop it. It goes round and round in my head. I see her when I'm sleeping – the blood oozing from her. She says, 'Daddy, daddy.'

'No.'

'Help me,' she says. 'Help me daddy.' And I can't help her and she's reaching out to me, calling me.'

'No.'

'Yes. And it goes on and on. And sometimes I think as it's happening that it's just a dream and I try to wake up but I can't wake up and the crying goes on until I close my ears to try to stop hearing it. And then when I do wake up, sometimes for a moment I forget that it's real. Fleeting seconds when I believe that the nightmare is over, but the nightmare is never over.'

'I don't want to go the funeral.'

'What?'

'I don't want to go.'

'You have to.'

'No, I don't.'

'Do you think I want to go?'

Mary bit her lower lip. 'Robert,' she blurted out. 'I slept with Alexander.'

'What?'

'I slept with Alexander.'

'Fuck.'

Robert sat back down on the wingchair.

'It was when you were still seeing that woman. I didn't want to. He was there, helping me.'

'Helping his fucking self, you mean.'

'It wasn't like that. He told me he loved me. It was over as quick as it had begun.'

Mary got up from the settee and sat down on the floor in front of Robert. 'I told him that I loved you Robert. I've always loved you.'

'Did you spend the night with him?'

'No.'

'In our bed?'

'No.'

'Where then? On the floor? Standing up?'

'Stop it.'

'I just want the full picture, that's all. Fuck,' he said more loudly. 'I never even thought. When? When did you sleep with him?'

'It doesn't matter, does it?'

271

'Yes, it does. Tell me. When?'

'I didn't mean to Robert.'

'When?'

'Early November, a week or so before you finished your affair, before you came back to me.'

Robert stood up and grabbed her to her feet. 'Don't you know what this means?' he said.

'No,' she pleaded with him. 'It wasn't his child. It was your child.'

'You don't know that.'

'I know it,' she said.

'Jesus. Do you know what you're telling me? You're telling me that the child could have been Alexander's.'

'It wasn't.'

'It could have been.'

Mary shook her head.

'Who did Peter kill that day? My child or Alexander's?'

'I don't know,' she said as Robert's phone rang. He lifted it from his pocket and switched it off.

'I'll go to him and ask him, shall I? Oh, I know you've just buried Elsie, but do you mind telling me whose baby it was I buried? Maybe he'll have the right answer.'

'You can't,' she said.

'Watch me.'

He walked out the front door, turned the ignition in the car and headed in the direction of Milltown Cemetery.

Chapter 26

'I've never seen such rain,' said Mrs. Cullen to the driver. 'It's a dark day.'

The driver could not hear her properly though he was glad she'd chosen to stay in the car, for the rain fell down thickly on the mourners. He'd driven as close to the burial plot as possible so that she could hear the funeral proceedings through the partially opened window in the back.

Mrs. Cullen took her teeth from her woollen cardigan pocket and snapped them into place. 'You've your own teeth?' she said.

The driver laughed, displaying a heavily gold crowned tooth. 'More or less,' he said.

'Nothing like your own teeth. Elsie had all her own teeth you know. Right from when she was no age they called her Smiley. My Albert just loved her to bits. He said we'd have one of our own, just like Smiley, when he got home from the war.'

The driver looked in the mirror so that he could see her as she talked. 'My poor Albert,' she said. 'He wasn't the best looking of men. No, not Albert, but he was a good soul. Would have done anything for anybody.' Mrs. Cullen sighed.

'It's upsetting to see the young ones go before you,' the driver said.

'Aye. I'm only glad that Albert's not here to see it. He was a big softie, wouldn't have hurt nobody if he could help it.'

'In the war you said?'

'He was. He didn't last long you see. It was the 6th of May 1942 when they told me, but they couldn't tell me when he'd died for they never found my poor Albert. Missing in action he was. I waited to the end of the war. I kept thinking that Albert would be coming home, that he'd got lost. I prayed to St. Anthony, hoping he'd turn up. Even if he'd turned up drunk, that would have been alright too, for I missed him that much. I don't like the old drink though, no. There's many a good man, a good woman for that matter, has fallen foul with the old drink.'

'I'm sorry to hear that,' said the driver. 'About Albert.'

'It wasn't St. Anthony's fault. He was dead and you can't find the dead. Not in this life anyway. Has she gone in yet?' Mrs. Cullen tried to peer through the rain-drenched front window screen. The driver turned the ignition so that the wipers cleared it.

'I think so,' he said as he put his cap back on.

'I'll be glad to go myself,' said Mrs. Cullen. 'Fed up waiting around.'

'Glad to see Albert again?' said the driver.

'Aye,' laughed Mrs. Cullen. 'Though God knows what he'll think of me. Your body lets you down in the end. He died a young man, you see.'

'It'll be different up there,' said the driver.

'You think so?'

'Age won't matter,' he reassured.

'I hope you're right. For my Albert, he wasn't good-looking but he was fit.'

'What age was he?' A huge grin spread across Mrs. Cullen's face.

'Nineteen,' she said. 'We were only married six months. He was younger than me, even then.'

'I'm sorry.'

'Oh don't be sorry,' said Mrs. Cullen. 'It was the best six months of my life. Here,' she said, withdrawing a black and white picture of Albert in uniform from her handbag. She held onto one side of the photograph so that the driver had to turn around awkwardly to see it properly.

'Looks like a good-looking man to me.'

'You think so?' said Mrs. Cullen, turning the photograph around to look at it. The driver nodded. 'That'll be the uniform. Smartened them all up.'

'No, he is.'

'Well now, they say all things come to those who wait and no-one ever called my Albert good-looking before,' said Mrs. Cullen. The driver laughed and tipped his cap. 'Up in heaven smiling at that one, he'll be,' she said.

'They're starting to leave.'

'Aye,' said Mrs. Cullen. 'Smiley's gone then.' She took a hanky from her pocket and blew her nose when she saw Maisie heading back towards the car. 'Do you mind if I take my teeth out?' she said hastily to the driver. 'They're starting to hurt.' The driver suppressed a laugh.

'Not at all,' he said.

She put the photograph carefully into a sipped compartment of her handbag, took a pound out of her purse and slipped it into his hand forcefully so that he could not argue with her. 'Thanks son,' she mumbled, 'for bringing me. God knows but my Albert will be glad to see Smiley again.'

****

Robert parked the car at the front gates of Milltown Cemetery and walked through the pathways until he got to Elsie's grave. The mourners had largely dispersed, leaving Tommy and Lily at the graveside.

'You think you could have made it,' said his mother. His father looked away from him and back at the grave.

The grave was open, covered in a green felt cloth, waiting to be filled in. Elsie's mother and father were buried in the same plot; Rosie was also buried there; her coffin set into a niche in the wall of the grave. Her other brothers and sisters were in the poor graves, further up the slope, but the poor graves were being dug up. Temporarily, as they buried Elsie, the diggers had stopped digging.

'Where is he?' said Robert. Lily pointed to Alexander who was tipping the gravediggers.

'Keep your money,' said the gravedigger. 'We're only sorry that we misjudged.' Alexander shrugged and put the money in the gravedigger's soiled pockets.

'No harm,' he said.

'It's never happened before,' said the gravedigger, putting his hand consolingly on Alexander's shoulder. 'We thought it was wide enough, but it was dug yesterday and sometimes, with the weather, the sides fall in. But we should have checked it this morning. Having to lift her out

276

like that to widen it and then lower her back in again. I'm ashamed.'

'Don't be,' said Alexander. 'Elsie would have seen the funny side of it. She'd have said something like, 'I was going to change my mind and come back and sort you all out.'

The gravedigger apologised again: 'It wasn't right though. Take your money,' he said, pulling it out of his pocket, 'for I can't take it from you.' He held out the twenty-pound note, just as Robert tapped Alexander's shoulder from behind. As Alexander turned Robert landed a punch.

'You fucking bastard,' said Robert, as Alexander lay on the ground.

Both Tommy and Lily ran towards them. Lily bent down and gave Alexander a clean hanky, to wipe the blood on his busted lip

'What do you think you're doing?' said Tommy to Robert.

'He slept with my wife,' shouted Robert as he put his right foot into Alexander's lower back.

'That's enough,' said Tommy.

'Get up, you piece of shit,' said Robert.

'I said that's enough.'

Alexander stood up. Robert threw a second punch but his father, standing a foot taller, blocked the punch by grabbing his arm mid-air.

'We have just buried Elsie,' said Tommy.

Robert tried to pull his arm away but Tommy's strength defeated him. 'There'll be no more fighting,' said his father.

'No,' said Lily, shaking her head from side to side.

277

'You will take this thing out of this graveyard. For I'll not have Elsie's memory marred by it.'

'Did you?' said Lily as she helped Alexander to his feet. Alexander nodded and dropped his head forward, shame-faced.

Robert struggled to free himself from his father's grip, but it held firm.

'You're a lying bastard,' said Robert to Alexander.

'You cheated on her first.'

'What?' said his mother as she turned her solemn gaze towards Robert. 'You cheated on Mary?' Tommy released Robert's arm.

'Go home Robert. You can sort this out tomorrow. You can do whatever the hell you want tomorrow, but this is Elsie's day and we're going to go to the pub and give her a proper send off. Besides, you made your position clear when you couldn't even be bothered turning up for the funeral.'

'I'm sorry,' said Robert.

'For what?'

'For not being here. I should have been here.'

'Go home Robert,' said his mother.

'This isn't over,' said Robert to Alexander as he left.

****

Tommy had helped Alexander arrange a full set-down meal in The Rock, bringing in outside caterers, but he wanted to pay for it too.

'She was my mother,' Alexander said. Tommy looked offended. 'I don't want you to feel that Tommy. I don't mean any harm. It's just that I wanted to do so much for

278

her, but she didn't live long enough. She just didn't live long enough.'

'We all wanted to,' Tommy said.

'Even the bathroom that we put in last year. It caused so much disruption. If I'd have known that she was ill then.'

'You wouldn't have done anything different,' said Tommy.

'I'd have done a lot different,' Alexander said.

'Aye,' said Tommy, trying to console.

'But she loved it. She loved having her own bath. Sometimes, y'know, she'd go out and clean it, when it didn't even need cleaned. She kept buying towels, couldn't seem to get enough of them. God, she loved that bath. It was like all her dreams had come true. And bubbles, she loved those too. After she'd filled the bath and was still in her dressing gown she used to call me. 'Your job,' she said. I'd pour the bubble bath in and mix it up so that the bath was almost overflowing with them. She said that every time she put the stuff in she couldn't get it mixed up properly.'

'She loved her name above the bookstore,' said Tommy.

'She didn't half,' said Alexander. 'At the beginning when it opened she would come round during the day, sometimes after mass. She used the stick then, after her fall, but she'd come round. "Still that old name," she'd say. You know the way she had that dry wit of hers. But she loved it, yes, not as much as the bath though. I just wish that it had started earlier. I just wish that I'd have got my life together earlier.'

279

'It takes time,' said Tommy. 'Elsie didn't hold it against you.'

'No,' said Alexander. 'It wasn't in her nature. She didn't hold anything against anybody.'

'She just wanted the best for you Alexander. In a way, you became her life.' Alexander started to cry. He leant against Tommy. 'You're like a son,' said Tommy. 'You do know that.' Alexander wiped his eyes, failing to notice that Tommy too was crying.

During the meal Lily said that she wasn't feeling well. She stayed until it finished and asked her husband whether or not anyone would notice if she left. He asked her to stay a while longer.

She could not look at Alexander, though she tried. Yet if Robert had cheated on Mary then he was as much to blame. She tried not to feel angry, but gradually her anger gave way to a deeper pain inside her.

'It's alright now,' said Tommy. 'They've all had a bit to drink and won't notice you leaving.' Lily wanted to say, 'We did our best by her,' but she knew it wasn't true.

'I'll walk you up if you like,' said Tommy. 'But I'll have to come back. Alexander's in no state to...' But his voice trailed off.

'I want to be alone for a while anyway,' said Lily.

As she walked up Rockdale Street and looked at the outside of Elsie's house she remembered the day when she'd been given the letter:

'Here,' said Elsie's mother, handing it to her. 'I've kept that some time. Don't know why she posted it to this address in the first place. Always was a bit of a skinflint. She put it inside a letter to me and asked me to pass it on.'

'Maybe she didn't have Tommy's address,' Lily volunteered.

'Maybe.'

'You said you've kept it some time?'

'I have.'

'Why?' said Lily.

'Forgot about it. Now I'm busy if you don't mind. But I just found it and thought, since you're hanging out with Tommy these days, that you might like to pass it on.'

Lily took the letter. She was meeting Tommy later that night and could give it to him then, but as the night wore on the letter remained in her handbag; she determined that she would give it to Tommy before the end of the week, but one day led to the next and the letter stayed in her handbag. At the end of the week she took it out and hid it in the bottom of her dresser drawer.

****

Tommy locked the pub up early. When he arrived home Lily was still up. She was sitting at the kitchen table, fully dressed. A suitcase lay in the hallway at the front door.

'What's going on?' he said. Lily handed him the unopened letter. 'What's this?'

'It's from Elsie.'

'Elsie?' The letter was old and yellowed and crumpled, but the seal, as Lily said, was unbroken. 'But how?' said Tommy.

'I kept it,' said Lily. 'All these years and I kept it from you. Open it,' she said.

'I don't want to,' said Tommy, setting the letter on the table.

'Open it,' she said. 'Or I'll do it for you.'

Tommy opened the letter.

'She said yes, didn't she?' Tommy nodded, but he felt angry too. 'I kept it from you Tommy. Do you understand that?'

'But why?' he said.

'Because I loved you. That's why. Elsie's mother kept it from you first and then I did. I was no better. She gave it to me after we started going out.'

'Why did she do that?'

'I don't know Tommy. She was bitter. She was bitter about all the children that'd died. She was bitter about her dead husband and she was bitter about Elsie leaving. Maybe she'd a right to be.'

'But she gave me Elsie's address.'

'I don't know Tommy. I can't go back in time and read her mind.'

'No,' said Tommy.

'But I can read your mind. At the graveyard it was you who mourned the most. Not me, her best friend, not Alexander, her son. It was you Tommy. You grieved the most.'

'That's not true,' said Tommy.

'Do you know what it's like to have spent a lifetime with someone who doesn't love you the way you want them to? Do you know what that's like? You loved her Tommy, and she loved you too. I kept you apart. Do you know what that feels like? To have carried that sin all my life. To be carrying it now as I'm standing in front of you.'

'What's the suitcase for?' he asked, furrowing his brow.

'I'm leaving,' she said.

'Leaving?'

'What else can I do Tommy? Do you think I can spend the next months, years, watching you grieve, knowing what I did?' Lily walked into the hallway and lifted the suitcase. 'I'm sorry Tommy. Truly I'm sorry. You two were meant to be together. If I hadn't hidden that letter then you would have been together and you would have been happy.'

Tommy set the letter back down on the table. 'She said no Lily. Not there,' he said pointing to the letter, 'but she turned me down. Y'see I asked her again, when she got back from the nursing. She said no.'

'You stupid bloody fool. Why do you think she said no? Elsie knew that I'd fallen for you. I made sure she did, 'cause I got to her on the first night she came home. I knew she wouldn't cross me.'

'She did love me then,' said Tommy.

'Yes Tommy. She loved you.'

'She told me to take care of you, after she'd gone.'

'It's not enough Tommy. To love and to know that you've always been second best. I should have known that years ago. I should have put it right, at least tried to before now. I should have given you the letter.' Lily tied the belt of her beige overcoat and walked down the hallway. 'I'm sorry,' she said as she got to the front door, 'I'm so sorry.'

'Hold on,' he said, standing up from the table. 'Do you think you've done all that lying to walk out on me now?'

'What?' she said.

'Think about it. You fought, lied to marry me, and if what you said is true Elsie stood aside.'

283

'It is true.'

A taxi pulled up outside the door and beeped its horn. Lily opened the front door.

'Where do you think you're going?' said Tommy.

'I don't know,' said Lily, 'but I do know that I can't stay.'

'Can't you?' he said.

He lifted the suitcase from her, set it back down on the floor and walked outside to the taxi driver. 'A change of mind mate,' he said to the cabby as he paid him. The taxi pulled away.

Lily stood outside the house, on the doorstep. 'Go in,' he said, but Lily didn't move. Tommy walked back to her and lifted her off her feet. 'I've lost one woman in my life today,' he said, 'I may have lost a son too, but I'm not going to lose my wife.'

'But the letter,' said Lily.

'That was then,' he said, 'we can't change that.'

He kicked the front door shut with his heel and lifted her upstairs.

Chapter 27

The early January street was dark though it was morning and the wind clawed. Alexander stood in the street in an old beige duffle coat rubbing his hands, numb with waiting. Gate after gate clanged as the milkman delivered bottles to doorsteps, unhurried, as though it mattered little whether his round took a week or a month or a lifetime to complete.

The white of the milkman's coat made the industrialized brick of the street blacker still. 'It's cold,' the milkman said to Alexander. 'Are you wanting something?'

Alexander shook his head. 'I mean yes,' he said, 'sorry. Can you leave two bottles in future?'

The milkman etched the order in pencil in a hard-backed notebook that he pulled from an inside pocket, replaced the notepad and lifted two bottles of milk from the open-backed milk-float before leaving them on Elsie's doorstep; he coughed and climbed back into the vehicle that spluttered as it was switched on. With the milkman gone the street returned to empty.

Alexander rubbed his hands together and pulled his collar up. He did not want to go back inside. Yet Mary and the children were not due to arrive until eleven. He had wanted to pick them up himself, but Mary had insisted that she wanted to come by herself. 'It is better that way,' she said. 'I will have ghosts to bury.'

Alexander nodded. It had been seven years since Robert had left, returning to his home on the day of Elsie's funeral and taking his passport and a single bag of belongings before walking out. Mary had rung Alexander, 'I can't stop him,' said Alexander, unsure as to whether or not he wanted to; but even if he could have stopped Robert from leaving, he would not have deserted Elsie's final farewell, he owed her that at least.

After the day of the funeral, Mary had leaned on him and Alexander had gone to her. As the weeks and months and years moved forward, they both knew that Robert was never coming home. And when, unexpectedly, Mary received divorce papers through the post, she felt, not anxious about letting go of him, but only glad that he was still alive, for she had not heard from him in those seven years and the not knowing was harder. He was alive, he had moved on and she must move on too, if she could.

She had picked herself up gradually, been picking herself up, and Alexander made her laugh even on a bad day; he had always made her laugh.

He was good with the kids too. She had always been fond of him, but over the years she had grown to need him, grown to love him, and so when he asked her to marry him she said yes.

****

Lily came out into the street. 'So it's today?' she said. 'Mary and the kids are moving in with you today?'

'If they come,' said Alexander.

286

'Be patient,' said Lily.

'I have been,' replied Alexander abruptly.

'We can't give our approval Alexander,' she said, hurting.

'No,' he answered.

'But I can wish you well,' said Lily. 'I can do that,' she said. 'You've been good to the kids Alexander. I know that.'

'Perhaps it would have been easier for you if we'd have gone elsewhere?'

'Perhaps,' said Lily.

'But I won't leave Elsie's house. No Lily, I can't do that. Not for you, not for Tommy. It is my home, too hard won: for me, for Elsie. I won't leave it.'

'Tommy says it'll be good to see more of the grandchildren; he's mellowed in his old age.'

'He did?' said Alexander.

'It's Tommy's way. He doesn't say a thing direct.'

'No,' said Alexander. 'I know that.'

'Go in Alexander,' said Lily, 'she'll come soon enough.'

'Aye,' said Alexander, but he could not go in.

Lily closed her front door, leaving Alexander in the street alone, watching the corner at the bottom, hoping. He was full of optimism: for Mary, for the arrival of the two kids, for the dream of a family of his own, but he was full of anxiety too.

If only the taxi would pull up soon and the beginning would begin. He planted his hands in his duffle coat pockets and went back to waiting.

But the morning wore on and still Mary and the children did not come. 'It'll come to no good,' he heard

Elsie say. 'Love does not expect,' he heard her say. But love does expect, it expects to love, to be allowed to love, and it hopes to be loved back. It was a stupid thing she'd said.

But suddenly the wind lifted a white plastic carrier bag from the ground and in a forceful blaze it smacked against Alexander's face, sticking to him before dropping to the ground.

'Serves me right,' said Alexander smiling. He picked the white carrier bag up from the ground and held it, and for a moment it became a flag in his mind that he lifted and waved: a flag of peace between Elsie and himself and his unkind, now sorrowful thoughts. He brought the carrier bag inside, sat down and picked up yesterday's newspaper, but he'd already read it thoroughly and the words filtered away: sound without meaning. He wished he had been kinder to Lily.

****

Mary sat on the porch with her head held between her hands. The house was packed up, she had only to ring a taxi. But she had been sitting in the porch for some time.

'Go and play,' she said to the children. But Emily was too old to go and play. 'I'll take Peter to the park,' she offered instead. 'We'll go for a walk and come back.' Mary nodded.

We had such hope, Mary thought, remembering the first day Robert and she had got the keys to the house.

We had such dreams, she thought, remembering how they'd sat on a decrepit armchair after lovingly painting the first room of their new home – vermillion and white and two weeks later a gentle beige repainting.

288

We had so much love, she thought, remembering how they'd held each other and cried when Emily was born; sitting in the Royal Victoria Hospital as the night wore in; rocking each other and sleeping side by side, Mary in the bed, Emily in the cradle and Robert in an armchair. The moon had seemed to smile at them through the dusty window.

We were so young, she thought and heaved in her gut, restraining a tear that fell anyhow, a solitary tear that Mary moved her foot towards and crushed as though it were a cigarette butt.

'Are you alright love?' said her gossipy next-door neighbour.

He used the wall that parted their two houses like a gateway, hopping over it, back and forth, to ask about the weather, the children, the paintwork; to tell about Mrs. Moon up the road; Joe Swilly who got done for not having car tax; the drug dealer in the corner house who was temporarily living in Spain; and the end house where a prostitute lived with a child from as many men as he'd had hot dinners. The gossipy next-door neighbour had a young woman who called to his house; she looked shoddy and stumbled with the sway of drink, but he did not talk about her.

'Robert's been away quite a bit now?' the gossip said. 'So is that guy who's always hanging around. Alexander? That's what you call him, isn't it? Is he your new bloke?'

'I've a lot to do today,' said Mary.

'Aye, but you've been sitting there a while,' the gossip said. 'I just thought I'd come out and ask if you needed anything.'

'Nothing,' said Mary.

'Where are you going to anyway?' the gossip said. Mary didn't answer. 'Can't say that I'm glad to be having new neighbours; it's always a hassle to begin with, wondering what nonsense they'll bring with them. The new owners. What are they like?'

Mary shrugged.

'Did you know Margie has been given six months? Eddie and she got together late in life. Too late,' he said. 'They've no kids as you know. I've four kids,' he said, 'all grown-up now. I go and visit them sometimes,' he said.

Emily and Peter came back from their walk and stood in front of Mary and the gossip who had sat down on the front porch beside her.

'I'll be going then,' said the gossip getting up. He took out a fiver from his pocket. 'Don't imagine I'll be seeing you again, young man,' he said to Peter as he held out the money. Peter shrugged. 'Take it,' he said, 'and look after your mummy.' The neighbourly gossip hopped over the wall and shut his front door.

'Can we go?' said Emily. 'It's cold in the park.'

'Yes,' said Mary. 'But I have to say goodbye to Eddie and Margie.'

'Shall I ring for a taxi?' said Emily. Mary looked back at the house.

'Yes,' she said.

****

Alexander put down the newspaper. What was he doing reading yesterday's news? What did it matter? He went out to the scullery and put the kettle on the gas stove. He pulled the curtains open and the net curtains, underneath them, up. If he wasn't going to wait outside, at least he

290

could see the taxi, if it came, when it came. As the kettle boiled he kept walking from the scullery to the window and back again, occasionally opening the inner stained-glass door to peer down the street, for he'd left the front door open.

Eleven o'clock came. He went back into the street. Mary was due to arrive at eleven. But at twelve o'clock Alexander returned in-doors.

He boiled the kettle again and thought to ring her: he lifted out his mobile phone and brought forward her number on the display, but he pressed the red button. It was her decision; he must not force it.

It was three o'clock before Alexander closed the front door. The waiting was over, Mary would not come.

He went inside and reached up to a bookshelf, hoping that he might yet divert his thoughts, assuage his pain. But as he pulled the book from the shelf, Elsie's church missal that lay shelved beside it fell onto the floor. A prayer card tumbled out and landed at Alexander's feet. He picked it up and read it:

'*Thou hast made us for thyself, O Lord, and our heart is restless until it rest in thee...*'

Alexander sat down on the settee, shifting the cushion behind him to read on:

'*But the love of God lifts them up, and carries them even to a desire of suffering more. They are determined to suffer as long as it shall please God, without allowing themselves the liberty to wish for an end, or even a diminuition of them. Thus do they find in pain, their peace, their repose and their delight.*'

He lifted the missal from the floor and put the prayer back into it. It was strange how it had fallen out.

Sometimes, he thought, just sometimes, it was hard not to believe, for the signs often seemed so clearly posted, and Alexander, like Elsie before him, did not hold sway with coincidence. But even so, he did not believe and yet, for the prayer and the comfort it gave him, he felt grateful. To whom? He did not know. Perhaps to Elsie for having kept it, though in that moment as he picked up the prayer and read it she was alive, as though she sat beside him and offered it up. Perhaps it was not the prayer, but Elsie's presence, alive though she was dead that had comforted him.

Alexander put the missal back on the shelf, rolled a joint and went out into the yard to smoke it. He could not change what was, and he accepted that; but just as he had all but given up the ghost his waiting ended: his mobile rang.

'Alexander,' Mary said. 'I will be there in half an hour.'

Yes, Alexander thought, the waiting is over, for today at least, but he knew that tomorrow there would be other waiting games, that tomorrow there would be other stories to live and other stories to tell.

Epilogue

Robert threw his walking stick down on top of the grave and arranged the flowers in front of the headstone. He hadn't been home since his mother was buried nine years before. He was glad that she had come to visit him in Edinburgh after he had left. And when he'd got married again and had children she had come too. But his father had stayed at home and never forgiven him for leaving. Robert regretted that.

It was always cold in the graveyard. It sloped down, overlooking the M1. Its still, sombre presence at such odds with the fast cars and busy lives of those it overlooked. He supposed that the graveyard's situation summed up all of life – a place where the present and the past, the living and the dead, were juxtaposed, and where sometimes too the demarcations blurred.

Robert lifted the stick and leant against it. He rubbed his shoulder, for his arthritis was playing up and his gammy hip ached. He buttoned up his long, dark grey overcoat and turned the collar up. He was glad his mother and his father had never known about the child he had

293

buried. His mother would not have been able to forgive him for that and, as long as the secret remained hidden he had been able to keep her love.

****

'Why the secrecy?' Alexander said. 'Why won't you tell me why Robert's flown home from Edinburgh?'

Mary took his hand and squeezed it. He let go and walked to the window.

'I wouldn't change anything,' he said. 'Even though Robert got hurt.'

'He left me Alexander.'

'Yes, I know. But still, it didn't make sense to me. When he busted my face at the graveyard he said that it wasn't over. But after that, he left. It wasn't like Robert to lie down. Angry, yes. I expected that, but to walk out and leave it all, leave you all. To walk out on his two kids.'

'It was better that way. He couldn't cope,' she said.

'Cope?'

'Not just with you and what had happened between us.'

'With what then?'

'Get my pills,' she said. Alexander lifted the box of pills from the dressing table and went downstairs to get a glass of water.

'Better?' he said.

'It'll take a minute for them to work.'

'When will Robert be here?' said Alexander as he stared out into the street.

'Soon,' Mary said as she looked at the clock on the bedside locker. 'I should get up and get dressed.'

'Can I get you anything?' he said.

'You've always looked after me,' said Mary. 'I didn't fall in love with you Alexander, you know that, but I grew to love you and that sometimes means more.'

'Sometimes?' he asked.

'No, not sometimes.'

'Can I at least read the letter he sent? Does he want you back after all these years?'

'No Alexander, he doesn't want back with me. You know he has his own wife and kids. And even if he did, I'm with you and that's not going to change.'

'It wouldn't be the first time he's left a wife and kids.' Mary sighed.

'That was harsh,' said Alexander, 'I'm sorry.'

'Don't be sorry Alexander; you haven't done anything to be sorry for. And even if he did want me, and he doesn't, I wouldn't go. I've spent the guts of my life with you Alexander, not with Robert.'

'Then why's he calling? Does he explain it in the letter?'

'Wait Alexander; it's best it comes from Robert.'

'Jesus Mary, best what comes from Robert?'

He snapped the letter from her and opened it, but he had only begun to read when Robert rapped the front door. He put the letter down on the bed and went downstairs to answer it.

Robert's hair was still dark, though flecked with grey. Alexander had expected to see an older man.

'You'd better come in,' he said. Robert took off his coat and gloves and held them.

'It's been a long time since I was in this house,' he said.

Alexander cast his eyes around the room.

'It looks well.'

'We knocked the two downstairs rooms into one after the kids grew up. The back room was Peter's. Alexander's voice trailed off.

'It's okay,' said Robert. 'It's been so long now. I've learned to live with it. He didn't leave a note. You'd have expected that. Most suicides leave a note. Don't they?'

Alexander shrugged. 'Take a seat,' he said. 'She's still a bit slow after the operation. It takes her time to get dressed. I'll leave you both, for a while, when she does.'

'No.' said Robert. 'We won't need that.'

'No?'

Robert shook his head.

'Right then.'

Robert was still standing up. 'Is it okay if I sit down?' he said. Alexander hastened to the armchair and lifted a magazine off it.

'Here,' he said. 'Sit here.'

'Thank you.'

'I'd offer you a drink,' said Alexander, 'but believe it or not there's nothing in the house.'

'I didn't mind...'

'What?'

'When Tommy left you half of the pub.'

'Is that what this is about?'

'No.'

Robert took a hip flask out of his inside jacket pocket. 'If you get a couple of glasses,' he said. 'It's whiskey.' Alexander shook his head. 'For old time's sake Alexander. For we had some good times,' he said, 'before ...'

'I don't want to rake up the past,' said Alexander, 'if that's all right with you.' He moved across the room to the

296

old china cabinet, crouched down to open the doors and lifted out two glasses. 'But I don't mind sharing a drink with you Robert. I don't mind that,' he said.

Robert poured a large whiskey into each glass and sunk his own back in one go. He was pouring a second glass when Mary came down the stairs.

She wore a black pinafore with a white blouse beneath it. She sat down beside Alexander and took his hand.

'You have something to tell me?' said Alexander.

Robert began to speak. He asked Alexander whether or not he remembered the year when a baby was found in a walkway. 'It was badly damaged,' said Robert. Alexander shrugged.

'Tell him,' said Mary. Robert poured himself another whiskey and told Alexander about Mary's pregnancy.

'Mary wasn't even pregnant then,' said Alexander.

'I hid the pregnancy,' she said.

He told Alexander about coming home from work and finding her on the bed. He told him about finding Peter in the tree house and he told him about burying the child.

'Recently,' Robert said, 'I was in a bit of a scuffle. Some bloke had been winding me up and I hit him. Happen he fell and was badly cut. There were witnesses present who called the police and I was taken in and charged.'

Alexander put his arm around Mary's.

'They linked up my DNA and have identified Mary as the mother. They hauled me in; it's why I'm home. I'm on bail.' Robert pulled up his trouser leg, 'and tagged.'

Alexander couldn't believe what he was hearing.

'Anyway,' said Robert. 'It's not why I'm here.'

'Tell him,' said Mary.

'I've told him enough,' he said. 'I want you to say it.'

'I can't,' Mary said.

'Can't tell me what?' said Alexander, still holding her hand, not knowing. Robert sighed.

'The child I buried that day was your child Alexander.'

****

The case came to trial. Robert had a motive: for his wife had committed adultery, and the child was not his. His DNA was at the scene of the burial. On this evidence alone the jury may have convicted him.

On the day of Baby Clare's death, when Mary had cleaned up the floor of the tree house, she had wrapped the scissors in a muslin cloth, covered this with a plastic carrier bag and put them in a Tupperware box that she sealed with an entire roll of brown masking tape; turning the box over and over so that even the plastic exterior was completely concealed. She had never been able to look at the scissors again or, for fear they would be found, dispose of them. And so they had gone with her, in the bottom of a wooden trunk, to Rockdale Street and had lain in that trunk, in the attic, until now.

As the trial proceeded Mary believed that the scissors she had kept would prove that Robert had not killed the child. But Robert, when questioned by the prosecution and made to relive the day he had lifted Peter from the tree house, remembered that he had taken the scissors from Peter's sleeping hand and laid them on the floor before lifting him. The prosecution's final forensic submission proved that his fingerprints were on the murder weapon. The jury returned the unanimous verdict of 'Guilty'.

In the judges final statement he described Robert as a fiend, who without remorse had blamed his own son on a murder he did not commit. 'How could a child,' the judge said, 'so small, so incapable, have the strength to carry a baby, never mind to kill it.' He described Robert's flight, leaving his wife and two children without a father, as further evidence of 'a selfish mind and a cold, evil heart.' The judge stated that, 'He embodied everything that was hellish and inhuman.'

Alexander did not know, for sure, whether Robert's story was the truth. He accepted it as being so because Mary confirmed it and he did not wish to set himself against her. Throughout the trial he grieved for his child whom he had never known, would never know, and he grieved for Mary. But he grieved too for his friend, whom he had wronged.

As Robert left the dock to be taken down he looked back towards Mary, and as she said his name, extending her arm out to him, Alexander knew that she was still in love with Robert.

He took Mary's hand and led her from the courtroom. And as he looked up at the blue sky and at a lone seagull perched on a rooftop, he heard Elsie's voice, 'Love does not ask,' she said. 'It gives without expecting anything in return.' The words strengthened him, for even as he grieved he knew that he had his own sin to carry and he knew he had to be brave.

5946832R00171

Printed in Great Britain
by Amazon.co.uk, Ltd.,
Marston Gate.